THE UNDERDOG

A true story

THE UNDERDOG

A true story

(Most names have been altered)

JANETTE HIRST

Janette Hirst left school at 16 with no career plan.

She started work as a gym instructor, then became an apprentice electrician, electrician, Lecturer of Electrical Installation and is now an NVQ assessor for apprentice electricians.

Janette lives in Brighouse, West Yorkshire, England with her husband.

THE UNDERDOG

JANETTE HIRST

For anyone who has gone through, or is going through a bad time at work.

INTRODUCTION

I'll be brief, so I can get on with the story:

- I taught Electrical Installation for 12 years at Kirklees College
- My work record was impeccable
- The section (Electrical and Plumbing) was a good, hardworking section
- The colleagues in the section all got on, and we had a good manager

Then:

- We had a college restructure. The college changed its name and our manager took voluntary redundancy
- We got a new manager who demoralised and intimidated staff
- People left the section to escape him
- It became a horrible place in which to work

………then it became my turn to be the object of my manager's intimidating regime.

Previously.

The person who took over the Electrical and Plumbing Department at Kirklees College was called Ron Atler. Ron Atler was already the Plumbing Co-ordinator. I had always got on well with him, but I knew his reputation – if he didn't like you, he was vindictive and a bully.

I got on quite well with Ron Atler for the first few months when he took over management of the section – probably because I was quite valuable to him as he knew very little about Electrical Installation, what courses we ran and how we ran them.

I ended up doing all the electrical lecturer's timetables and rooming. I organised the apprentice's block pattern when all the assessments would be run etc, Generally, doing his job for him as well as teaching fulltime.

In December 2010, I went out with my colleagues and was talking to Tanya Brown. She had previously worked in our section teaching functional skills until Ron Atler had fallen out with her and had made her life so difficult that she had moved to another section of the college to escape from him.

Tanya was telling me to be wary of Ron Atler.

I remember saying, "I know you're right, I've seen how he is with certain people, but I've got to be right with him, as he's being OK with me at present."

Things then started to deteriorate throughout 2011.

Both the Electrical and Plumbing staff started to call Ron Atler 'Jekyll and Hyde' as you never knew what mood he would be in. Another common name for him was 'Hitler'.

My relationship with Ron Atler started to 'go down-hill' in the last three months of 2011. Most of the Electrical and

Plumbing section were very unhappy, but felt they had no control as Ron Atler was very friendly with the Head of Construction Dale Rolland; so, there was no one to complain to. Ron Atler had driven good lecturers out of the college.

I decided that I would try to stand up to Ron when he behaved unprofessionally and when he tried to bully and intimidate me. This ended up infuriating Ron and making his behaviour worse which gradually wore down my mental health and ability to function.

<u>7/12/11</u>

<u>One example of the beginning of my crisis</u>

Ron Atler called me and Jack Booth (another electrical installation lecturer) into his office at 2.15 pm. Dale Rolland (the Head of Construction) was in his office when we walked in. Ron Atler stated that he felt there was 'negativity' within the section, and he wanted to know why.

It seemed as if this 'scenario' had been planned and that Ron Atler was intentionally trying to make us feel intimidated by having Dale Rolland present.

I was furious about this and decided to 'speak my mind'. I felt that I (and the rest of the section) had taken enough from Ron over the past few months with his erratic, intimidating style of management.

I replied (mainly addressing Dale Rolland) "Most of the people in the Electrical and Plumbing section feel very stressed and under pressure. Ron has no communication skills, he's moody, and it depends what mood he's in, as to how he behaves." I finished with, "Ron does not have the word 'thank you' in his vocabulary either."

Ron made no reply to this. I think he was amazed that I had dared to stand up to him in front of his line manager (Rolland) when the reason for him calling this meeting was for him to intimidate me and Jack in front of Dale Rolland.

The meeting went on about 45 minutes. Ron Atler lied and told Dale Rolland that we weren't doing admin/reports/student trackers etc; I disagreed and 'stood my ground' throughout the meeting. I had an answer for everything that Rob 'threw' at me which wound him up.

He told us he wanted us to work the first 2-3 days of our Christmas holiday to prepare for the Ofsted visit in April. I told him that I was taking the full Christmas break and that I would be ready for Ofsted. Ron reared up and snarled "I know you'll be ready, but I still want you in!" (meaning he wanted me in to organise others in section). I repeated that I was taking the full Christmas break off to which he said, "Do you think it would be acceptable for all British Home Stores staff to take the full Christmas holidays off?"

I calmly replied, "No, because British Home Stores is open to customers during the Christmas period, but this college is closed to students over Christmas so therefore it's not a problem for me to take my full holiday entitlement."

Dale Rolland just sat there observing, whilst Ron was getting more and more annoyed. He finally dismissed us (after repeating that he expected us to work the first 2-3 days of the Christmas holidays).

Jack and I were very despondent. Two members of staff had suffered from 'bad health' and had left Kirklees College because of Ron Atler about a year previously. I didn't want to be the next one.

I went home and couldn't stop thinking about the meeting and Ron's behaviour. I didn't know what to do about it; but figured that I would either need to accept his behaviour, or make sure I 'logged' the meeting/issue with Dale Rolland (as he was Ron Atler's line manager), in case things deteriorated even further.

I wrote Dale Rolland an email the next day asking why the meeting had been called if there was a conclusion to the meeting, and if so, what was it?

I sent the email and then felt very stressed and nervous, wondering what response I would get.

Strange things began to happen. Dale Rolland did not answer my email. He printed it off and got me into the office and verbally went through it, then suggested I had a chat with Ron Atler to clear the air. I said to Dale that I had wanted a reply to my email (written), but he wouldn't – why?

Phil Newsome (the plumbing technician) found me and said, "I hear that you've had a 'run in' with our leader!"

Phil went on to tell me that Ron Atler had been slagging me off to all the plumbing department. He told them all about the meeting (no confidentiality) and that he couldn't believe what I had said in the meeting about our previous manager and that things had run better under him.

This just confirmed that Ron Atler was a terrible manager and that I was not his favourite member of staff.

Phil, and later Steve Clay and John Forrest (plumbing lecturers) all told me that I needed to watch my back as Ron would have it in for me.

John Forrest was laughing, saying that I had taken the 'heat' off him and that Ron would now focus on me and leave him alone a bit.

Anyway, things went from bad to worse for me. Ron Atler's behaviour became more and more erratic. He hardly spoke to me and gave me filthy looks.

I had always taken off the full Christmas holidays. Any lecturer will agree that you need the holidays to 're-group' and de-stress yourself after a hectic teaching term, and to recharge your batteries for the following term. And teaching 8 extra hours each week than I should have been doing, had compounded this need. I worked between 46-48 hours each week (when my contract of employment stated my working week was 37 hours), so I felt I was well within my rights to take my holidays to recuperate.

I decided that I would not give in to Ron Atler trying to intimidate me into working the first 2-3 days of my holidays. I felt if I gave in, he would just expect more and more. All the other lecturers in the plumbing and electrical section did as Ron Atler requested (through fear of retribution – not because they wanted to). I 'stuck to my guns'. I told Dale Rolland at my 'meeting' with him that I was taking my full Christmas holidays off and he said that that was fine.

This annoyed my line manager greatly and I came back to work in January to an email (to all staff in the section) from Ron Atler thanking all the staff who had worked the first 3 days of the Christmas holidays – and stating that they would be rewarded with 3 days extra holiday as lieu time. I felt this was aimed at me but I had stood up to him, so decided it was worth it.

Chapter 1

My Crisis

I had emailed my manager Ron Atler before leaving work about concerns I had about course material for a new Level 1 group. I reminded him that we still didn't have a completed workshop booklet and Scheme of Work for the group and that we were being inspected by Ofsted in about two months.

I wasn't responsible for that group, but I had done the majority of the incomplete workshop booklet and I didn't want our section to perform badly at inspection by Ofsted.

Ron Atler had become completely unapproachable by now and I was worried he might 'shoot the messenger' so I felt it might be better to send an email rather than talk directly to him.

5/1/12

I went into work as normal and taught my first lesson of the day. When I came back into the staffroom for morning break, I noticed Ron Atler in his office typing away furiously on his computer. I checked my emails to see if I had had a response from Ron but had not, so I went to teach my second class.

At dinnertime, I checked my emails again and noticed that Ron had replied. I opened the email and was completely dumbfounded.

I read the email twice and felt shocked and surprised at the content. Ron had copied everyone in the electrical section into the email and Dale Rolland (the head of the Construction Department) <u>AND</u> Diana Brand (the Director of the Construction Department).

Instead of just answering my question, his reply seemed very lengthy, rambling and had a very 'angry tone' to it.

Ron for some reason felt the need to mention nineteen separate tasks that had been undertaken in the electrical section putting the initials of the different members of staff in the electrical section next to the tasks to show who had undertaken each of the tasks.

Everyone in the electrical section got a mention, except me.

I read this as Ron inferring that either:

- I had not done any work in the electrical section
- He was trying to exclude me from the rest of the team

I had a class to teach at 1 pm. I printed the email off and then struggled through my two-hour class. I kept having to take deep breaths to try to calm myself as I felt very tearful and anxious.

Luckily the class was a revision session for an upcoming exam, so my class delivery was less than normal. My colleague Andrew Smithy came in to see me during the session. He was just shaking his head saying he had read the email and wanted to know if I was OK.

After my class I grabbed my bag from the staffroom, then before leaving, I went in to see the secretary of the section. I asked her if she had read the email and she said that she couldn't believe that all the work I had done for the section had been omitted. I started to get upset, said I would have to go and left.

I drove home in shock, stepped into the kitchen and started crying. I got the email that I had printed out of my bag and read through it again. I was crying when Marcus (my stepson) came downstairs. He saw the state of me and asked me what the matter was. I told him about the email and that my boss had copied in the Head of Construction and the Director of Construction and Engineering!

I was so upset that I told Marcus 'I could fucking well punch the bastard (Ron)!' I hardly ever swore in front of Marcus (even though he is 24) so he could see how distressed I was and looked worried.

I felt too upset and sick to eat anything and just sat 'brooding' over the email until Robert (my partner) got in from work. I started trying to explain how Ron had copied the Director of Construction into the email and that he had made out that I didn't contribute to the section.... I couldn't speak properly as I was crying so much. Robert was trying to calm me down, but he couldn't. I seemed to be getting worse, crying uncontrollably. Robert said, "Come down here and cuddle Indie" (our gorgeous dog who was laid in front of the fire) - thinking it may calm me.

I did as I was told, but nothing could stop me crying.

Robert had commented previously that I had been getting more stressed about work and Ron Atler's behaviour for quite a few months and said, "Right, you're not going to work tomorrow, you need to go to the doctors!"

I replied, "I have to go to work tomorrow. What about my students?"

Robert's response was, "Never mind your students. What about you. You're a mess. You're not coping! Just listen to your breathing!"

(I didn't know what he meant about my breathing until the following morning at the doctors.)

Anyway, I just kept crying all night. When we went to bed Robert was cuddling me, trying to comfort me. As I lay there, it was like a video recorder playing in my head that wouldn't stop. The 'video' was running through all the stressful events that had happened over the previous few months – all involved Ron Atler and Dale Rolland.

Robert fell asleep, but I couldn't. I went into the spare bedroom so that I didn't wake Robert up. I couldn't stop sobbing. The 'video' in my head kept playing non-stop. I could feel my heartbeat pumping high in my chest and loud in my ears!

I felt scared. I couldn't understand why I wasn't able to stop crying and why my heart was pumping so loud and my breathing so heavy and irregular – I was healthy, what was the matter with me?

<u>6/1/12</u>

At about 4 am I went and laid on the settee. When Robert got up and saw the state of me, he said I needed to make a doctor's appointment and that he would ring the section secretary and HR at work to inform them that I wouldn't be going into work today.

I felt that terrible that I accepted Robert telling me I couldn't go to work. I always went to work, even when I was ill. I didn't know what was wrong with me, but I realised I wasn't physically or mentally able to go to work today.

I telephoned the doctors and managed to make an appointment for 11 am. I spent the morning crying. I couldn't eat anything and could feel my heart beating high up in my chest all the time and my breathing was loud and felt heavy.

I went to the doctors and was crying in the waiting room whilst waiting for my appointment.

Doctor Mattins called me in. As soon as I sat down, I started crying. I started trying to tell him what had been happening at work, but I seemed to be talking too fast. It was all disjointed 'Ron Atler this and Dale Rolland that' and then, suddenly, I couldn't breathe properly. I kept trying to gulp in air, but it wouldn't seem to go into my lungs!

I was gulping and gulping! I was panicking like mad, not knowing what was going on. It seemed to go on for a while. All I could think was that I would die if I didn't start breathing soon.

I looked across at Doctor Mattins for help, but he was calmly typing into his computer. I was staring at him, my eyes like saucers, tapping my hands on my chest as I tried to breathe. I don't know how long it went on for, but it gradually seemed to subside. Strange noises (weird gasps, groans) were coming out of my mouth that didn't seem to be coming from me? I got to the stage where I was gasping, "I think I'm alright now, I think I'm alright now!"

I started to breathe more normally but couldn't talk properly as I was shaking all over, my teeth were 'chattering' and I was sweating from every pore of my body.

I was in the doctor's surgery for an hour! When I had calmed down enough, Doctor Mattins said that I needed two weeks off work to enable me to calm down from the stresses of work and gave me a sick note. He said he wanted to see me in two weeks.

I went straight home and locked the door. I couldn't believe how I'd 'crumbled' at the doctors and gone from a normal and fully functioning individual to a complete wreck within twenty-four hours. I realised that I must have been close to having a panic attack last night when Robert had been saying 'Listen to your breathing!'

I telephoned Robert and told him about having a panic attack at the doctors and that I had a two-week sick note. I asked if he could contact the college to inform them as I didn't feel up to it.

As well as feeling terrible about my situation, I felt stressed that I hadn't gone to work and that I'd let my students down. I was thinking that I should be at work, teaching my students – not sat about at home. I was a mess and was also full of guilt, feeling like I was letting my students down and my colleagues (who would need to cover for me).

I couldn't just sit down and do nothing as the 'video' in my head was all I could focus on. When I sat down the 'video' (starring Ron Atler and Dale Rolland) just played continually. I started cleaning the house to keep myself busy and to try to distract myself a bit. Nothing worked.

When Robert came home, I don't think he knew what to do with me. I was just a tearful mess.

7/1/12

The weekend

Robert has tried to distract me today. He decided that I needed to get out of the house and took me to the cinema at tea time (which was the last thing I wanted to do). I was still crying on and off during the drive to the cinema and then clung onto Robert like a small, vulnerable child as we walked into the cinema!

The next two to three weeks were like 'Ground Hog day'. I went to bed exhausted at about 10 pm. It took me until about 11 pm to fall asleep and then I woke up between 11.45 pm and 12.15 am. I could never get back to sleep so I would get up, take the spare quilt and lay on the settee.

The nights are even worse than the days, it's dark and I am alone with my thoughts. I can't get my mind to stop – it just constantly played the 'video' of Ron Atler and Dale Rolland - tormenting my mind and not letting me sleep.

My house is the cleanest and tidiest it has ever been as I can't sit still during the day. I don't feel hungry (which is very unusual for me) and just eat bits when I can face it.

I have a mirror above the fireplace in the dining room. When I look at myself in it I wonder how I can look so ill and rough when I don't have a physical illness. I usually have a naturally pink complexion, but I am now pale and ashen. My eyes are just lifeless. They look like they are glazed over. As I look at myself in the mirror, it is as if a zombie is staring back at me.

I don't even feel comfortable when taking Indie (my dog) for a walk. I feel paranoid and that I should be at work. After my walks, I get back in the house, lock the door and sigh with relief. The only place I feel safe is at home.

Whenever the house phone rings, I panic and stop breathing, wondering who it is – but I never answer it. One day it rang, I didn't answer and then my mobile went off immediately afterward. The caller I.D. came up as Robert, so I answered it. Robert said, "I've just rung the house phone" I replied, "I'm not answering the house phone" and from then on, he always rang my mobile.

I also stop breathing if anyone pulls up in a car outside the house, worrying that it was someone from work. I feel panicky and just hold my breath for some reason?

20/1/12

I went to my doctor's appointment and explained that I felt no better, that I wasn't sleeping and that my head was just like a video recorder, playing over, and over again. I also showed him my hands that had broken out in eczema.

I think he could tell from just looking at me, at what a mess I was, and he gave me another sick note for Work-Related Stress for two weeks.

I telephoned Robert to ask him to contact the college to inform them as I couldn't face contacting them myself. I then sent my sicknote to college in the post.

I can't think clearly. I have no idea what is happening to me. I am stressed, confused and anxious. I have worked so hard, been so professional and conscientious, and now I am unable to work, or even simply function normally.

The thought of Ron Atler, being in control of me at work is sickening. Over the next week, I knew I had to do something. I couldn't be yet another statistic of Ron Atler – someone who had been run out of the college by a bullying manager.

I have decided that my only option is to put in a Formal Complaint against Ron Atler. The thought is terrifying as I have no idea what the outcome will be – just that it will probably get worse before it (possibly) gets better?

<u>31/1/12</u>

It took me all morning to pluck up the courage. At 12.10 pm I sent the following email to HR:

From: janettecastle@hotmail.co.uk

Sent: 31 January 2012 12.10

To: cwood@kirkleescollege.com
drolland@kirkleescollege.com

Subject: My Absence

Hi Carol,

As you know I am not in college at the moment.
I wish to put in a formal complaint about Ron Atler, but I do not know the process.
Please could you advise?

Regards

Janette

I felt physically sick as I pressed the send button! I knew it was the right thing to do, but also knew that my life would now get even more stressful.

I had copied Dale Rolland into the email (as Ron's boss – and unfortunately for me, his mate), so I knew Ron would find out immediately and that he would want my blood!

I felt sick all afternoon and kept checking my emails every half hour to see if I'd got a response from HR.

The next two and a half days I felt depressed but obsessive. I was checking my emails for a response about six times a day, then stressing that they were ignoring me. I couldn't understand why they were ignoring me, and this was adding to my stress levels.

3/2/12

I had another doctor's appointment in the afternoon. I told my doctor that I had decided to put a complaint in at work and that they still hadn't responded to me three days later and that it was making me feel even worse. I told him I was exhausted as I hadn't slept for almost a month now. The doctor prescribed me some sleeping tablets and gave me another sick note for three weeks.

When I got home, I checked my emails once more and there was still no response. I decided I would email them again as it was now Friday tea time:

From: janettecastle@hotmail.co.uk

Sent:03 February 2012 16:38

To: cwood@kirkleescollege.com drolland@kirkleescollege.com

Subject: Janette Castle (Electrical Installation)

1 attachment

Hi Carol/Dale,

I've been to the doctors today and he's given me a sick note for a further 3 weeks, a copy of which is attached, and I'll post you the original later today.

I would be obliged if you could respond to my earlier email request below and supply or advise on the College's Staff Complaints Procedure as I've not received either.

Regards

Janette

I had written this email and forwarded my one from Tuesday on the same email so that there could be no confusion.

Robert (who is in management himself) is surprised that college has not responded to me. He has advised me to have a paper trail in case they become awkward with me.

4/2/12

I received a lengthy letter in the post from Jan Weldon in HR this morning. The letter was dated 1/2/12 but was posted 1st class 3/2/12 – immediately after receiving my email I imagine. I think that realising I would be off work for another three weeks, they felt they should now reply.

The letter stated that due to the length of my absence, the college needed to meet with me to discuss support mechanisms to enable me to return to work. It mentioned my wish to put in a formal complaint and enclosed the College's Grievance Procedure.

The letter asked that I attend a meeting at the college on 7/2/12.

Robert read through the letter also. I told Robert that there was no way that I could go into college. The thought made me feel sick, and so I asked Robert if he would ring HR on

Monday and ask if they could come to see me at home instead.

So, another nightmare weekend. Stress levels through the roof!

6/2/12

Robert telephoned me from work to let me know that he had spoken to Jan Welden in HR and told her that I was not well enough to go into college and that I would like the meeting to be held at home.

Jan told him that they didn't have time to do that tomorrow, but that she would contact me to re-arrange.

7/2/12

I received an email from Jan Weldon informing me that the meeting with her and Dale Rolland could take place at my house at 11 am on 14/2/12.

I replied that that was fine and that I would like my partner Robert present at the meeting.

Nightmare - another week to wait and stress about the meeting. I want to start the Grievance Procedure. I have informed them of my intention and they seem to be ignoring that issue and concentrating on a meeting to get me back to work????

I kept reading through the College's Grievance Procedure. It explained Informal and Formal Procedure and how you could be represented by a Trade Union Official.

I'm not in the Union, so I'm on my own!

10/2/12

Robert came home earlier than usual. I was just checking my emails when I noticed that I had received one from Jan Weldon in HR.

The email was cancelling our scheduled meeting on 14/2/12 and rescheduling it for 21/2/12.

I just 'lost the plot'! I started crying uncontrollably, wailing, "Why are they doing this to me? Why are they making me wait?!" I was not myself at all. I just couldn't cope.

Robert seemed shocked at the state of me and was trying to calm me down.

All I could think was that I now had to wait another 11 days to go through the stress of the meeting and trying to start the Grievance procedure when I had already been waiting 10 days!

13/2/12

I have only been leaving the house to take Indie for walks and to go to the doctors. I feel bad as Robert works very long hours and he is now doing the supermarket shopping too. I decided I needed to go to the supermarket. I told myself that I wasn't physically ill, so I should be able to do it.

I drove down to Sainsbury's and got a small trolley. I began walking around the aisles and immediately found that my legs felt weak and shaky. I could feel my heart beating in my chest and my breathing felt very strange. I hardly had anything in my trolley, but it felt heavy and was an effort to push. I felt so weak, that I didn't know if I would be able to get around to the checkouts!

I continued slowly, half resting on the trolley for support and managed to get through the checkouts. I couldn't understand what was happening to me? I drove home, locked the door, and only then did I feel safe; as if no one could 'get me'.

16/2/12

People at work know what is happening now. I have received text messages from Judith, Kay, Tanya, Andrew and Phil Carter (from JTL).

Everyone is supportive and telling me to keep strong.

Tanya texted me this morning. She left the section because of Ron. She has warned me that Ron will have 'it in for me' (how comforting).

17/2/12

I started making a few notes about what I wish to discuss at next weeks' meeting in case I get upset and start getting flustered. If I have notes I will feel prepared and hopefully, it will help.

I am exhausted! I haven't slept now for the last seven weeks or more. The sleeping tablets are not working. Every night is the same. I go to bed at about 10 pm. I read and manage to nod off at about 11 pm – but every single night I wake up between 11.45 pm and 12.15 am. I'm then wide awake, fidgety and anxious. My mind just spins and plays the Ron Atler and Dale Rolland video in my head. I get up and lay on the settee downstairs. Everything feels so much worse at night, alone in the dark. The nights seem to drag on forever. It feels like a kind of Chinese torture!

Robert keeps telling me to try to sleep during the day, but my mind won't rest enough to allow me to sleep. I am so tired now that I seem to walk into a room, and then when I get there, I can't remember what I've gone in for. I am in a 'foggy', confused daze most of the time.

<u>21/3/12</u>

God. I'm stressed! Dale Rolland and Jan Weldon (from HR) are due to arrive at 11 am. Robert has gone to work but is coming home to be at the meeting with me.

They arrived slightly early before Robert had got home, so I felt panicky. I let them in, made them both a coffee and luckily Robert arrived home before the actual meeting began.

Dale and Jan were both polite and feigned concern. They said that they wanted to understand my concerns about Ron Atler, to enable them to 'help me'.

I was prepared for this and read through the notes I had written:

- That Ron Atler is aggressive and threatening
- That I had been dragged into a meeting before Christmas to discuss my 'negativity'
- How I had been falsely accused of not filling out student tracking sheets
- That other members of staff in the section felt intimidated by Ron – but were not confident to raise the issue
- That Ron Atler is not confidential – that he discussed the 'negativity meeting' with others in the section and divulged a colleague's poor lesson observation with me
- I mentioned the ranting email he sent me, that he copied everyone else in the section into the email, and that he had intimated that I didn't work as hard as the rest of the section

I mentioned that I did not feel confident that my Grievance would be taken seriously. I informed Jan Weldon that other members of staff had left the section due to Ron Atler's behaviour and that the section was not happy.

When I started discussing putting a Grievance in against Ron Atler, Jan Weldon replied, "I would always advise trying to resolve a grievance informally" Dale Rolland agreed profusely with Jan (probably because he's Ron Atler's mate, I thought). I replied, "This is far too serious, and it needs to follow the formal Grievance Procedure."

After I had made it clear that I wanted it to be a formal grievance Dale suggested that I attend a meeting at Brunel House on 24/3/12 to begin Stage 1 of the grievance procedure.

I could tell that they were both disappointed that I had not given in straight away and let them deal with my issue with Ron Atler informally.

Jan Weldon told me she would be making an appointment for me to see the college's occupational therapist (which I agreed to).

After the meeting, I had mixed feelings. I was glad the meeting was over – but had thought that the main purpose of the meeting was to start my grievance? I now need to wait another three days to start it – and go through the stress of doing so!

The College Grievance Procedure clearly states, 'that the line manager should deal with and try to resolve the Grievance at Stage 1 and inform the complainant in writing within 5 working days of receiving the complaint'.

I advised the college that I wished to put in a complaint on 31/1/12!! Three weeks have passed, and I haven't even started the procedure yet!

At least I should know the outcome by the end of next week at the latest.

<u>24/2/12</u>

I had another doctor's appointment at 9 am. I told Doctor Mattins that the sleeping tablets weren't working as I still wasn't sleeping.

I told him about only feeling safe in the house and that even walking my dog didn't feel 'right'. I also told him about 'my funny episode' at the supermarket, how I went weak, could feel my heart beating fast and that my breathing wasn't normal.

Doctor Mattins told me that taking my dog out, getting fresh air and exercise was exactly what I needed to be doing and that I needed to keep trying to do normal things like going to the supermarket.

I told him that I was finally beginning Stage 1 of my Grievance at 11 am this morning and that I was nervous. Doctor Mattins wished me luck and gave me another sick note.

Doctor Mattins also advised that I keep all emails and letters from college and that if I can still get onto the college system, I need to make copies of any emails relating to the issues I have been having. He went on to say that in his experience with other patients, he had found that some employers had deleted evidence when there were any disputes like mine.

Chapter 2

Stage 1 of the Grievance Procedure

I drove home from the doctors with stress levels even higher, thinking about my meeting to start the Grievance Procedure and knowing that I would be bumping into people from college who would know I was off work and that I was putting a complaint in.

I got home and quickly re-read through the document I have prepared for the meeting. My stomach is doing 'flips'. God knows how many times I've been to the toilet today – but there can't be anything left!!

I got my paperwork together and drove to my meeting at Brunel House. I tried to breathe slow deep breaths as I was shaky and anxious. My heart was thumping in my chest again.

I walked into reception and the receptionist gave me a sympathetic, 'knowing' smile (which told me that my issues were common knowledge).

I sat in reception briefly and then Dale Rolland called me into his office. Dale was polite and asked me to go through what my issues were.

I informed Dale that I was starting the Grievance Procedure not just for myself, but for the rest of the section.

I then read through my prepared document regarding my issues:

I, Janette Castle wish to put in a formal complaint against my line manager Ron Atler.

Ron Atler's management style is not conducive to a happy working environment.

Ron Atler at times behaves in a bullying, undermining and intimidating manner.

Ron Atler's behaviour caused me to feel anxious and stressed at work. I became unable to sleep, suffered from outbreaks of eczema and twice broke down in tears at work.

The 'straw that broke the camel's back' was the e-mail that Ron Atler sent to me on Thursday 5th January 2012, which was in my opinion, aggressive in parts and seemed to infer that I do not contribute within the section and that I am incompetent. This e-mail was copied to everyone in the section, Dale Rolland and Diana Brand.

I was affected so badly by Ron Atler's poor management skills that I ended up going to seeing my doctor who diagnosed Work-Related Stress.

I have worked for Kirklees College for over eleven years and have always proved myself to be a very conscientious, hard-working and competent member of staff.

In brief, Ron Atlers management style includes the following behaviours:

- *Aggressive/threatening*
- *Moody and non-communicative*
- *No confidentiality*
- *Treats people differently*
- *Can't accept there are problems (blames people for negativity)*

I wish to bring to your attention that it is not only me who has found Ron Alter's management style unacceptable. I hope you will speak with the rest of the team as I am sure that at least 90% of them will confirm to you that Ron Atler is a bully

Janette Castle

Dale Rolland remained polite and friendly. I gave him a copy of the above and he informed me that he would investigate my claims and that he planned to interview all staff in the electrical and plumbing department.

I left the meeting half feeling like something was happening at last but the other half of me knowing how friendly and close Dale Rolland was with Ron Atler – so not confident that it would be dealt with properly.

27/2/12

A work colleague telephoned me after dinner and told me that Dale Rolland had been waiting in the staffroom first thing in the morning and had started taking staff into the office to be interviewed one by one. They said that he asked questions about Ron Atler's behaviour, general questions about the section and took notes.

Seemingly all staff, (except James Tebb – Ron's mate), had been whispering about the investigation during the day, trying to find out if everyone was asked the same questions – and how they had answered them. Everyone in the section had been questioned today except John Forrest as he was on holiday.

Judith and Andrew telephoned me in the evening and confirmed they had been interviewed as part of the investigation. Andrew told me that he had asked Dale Rolland if the investigation would be confidential and Dale had assured him that it would be.

Steve Clay then rang me to say he had texted John Forrest on holiday to tell him that Rolland was investigating my accusations against Ron Atler. He said John had been ecstatic and had texted back 'Fucking brilliant! Bring it on!'

1/3/12

I received an email from Dale Rolland:

From: drolland@kirkleescollege.com

Sent: 01 March 2012 10:24:22

To: janettecastle@hotmail.co.uk

Subject: Investigation

Hi Janette

Sorry, I forgot to mention in my last email that I have begun the investigation with staff.

I have just one member of staff left to interview, and hopefully, this can be done early next week.

I'll then be in a position, to share my report with you.

Thanks

Dale

3/3/12

John Forrest telephoned me to say 'Well done' for bringing the Grievance against Ron Atler. He said that he was looking forward to going to work on Monday to be interviewed and that hopefully, Ron Atler would 'get what was coming to him'. We discussed whether Dale Rolland was the right man to investigate as he was 'bezzy mates' with Atler. Neither of us felt overly convinced.

5/3/12

I kept checking my emails to see if Dale Rolland had contacted me after interviewing John Forrest. A big fat NOTHING!

8/3/12

What a stressful week! Checking my emails every half hour and waiting for the post to arrive each day, expecting to hear from Dale Rolland.

Still not sleeping, though not surprising with what's going on (or rather what's NOT going on – as nothing seems to be happening).

So frustrating! Feel sick, anxious and exhausted. I can't believe I'm being treated like this, after all the hard work I've done for college!

People from work are also nervous and wanting to know if I've heard anything from Dale Rolland.

9/3/12

I had another doctor's appointment this morning. I told Doctor Mattins that I still haven't heard anything about my Grievance, even though the grievance procedure states that I should have heard within five working days. Doctor Mattins was sympathetic but didn't seem too surprised. He gave me another sick note for two weeks.

16/3/12

Another week and still nothing. I can't understand why it's taking so long! Why are they treating me like this when they know I'm ill??

20/3/12

I finally received an email from Dale Rolland.

From: *drolland@kirkleescollege.com*

Sent: 20 March 2012

To: *janettecastle@hotmail.co.uk*

Subject: Meeting

Hi Janette,

I hope you're feeling well.

I have completed the investigation with staff, is it possible for you to meet with me at Brunel House to discuss it on Friday 23rd March at 11.00?

Thanks

Dale

Glad I've got a response; but very worried as to what the outcome will be! Let's hope he does the right thing and sorts this problem out for me and the rest of the section.

By the time it gets to Friday I will have been waiting four weeks for Dale's response, so he hasn't followed the college's Grievance Procedure!

I was very apprehensive about my meeting, but also a bit relieved that I will find out what's happening to me (and more importantly to Ron Atler)!

The meeting began at 11 am with just Dale Rolland and me present.

Dale began by going through the answers staff in the electrical and plumbing section had given when questioned by Dale about Ron Atler's management style.

From reading through the questions, it was clear that my workmates had agreed with me about Ron Atler being intimidating, a bully and not being confidential with information. After Dale had read through their answers, I counted how many answers there were to the questions, to ascertain how many people Dale had interviewed. There were nine. Dale listed the names of the staff he had interviewed, and I stated that he hadn't interviewed Kay Ramsden or Tanya Brown. Dale replied that this was not intentional and that he had just interviewed full-time members of staff.

I replied, "Well I know what Tanya Brown's answers would be, had she been interviewed" (as Tanya had had issues with Ron). Dale didn't answer this.

Dale went on to tell me that Ron Atler has 'come off' some tablets, and it had 'not done him any good'.

I felt that this was an attempt by Dale to try to make me feel sympathetic towards Ron. Dale went on to say that Ron realised that he needed to change his behaviour and that he (Ron) wanted to make the changes.

Dale then asked me what I thought we could do to move forward!!!!

This was when I realised that he was trying to shaft me - and was trying to get me to help him to sweep it under the carpet!!

I started panicking, thinking, 'How am I going to get out of this one?'

I tried to remain as calm as possible and asked Dale "Have you written up your conclusion for me?"

Dale replied, "I wanted you to be involved in the process."

I replied, "I thought that I was finally going to get your written conclusion to the investigation today and that that was the point of this meeting."

Dale replied, "I have almost finished my conclusion. I can complete it this morning, and probably email it to you early this afternoon"

I replied firmly, "That's what I want, and when I get your conclusion, I will then be able to either agree or disagree with it"

Dale said that he would do that and that we could discuss it in our meeting on Thursday with Jan Weldon (HR – back to work meeting).

Dale then asked how I felt about coming back to work. I replied, "I'm happy to come back to work, but not with Ron Atler as my boss."

Dale replied "Ok" and I left.

Complete nightmare! Dale had just tried to back me into a corner! It was so hard to know what to do – and not just fold like a pack of cards.

Dale gave me excuses and no answers! He was hoping that I would help him sweep it under the carpet. That I would return to work and that his mate Ron Atler would just carry on as normal (and have it in for me and make my life hell).

I received an email from Dale Rolland at dinnertime saying that he hoped to send his conclusion in the early part of next week.

Next week! NOT happy!

Dale Rolland has not taken this seriously at all. He assured me that he would send me the conclusion in an email at dinnertime; instead, he has sent no conclusion and said that it will hopefully be next week.

He must have been confident that I would just 'roll over' and accept him turning a Formal Grievance into an informal chat!

So, another very anxious weekend to get through and still none the wiser.

<u>27/3/12</u>

I received two letters in the post from college today.

The first one I opened was from the Principle of Kirklees College. He wrote:

Dear Janette,

I would like to congratulate you on achieving a Grade 1 for Excellence in Teaching and Learning.

To formally recognise your achievement, I would be honoured if you would join me and other achievers at one of our lunchtime award presentations to receive your certificate and allow me to express my appreciation for all you are doing for the College.

There are three scheduled events, two at the Huddersfield centre and one at the Dewsbury centre. An invitation with all the details for these is enclosed.

Please confirm your attendance and the event date most appropriate for you on extension 7397.

Could you also indicate whether you are happy or not for your name and/or photograph to be used for marketing and publicity purposes. Also, please make us aware of any dietary requirements.

I look forward to seeing you at one of the events.

Yours Truly,

Paul McKant

I could not believe what I was reading. Was there no communication in the college? He wants to express his appreciation for all I am doing for the College, whilst his managers are causing me such anguish and stress!!

You couldn't make it up.

The second letter was from Dale Rolland. It read:

Dear Janette,

Stage 1 Grievance

Further to the recent grievance which I heard under the formal procedure at Stage 1 on 24th February 2012, I am now writing to inform you of the outcome of my investigations to date.

Your grievance was centred around allegations relating to Ron's behaviour and management style, specifically that:

- *He is not operating in a way that is conducive to a happy working environment*
- *There is a perception in the team that people are afraid to voice their opinion*
- *He doesn't always listen to the concerns of staff or take on board other people's opinions*
- *At times he behaves in a bullying, undermining and intimidating manner*
- *Has acted in a belittling and undermining way (example of email)*
- *Is often non-communicative*
- *Doesn't always deal with issues in a confidential manner*

We discussed in the meeting that I would speak to other members of the team to ascertain their views of Ron's behaviour. My investigation has revealed that several of your colleagues share similar concerns about Ron's behaviour and I will, therefore, need to deal with this on a more formal level.

Yours Sincerely

Dale Rolland

Head of Construction

So, over a month later, Dale Rolland is telling me that several of my colleagues share similar concerns (you don't say!), and so he needs to deal with it on a more formal level!

I felt it was beyond belief! I was promised an outcome! He knew my colleague's views a month ago and he knew that it was a **Formal** grievance. He should be following the grievance procedure? It's the College's procedure, not mine; what's the point of having one if they're not going to adhere to it?

He thought he could resolve it to his and his mates (Ron Atler's) satisfaction – and not mine. It seems that birds of a feather do stick together. Goodness knows what he's going to do now. Are he and Ron hatching a plan right now and are they at all worried? – and will Dale have to forget his close friendship with Ron??

I have to attend a 'back to work meeting' in two days'. I'm not looking forward to that. They are so keen to discuss me returning to work – but don't seem to be so keen to resolve my grievance; even though I have given them eleven and a half years of 100% work commitment.

29/3/12

Another nerve-racking day ahead, as I need to attend a 'back to work meeting' at Brunel House with Dale Rolland and Jan Weldon (from HR).

Back to Work Meeting

Jan did most of the talking during the meeting.

We discussed my coming back to work, and it was decided that I would return after Easter, on the 16th of April, and that I would spend the first two weeks at Brunel House. I would then return to the Electrical Section on week three (30/4/12).

I stated that I did not want to see Ron Atler; that I would feel uncomfortable every time I was required to walk past his office to leave the staffroom, to teach or go to the toilet.

I told them that I thought that my grievance should have been dealt with by now. I explained that still not knowing the outcome of my grievance (after all this time), was harming my health; I still couldn't sleep and I was anxious all the time.

Neither Dale nor Jan seemed bothered by this statement.

Jan said that at the beginning when I returned to work, Dale would be my line manager and do my next PDR, which was imminent – but in the longer term, I would have to re-establish a working relationship with Ron Atler, as eventually, Ron would go back to being my line manager.

I was unhappy about this but did not make any comments. I didn't see how this could be so certain when my grievance had not yet been addressed.

I asked Dale if he was taking the full two weeks off for Easter. Dale replied that he was, so I said, 'So if I don't get the conclusion to my Grievance tomorrow, I will have to wait for another two weeks.' Dale replied that he was seeking guidance from Joan in HR on the matter and that he had a 'tender' to deal with, and so he didn't think that he would have time to finish his conclusion to my Grievance before Easter!

During the meeting, I mentioned my grievance at least five times and stated that I was disappointed that I still didn't have an outcome. No response from either of them! Dale seemed quite distracted during the meeting. He left the room at one point and I took this opportunity to begin telling Jan that I had been kept waiting too long for the outcome of my grievance and that I didn't think it was acceptable. Jen started to reply but then Dale walked back in, so we stopped talking.

I left the meeting feeling seriously disappointed that I had agreed to come back to work, but that they didn't seem obliged to complete my Grievance - when I had made it clear that it was affecting my health, and that I wanted it resolving before returning to work.

Later that day I received an email from Jan Weldon about the 'back to work' meeting. She stated what had been discussed in the meeting (but not about my concerns about my Grievance outcome).

30/3/12

Jan's email has wound me up, so I decided I needed to email her, to make it clear that I was not happy and to get my concerns documented.

From: _janettecastle@hotmail.co.uk_

Sent: 30 March 2012

To: jweldon@kirkleescollege.com

Subject: Yesterday's meeting

Hi Jan,

Thank you for your report on yesterday's meeting. Something that has not been mentioned in your report is that I, on many occasions stated that I was concerned that my grievance had not yet concluded.

To date, I have already been waiting five weeks for a conclusion, add to that the two weeks over Easter when no progress will be made – it will be over seven weeks!

I was promised a conclusion by Dale for dinnertime on 23/3/12, then it was altered until early the following week, and now I am expected to wait for over a further two weeks whilst Dale seeks advice from Human Resources.

Can you assure me that I will have a conclusion in writing during the week commencing 16th April 2012 as

You state the long-term goal is for me to re-establish my working relationship with my current line manager.

I think this statement is a bit premature, as it seems to indicate that the outcome of my grievance has already been decided – and that Ron Atler definitely will remain my line manager.

*This is after, in a letter sent to me by Dale Rolland (26/3/12) where he states that his investigation has revealed that several of my colleagues share similar concerns about Ron's behaviour and that he (Dale) **will, therefore, need to deal with this on a more formal level.***

Regards

Janette

I received a reply from Jan Weldon

From: jweldon@kirkleescollege.com

Sent: 03 April 2012 15:25:01

To: janettecastle@hotmail.co.uk

Subject: Yesterday's meeting

Hi Janette,

Thank you for the points you have raised in your email that were omitted from my original correspondence regarding your concerns about your grievance.

My understanding is that you will be informed of the conclusions of your grievance week commencing 16th April 2012 by Dale. I will contact Dale after Easter to ensure this will be the case.

Regards

Jan

Yippee. I can wait another two weeks for my conclusion! They either can't understand how bad I'm feeling or, they simply don't care; the latter I suspect.

The next two weeks were absolute torture. The stress of knowing that I was returning to work when I had not yet received my conclusion was terrible. Yet again I'm being the conscientious employee – whilst Dale Rolland seems to be unaccountable.

15/4/12

I return to work tomorrow! I am being sent to a different building, where I don't know the staff, (but I assume they all know who I am and that I will be the topic of conversation). At least Tanya Brown and Amy Lamb will be there, so that's a massive plus.

16/4/12

I felt so nervous! I drove down to Brunel House. I sat in the car park and took slow, deep breaths to psych myself up, before walking into reception.

The receptionist gave me a sympathetic, knowing smile and asked me to sit down whilst she informed Dale Rolland I had arrived.

Dale Rolland came out, all friendly and polite. He told me he would take me to where I would be working for the next three weeks. I had assumed that I would be put in a quiet room out of the way somewhere; but no! He took me into the massive staffroom and showed me to a desk and introduced me to a couple of staff.

I just wanted the floor to swallow me up! I could feel everyone's eyes on me (and could imagine the tittle-tattle of 'that's her…').

I sat down, got my stuff out of my bag and tried to get some of my preparation done.

A little later Tanya and Amy came in. Tanya came across and gave me a big hug, and it was a relief to see them. They started asking me if I'd got my conclusion from Dale Rolland yet and I told them 'No'. They were shaking their heads in disbelief.

At about 11 am, Dale Rolland walked up to me, handed me a letter and then just walked away. I opened the letter and read it about three to four times. I couldn't understand that this could be the conclusion, as it didn't seem formal, and it seemed to me, to be completely contradictory:

16 April 2012

PERSONAL

Janette Castle

(My address)

Dear Janette,

I have investigated the concerns that you have stated in your grievance. Here are my conclusions:

Management style not conclusive to a happy working environment – Upheld

It is apparent from the investigation that at times the management style of your line manager proves uncommunicative and unpredictable. There is evidence to suggest there is an inconsistent approach and at times they can display defensive behaviour.

Bullying, undermining and intimidation behaviour – Not upheld

There is some evidence to suggest some team members find their line manager behaving in an intimidating and undermining way, in particular when they may disagree with what has been said, and that as a team, you are often referred to as being negative if you propose any ideas that are in contrast to their own. It is apparent that some members of staff feel their line manager is unapproachable and difficult.

There is a common theme from team members that the line manager is unable to take on board alternative points of view and this often leads to a negative working environment.

However, there are other members of the team that do not fully uphold this behaviour but do acknowledge that there are times when your line manager can come across as a bit forceful and unpredictable, on the whole, they do not feel *they display this behaviour. There is evidence that they can be direct but is reasonable and very accommodating.*

There are elements of the line managers behaviour which relying on the evidence is unacceptable and their behaviour is intrinsically linked to their management style and with bullying, we would look at consistent, regular patterns of behaviour – some of the staff allude to them being 'Jekyll and Hyde' and inconsistent in their behaviour which could therefore potentially indicate that the behaviour is not wholly consistent.

Poor communication – Upheld

There is evidence to suggest that overall, there is poor communication with the team and what is communicated can be very defensive and is unwilling to take on board different points of view. There is evidence to support that the line manager does not always act in this manner, it can depend on the issue.

Confidentiality – Not upheld

The findings suggest that on the whole team members do feel that their line manager upholds confidence.

Treating everyone the same – Upheld

Looking at the information gathered the evidence suggests that their line manager does not treat all staff the same and there are favourites.

Bullying of students – Not upheld

From the investigation, there is no substantial evidence to support this statement.

Where issues have been identified they will be dealt with under appropriate management procedures.

Yours Sincerely

Dale Rolland

I didn't know what to do! The letter seemed to indicate that nothing serious was going to happen and that most of my claims had been dismissed.

After about twenty minutes I decided that I needed to go and see Dale Rolland and clarify if the letter meant that Ron Atler would remain my boss. I walked down to his office and when I got there I asked Dale, "Does this mean that Ron Atler will still be my boss?"

Dale Rolland started to explain that he (DR) would be my line manager in the interim period, but that yes, Ron Atler would later become my line manager again.

I started to get tearful and got up to leave his office. Dale asked me if I wanted a drink of water, but I declined and walked out.

Amy Lamb was in the classroom across from Dale Rolland's office (luckily, she was alone). I went in, closed the door and started trying to tell Amy that I'd had my conclusion and that Ron Atler was still going to be my boss.

I was crying by now. I couldn't speak properly and then suddenly started having a panic attack! I don't think Amy knew what to do. Luckily for her, I eventually got to the point where I began breathing more normally again, but I was crying, sweating and shaking all over.

Amy said, "You shouldn't have come back to work, look at you. You're a mess, you're not ready".

I replied, "I just want to do the right thing", to which Amy responded, "College isn't doing the right thing by you and you should go home."

I didn't know what to do. I had only been back at work for three and a half hours!'

Amy suggested that I telephoned Robert, so I went outside into my car and rang him. I was a sobbing mess and he said he would come across to me (he only works down the road from Brunel House).

Robert turned up about five minutes later. I went to his car and showed him my conclusion letter. After reading it he said he thought it was 'a load of crap and not professionally done at all'.

I don't think he knew what to suggest and left a little later after I said that I was going to go home.

I went back inside, and Amy said she would go into the staffroom and get my belongings. I then went to see Dale Rolland again and told him that I'd had a panic attack and that I would have to go home. He said "OK" and I left.

I went home feeling weak and useless. I hadn't even managed half a day at work – but Dale Rolland's conclusion had completely dumbfounded me!

I was tearful and stressed for the rest of the day and I felt physically sick.

I kept reading the conclusion letter, through all the contradictions, and wondering how anyone could be classed as intimidating, but not a bully? Surely, it's the same thing?

I spent another sleepless night wondering what I was going to do!

17/4/12

I got up feeling sick, upset and still tearful. I also felt frustrated as I had wanted to go back to work. I knew I couldn't go into work today as I couldn't stop crying, so I decided to send Dale Rolland an email. In the email, I told him that I wasn't well enough to go into work today and asked if I could go in on Wednesday and 'try again'.

Dale responded that that was fine and that he would see me on Wednesday.

18/4/12

I went to work feeling embarrassed as everyone must have known that I had gone home on Monday. I kept my head down and prepared some power points and handouts for when I was due to return to teaching in two and a half weeks.

As I was working away, I made the decision that I needed to move to Stage 2 of the Grievance procedure as there was no way I could accept Dale Rolland's conclusion.

CHAPTER 3

I went home and read through the Grievance Procedure and the Grievance form that I had to fill out for Stage 2.

I filled out the grievance form and attached it to the following email:

From: janettecastle@hotmail.co.uk

Sent: 18 April 2012 20:18:23

To: jturrand@kirkleescollege.com jweldon@kirkleescollege.com

Subject: Stage 2 of Grievance Procedure

4 attachments

Hi Jean,

My name is Janette Castle and I am a lecturer in the Electrical Installation section.

I have recently been absent from work due to Work-Related-Stress and put in a formal complaint about my line manager Ron Atler.

I am not satisfied with the outcome of Stage 1 of the Grievance procedure and therefore wish to move to Stage 2, where I believe you will be involved.

I have attached Appendix 2 of the College's Employee Grievance Form.

I look forward to hearing from you.

Regards

Janette

I felt sick as I pressed the send button. The thought of having to start the process all over again was nerve-racking. Jean Turrand is the new Director over the Construction Section. Surely it will be taken more seriously now it's at Director's level?

19/4/12

I went into work feeling extra stressed, waiting to see if I was going to get 'pounced on' by Dale Rolland or Jean Turrand. I checked my emails and was surprised to see that Jean Turrand had responded to my email the previous evening at 21:03 pm

From: jturrand@kirkleescollege.com

Sent: 18 April 2012 21:03:11

To: janettecastle@hotmail.co.uk

Subject: RE: Stage 2 of the Grievance Procedure

Hi Janette,

I just wanted to confirm that I have received your email, I will get back to you in more detail once I have discussed with HR.

Kind Regards

Jean Turrand

So, the ball was in motion again – or so I thought……

I kept checking my emails throughout the day, the next day, next week and so on…..and heard nothing more!

The stress levels were ramped up even higher. I couldn't understand why I was being ignored again. I was trying to do the right thing by going back to work and they didn't give a second thought to my health and wellbeing.

I had expected that the Grievance would now be dealt with in a more professionally. Jean Turrand is a Director for one of the biggest further education Colleges in England for goodness sake! Surely, she will follow the Grievance Procedure?

The Grievance Procedure states in 4.3.2 *'A panel will convene to hear the Grievance within 10 working days of receipt of the Grievance form'.*

The 10 working days came and went. I felt like I was losing my mind!

After three weeks working down at Brunel House, I knew that I was due to return to the Electrical Section in the main Kirklees College building (where Ron Atler would be) and begin teaching again.

I would have to face Ron Atler – who knew I had escalated my Grievance to Stage 2. I would have to walk past his office every time I came in and out of the staffroom. I would come face to face with him every day!

I wondered why Jean Turrand was keeping me in the dark - was she trying to 'break me' and make me give up?

30/4/12

I went back to work in the Electrical Section. Very stressful! I tried to appear chilled and relaxed and went and taught my first class before Ron Atler arrived in the section.

During morning break Ron Atler came into the staffroom and said, 'Good to have you back Janette'. I just kind of grunted a response. My back was towards him and I didn't turn around.

Kay, Judith, Julian, Andrew, all the plumbers and the technicians Phil and Paul were very supportive. It was very difficult, as I was back to teaching my students, but I couldn't tell them why I had been off for the past four months (as I wanted to remain professional).

I managed to get through the first week back teaching, but by the end of the week I felt completely exhausted – I think because I had been trying to put on a brave face and make out that I was OK when I was crumbling inside.

Jean Turrand still has not got back to me, and when I finished work on Friday, I decided that enough was enough. She is now not following the Grievance Procedure herself, and she is a Director of the College. Her deadline has passed, and my patience has run out.

I sent her an email when I got home.

From: *janettecastle@hotmail.co.uk*

Sent: 04 May 2012 16:40:54

To *jturrand@kirklescollege.com*
janweldon@kirkleescollege.com

Subject: Grievance Procedure

Hi Jean,

I am concerned that Kirklees College is not following the Grievance Procedure.

It was not followed by Dale Rolland at Stage 1.

It has not been followed at Stage 2, as I still haven't been given a date for Stage 2 to begin after I gave you notification on 18/4/12 that I was not satisfied with Stage 1 and wished to move to Stage 2.

As you know I have been off work due to Work-Related-Stress. The length of time this grievance is taking is causing me further stress and I can feel my health deteriorating again.

Can you please give me a date when Stage 2 of the grievance procedure will officially begin?

I have sought legal advice, and they have informed me that I can bring anyone I wish to meetings as my witness if I give you 24 hours' notice of who my witness is.

Regards

Janette

So now I have another stressful weekend to get through wondering what response I will get to my email.

7/5/12

I went into work feeling very depressed and despondent. I didn't know what to do. Nobody at work could believe that college was ignoring my request to have Stage 2 of the Grievance heard.

I checked my emails that evening and found that Jan Weldon had responded at 4.55 pm (just so I could stress for another day – or because she didn't know how to respond??)

From: jweldon@kirkleescollege.com

Sent: 08 May 2012 16:55:34

To: janettecastle@hotmail.co.uk

Cc: jturrand@kirkleescollege.com

Subject: RE: Grievance procedure

Hi Janette,

Thank you for your email. Please see responses below concerning the points you've raised:

- *I am unclear as to why you feel Dale has not followed the grievance procedure at stage one so could I suggest that this is discussed during an informal meeting with myself and Jean tomorrow?*
- *In terms of not confirming a date in line with stage two of the grievance, I thought it more appropriate to arrange following the informal meeting with Jean and myself, as following this meeting we aim to have a clearer picture of your specific reasons for escalating your grievance to the next stage, so we can ensure whoever is appointed to hear your grievance is fully aware of all the information. I would like to reassure you that date of stage two grievance will be confirmed asap following tomorrow's meeting*
- *In terms of bringing any witnesses to the hearing, you do have a right to do so – however in line with college policy (see attached – Appendix 1), you are requested*

to give us at least five working days' notice of anyone you wish to call as a witness

I look forward to seeing you at the meeting tomorrow.

Kind Regards

Jan

How could they not understand why I think Dale Rolland didn't follow the Grievance Procedure!!!

And now they want an **informal** meeting about the **formal grievance procedure** they are supposed to be following!!!

Kirklees College is one of the largest Colleges in the UK. It is hardly a small company that has just set up and doesn't understand Employment Rights. Unbelievable!!!

9/5/12

Exceptionally stressed! I had felt better before returning to work and had believed that once I took my grievance to Stage 2, I would be taken seriously and treated professionally, but today I just felt like a complete wreck.

At 10.30 am I went to my 'informal meeting' with Jean Turrand and Jan Weldon. I took Judith Hamilton with me for support and to take notes.

I had become really worked up and anxious again over the last few days and couldn't understand why I had to attend this informal meeting when I wanted Stage 2 grievance to begin. I felt unable to cope and started crying as soon as Jean Turrand arrived at 10.30 am.

We had the meeting and I managed to answer most of their questions.

Jan Weldon asked me why I thought that Dale Rolland hadn't followed the grievance procedure. I replied that the grievance procedure stated that I should have received a written conclusion within five working days and it had taken seven weeks.

Jan then asked why I was not satisfied with the outcome of Stage 1 of the Grievance Procedure. I asked Jan if she had read Dale Rollands' report. Jan replied that she had read his letter.

I told her that I had made accusations and that Dale Rolland had investigated them; the investigation had proved that my accusations were correct, and yet nothing was being done about it.

I told them that I didn't think I was being taken seriously. That I had an unblemished eleven and a half year career with the college, and that I was suddenly off work due to Work-Related Stress. I said that I thought that because of my impeccable work record, the college would have investigated the situation quickly and taken it seriously.

I then complained that I was now back working in the same environment as Ron Atler and that I didn't think that was fair. I stated that in other organisations if accusations of this nature had been made, that the perpetrator would have been given 'garden leave' until the investigations were complete.

Both Jean and Jan started to suggest ways where I would be more comfortable at work (ie going back to Brunel House). I said that this wouldn't be suitable as I needed to be where my students were, to be able to teach them.

I told them that I hadn't slept for days and that I couldn't function properly.

Jean started making excuses for the reason I hadn't been able to start Stage 2 of the Grievance Procedure within the correct time scale as she had wanted to introduce herself to me as she was new to the section.

Jan Weldon was backing this up by saying they thought I would feel more comfortable if I had been introduced previously. They both repeated that they also wanted to find out the reasons for me not being satisfied with Stage 1 of the procedure.

I felt these were all excuses and that they were 'backtracking'. They confirmed that I could take any witness I liked to any further meetings. Jan Weldon told me I would have to give the college five days' notice (of my witness).

I replied that legally it was 24 hours' notice. Jean Turrand said 'Yes, she thought 24 hours' notice was correct' and then Jan Weldon said, 'Just give us whatever notice you can'.

Jan Weldon then said that they would get a date to me today for when Stage 2 of the Grievance Procedure would begin.

I was too upset to continue at work after the meeting, so I went home and made a doctors' appointment. I sent an email to Jen Walden when I got home:

From: janettecastle@hotmail.co.uk

Sent: 09 May 2012 14:17:40

To: jweldon@kirkleescollege.com
jturrand@kirkleescollege.com

Subject: This morning's meeting

Hi Jan,

As you know I was very upset at this morning's meeting. I did not feel able to continue at work today, so I am contacting you to let you know that I have come home.

Before I returned to work, I was feeling a lot better and felt that I had regained my strength. I thought I would be able to cope with my job as I had done before my absence, but unfortunately, this has not been the case.

The length of time my grievance has taken and the fact that I am now in the same environment as the person who made me ill in the first place has been detrimental to my recovery.

I am back to not sleeping and feeling anxious. The lack of sleep and feeling continually stressed is making it impossible to function as I did before my time off work.

I have telephoned the doctors, but there are no available appointments today, so I have been asked to telephone to make one tomorrow.

I will inform you tomorrow of the outcome.

Regards

Janette

10/5/12

Back off work! I tried! I have worked for twenty-six years. I have never felt like this before. I am a grafter and I want to work, but they are making it impossible for me.

When Robert saw the state of me last night, he started looking on the internet about legal advice for issues at work. He found a place that advertised giving free advice on Wednesday evenings between 6 pm and 8 pm at Beeston. I have written down the address and phone number and Robert has suggested I go tomorrow to see if they can advise me. Robert is in management and says he believes that how college is behaving is making him believe that college management is going to stick together (against me).

I don't see how this can be right when I haven't done anything wrong and am the victim, but Robert has experience in management and has perhaps seen the other side?

11/5/12

I went to Beeston to the free legal advice center. I made sure I was there half an hour early so that I was the first person to be seen. The female solicitor I saw made a brief file about my 'problem,' so they could keep track of it if I went to further sessions. I showed her my conclusion letter for Stage 1 of the Grievance and she immediately said that 'intimidation' and 'bullying' were the same thing and that they couldn't claim he (Ron Atler) was one and not the other. This made me feel so much better - for a person with an understanding of the law to confirm my own belief and it gave me some confidence. I then showed her the Grievance Procedure timescales which College didn't follow and told them that I wasn't in the Union so I had been to the Stage 1 meetings on my own. The solicitor told me that College should have followed their Grievance Procedure. She told me to make sure I documented every meeting, kept all documentation sent from college and that I needed to take a witness to every meeting, and that the witness could be anyone; not just a union representative.

I drove home feeling a bit better. I had always known that I was in the 'right'. I also knew that Kirklees College was treating me badly, but didn't know if I could do anything about it. The solicitor gave me the confidence to keep going.

12/5/12

I finally received a letter to say that my Stage 2 Hearing would be on the 18th of May. So, another week to stress about that (and a full months' wait since I informed them (college) that I wanted to move to Stage 2).

I prepared for my Stage 2 Grievance Hearing. I typed up everything that I wanted to discuss and put it in a folder with all other evidence that I felt I may need. I feel I need everything written down, as I know that if I 'fall apart' on the day of the hearing, my mind might go 'blank' and I won't know what to say. As I was typing I looked down at my right wrist and noticed that my eczema which had started as a small patch, had enlarged considerably and was working its way up my wrist, all red and angry.

15/4/12

I am feeling seriously stressed about my Grievance Hearing in a few days from now. I woke up this morning to a nervous twitch in my right eye. I can feel it twitching, but when I look in the mirror, I can't see it twitching. Strange – and no doubt another symptom of the stress that my (not so nice employers) are putting me through.

18/5/12

I felt sick with worry. I drove to college and met Judith Hamilton. I had asked Judith to take minutes of the meeting for me, so I got a full accurate account of everything College said at the meeting (Judith does shorthand - so won't miss anything).

Present at the meeting were Alan Wiley (Chair – and another Director), Jean Turrand and Linda Anison (H.R)

I felt that I handled myself quite well under the circumstances. I was tearful at times and felt shaky, but I managed to keep going.

I found Alan Wiley to be very dominant. I felt he was trying to resolve issues (to Kirklees College's best interests) by trying to insist that Stage 1 had been investigated and that procedures had been put in place to improve Ron Atler's management style. He was trying to make me accept and agree to things 'there and then,' but I managed to 'stick to my guns' insisting that the 'investigation' at Stage 1, and the conclusion were flawed and that my claims needed to be investigated properly.

I think he found it frustrating that I wouldn't 'roll over' but I think the fact that he could see that Judith was taking copious notes about every word spoken in the meeting, made him realise that I was deadly serious and that he had to be seen to be impartial and to follow the Grievance Procedure. I also told them at the meeting that I had sought legal advice, and I think this may have helped his decision to agree to another investigation of my claims being carried out.

I left the meeting feeling drained but happy that I had been listened to.

21/5/12

I received a letter from Linda Anison in HR:

Strictly Private and Confidential

Dear Janette,

I am writing to confirm the decision of the panel who met on Friday 18th May 2012 to hear your appeal at Stage 2 of the grievance procedure.

The appeal was heard by a panel consisting of:

Alan Wiley (Chair) - Director of MIS, IT and Risk Management
Jean Turrand – Director of Higher Education, Development and Innovation
Linda Anison – HR advisor

At the appeal meeting, you were given the opportunity to outline the nature of the issues in your own words and to state why you disagreed with the Stage 1 outcome. You clearly stated the nature of your initial complaint, the circumstances surrounding the behaviours in question and, also the areas you wished to challenge from the Stage 1 report.

It was made clear during your account, that your main reasons for not feeling the grievance has been resolved to your satisfaction at Stage 1 are:

- *Issues that were not upheld at Stage 1 of the grievance, which you feel should have been upheld. In particular, point 3 of your grievance, which was concerning your Line Manager displaying bullying, undermining and intimidating behaviour*
- *A lack of confidence in the way in which the investigation was concluded.*

- *Concern regarding the length of time taken, following you submitting your grievance*

Discussions were held regarding what actions the college has taken to address the points which were upheld at Stage 1 of your grievance. These include further support and training for your line manager, to work towards making positive changes to his attitude and behaviour, which you outlined as potential outcomes to the grievance. As we further discussed, there needs to be a period of time to measure if the support put in place has been successful.

To try and satisfactorily resolve your grievance, the panel has carefully considered the case previously heard at Stage 1 of the procedure, and the points highlighted by yourself during the Stage 2 hearing.

Following the meeting, considering the information provided the panel has concluded that the following actions need to be taken forward before the panel is in a position to present their findings:

- *Commission a thorough investigation, in line with the Colleges' investigation procedure – paying particular attention to allegations of bullying, undermining and intimidating behaviour*
- *Seek clarification regarding timescales following submission of your original grievance*

I will ensure that you are kept up to date in terms of timescales of the investigation and will communicate our findings once the investigation has been concluded.

Thank you for attending the meeting, I appreciate it was a difficult situation for you to be in.

Yours Sincerely

Linda Anison

HR Advisor

So, Linda has promised that she will keep me up to date with a timescale of the investigation and conclusion – I would hope so; now that it is being dealt with by two Directors of the college!

I've had a few phone calls from people at work. John, Kay, Tanya and, Andrew were happy that it sounded like it might be taken seriously now, although John and Andrew were concerned that Ron Atler was behaving as unpredictable as ever and that James Tebb was 'wiz-whazing' with Ron. Andrew told me that Ron Atler and Dale Rolland spent a lot of time together in Ron's office and James is invited in – but the door is closed to everyone else.

<u>27/5/12</u>

I received a letter from someone else in HR:

25 May 2012

PRIVATE AND CONFIDENTIAL

Dear Miss Castle,

<u>**Re: Management Investigation at Kirklees College**</u>

I am writing regarding an on-going management investigation at Kirklees College. As part of the investigation, we would like to meet with you to ask you some questions.

*An investigation meeting has been scheduled for **Monday 11th June 2012 at 2:00 pm**. Please report to the HR Office (F135) at the Huddersfield Centre in the first instance.*

The meeting will be conducted by an independent Investigating Officer (Jane Davis – Childcare Support Manager). I will be the HR representative present at the meeting to act in an advisory role capacity.

Should you wish to be accompanied at this meeting we would appreciate it if you could notify us in advance of who this will be.

Yours Sincerely

Karen Watkins

My Stage 2 Grievance meeting was on 18th May and I have to wait until the 11th of June for my investigation meeting. That's over three weeks – so they still aren't following the Grievance procedure time scale!!!!

More torture! I feel even more exhausted as I have now not been sleeping for over five months. I wouldn't have believed that it was possible to survive without sleeping if I wasn't going through it right now. I don't know how long I can go without sleeping though? I toss and turn in bed and then end up getting up, going downstairs and laying on the settee so as not to disrupt Robert's sleep. The nights feel so long. It's so much worse in the dark; alone with my thoughts. Some nights I am pulling my hair (I'm surprised I've got any left).

Doctor Mattins is being very supportive. I keep him informed of my (lack of) progress with college. He seems confused as to why they are 'stringing it out'. He has given me some stronger sleeping tablets, but these, unfortunately, don't work either. I told him about my twitchy eye and he said it would be because of the stress I'm under.

Doctor Mattins keeps trying to encourage me to go for counseling and to take anti-depressants. I have politely refused the anti-depressants in case they slow down my brain even more than the lack of sleep already is. I feel like I need to keep my wits about me (whatever's left of them anyway) for the meetings I need to attend college.

<u>11/6/12</u>

The investigation day has arrived, and I have asked Judith Hamilton to be my witness and take notes again.

I felt extremely nervous, but at least the investigating officer Jane Davis seemed friendly and impartial/professional.

The meeting went on for over an hour. Jane explained that the main four items she wanted me to explain were about me stating that Ron Atler was unprofessional, undermining, intimidating and bullying. She went through them one by one and I answered why I felt Ron has all these traits. I gave her examples of things he had done and said, to prove my claims. Karen (from HR) was taking notes (and so was Judith for me).

Jane then asked me why I had stated that Kirklees College had not followed the grievance procedure so far. I was prepared and had everything written down, so I was able to look at my notes to give them the dates I had initiated the Grievance Procedure and my conclusion date. Jane seemed quite surprised that I had had to wait ten and a half weeks for Stage 1 to conclude when the grievance procedure states it should be ten working days from start to finish.

I told her I had initiated Stage 2 on the 18th of April and that was almost two months ago, so it should have been started and concluded weeks ago.

Jane Davis ended the meeting by informing me that she would send me Karen's notes to my home address as soon as possible. She said I should read through the notes and sign them to say I agreed that this was a true account of the investigation meeting. The rest of my work colleagues would do the same with their notes, and then the Stage 2 Grievance Panel would make their decision based on everyone's investigation notes.

I agreed that this seemed fair. Jane then thanked me for attending the meeting and assured me that they had received many positive comments (about me) from my work colleagues during their interviews.

So, I have been promised my notes back to read, sign and send back by the end of next week. I was the last person to be interviewed so I should get my conclusion by the end of June – not following the Grievance Procedure still; but if I get the right outcome (Ron Atler sacked or demoted), then it will have been worth all the stress.

16/6/12

Andrew Smithy telephoned me to tell me that yesterday, Ron Atler asked Andrew to go into his office. Andrew said that as soon as he was in the office that Ron started saying "What have you said about me to HR?" (regarding his investigation meeting). Andrew said that Ron was very aggressive and that his face was purple with rage! Andrew said they ended up having a heated argument, and that

Ron was shouting at him! Ron finished the meeting by saying that he would now have a weekly meeting with him to make sure that Andrew was happy?

Andrew was particularly cross as he has been miss-quoted regarding what he had said in the investigation meeting (from what Ron said to him).

Andrew told me that he had emailed HR about the incident to ask how it could have occurred. During his investigation meeting on 11/6/12, he asked Karen Watkins and Jane Davis for reassurance that everything he said would be confidential and was assured that it would be. How then could Ron have been informed about what had been said in the meeting? Andrew has not yet received a reply from HR.

18/6/12

John Forrest and Steve Clay rung me to say that work is going from bad to worse! Ron Atler's behaviour is more intimidating than ever and he seems to know everything that was said in their 'confidential' interviews. Both John and Steve say that no one in the section has received their interview notes back yet. I haven't received mine either. Jane Davis came across as professional, so I am both surprised and disappointed.

I feel guilty about my colleagues and friends at work. I started my grievance as I believed it would work out better for the whole of the section – BUT it seems my Grievance is making it worse for everyone else in the section!

19/6/12

Andrew telephoned me to tell me that he had received a reply email from HR and that he would forward it to me. He also said he thought I should know that I didn't have a timetable for September, but that everyone else in the section did!!! Andrew said that he had more teaching on his timetable than he should have and that Ron Atler told him that this is because he didn't know if I would be returning to college!

I am 'pig sick' of this! This is more proof that the Grievance Procedure is not being followed as no information should have gone to Ron yet. I was told at my 'confidential' investigation meeting that after everyone in the section had sent their interview notes back signed to the Panel, they would then decide the outcome. If the Panel decided that action needed to be taken against Ron Atler ONLY THEN, would he see the nature of the things discussed at the interview meetings?

It seems that I have been disregarded as a lecturer in the Electrical Section; that they don't expect me to return, and that can only mean that the outcome of my grievance must be in favour of Ron and not me.

Anyway, Andrew has forwarded me emails between himself and HR about a lack of confidentiality throughout the investigation procedure. I have printed them off and put them in my ever-expanding evidence folder:

From: asmithy@kirkleescollege.com

Sent: 18 June 2012 08:11

To: kwatkins@kirkleescollege.com

Subject: Management Investigation

Hi Karen,

I was interviewed on 11th June over a matter relating to management in the electrical section.

At this interview, I expressed concerns about the investigation procedure and received several assurances. You assured me and the other interviewees that we would have a chance to see our interview notes and agree with what we said at the interview meetings before this information was passed on to anyone else.

On Friday 15th June I was called into Ron Atler's office. He asked me questions that confirmed that he had already seen these comments.

To cap it all I had been misquoted.

I would appreciate a written reply which includes a copy of the college procedure which applies to this type of investigation.

Regards

Andrew

From: kwatkins@kirkleescollege.com

Sent: 18 June 2012 11:11

To: asmithy@kirkleescollege.com

Cc jdavis@kirkleescollege.com

Subject: Management Investigation

Dear Andrew,

I can assure you that no one has seen any information from the interview on 11th June. As we stated in the interview, I *will be writing up my notes and sending them to you to sign, once you do you are welcome to contact me if you feel there's any discrepancy between the notes and what you believe was said in the meeting. Please do let me know what comments have been made to lead you to believe that the notes have been seen.*

I'm attaching a copy of the grievance procedure.

I hope this helps

Best Regards

Karen

From: asmithy@kirkleescollege.com

Sent: 18 June 2012 11:32

To: kwatkins@kirkleescollege.com

Subject: Management Investigation

Dear Karen,

The main point Ron raised with me on Friday was the arrangements for my NVQ. As I had explained, both he and Dale Rolland had told me at the interview that time would be found for me to do my NVQ during the working week.

The conversation last Friday started like this....

RA 'Can you come into my office please Andrew'

RA 'Why have you told HR that I expected you to do your NVQ over summer without any pay?'

This could only have come out of our conversation on Monday 11th June.

Furthermore, it was misquoted because I told you he expected me to do it in my own time (not without any pay).

I don't know if the information was **intentionally** passed on to Ron who then **accidentally** let the cat out of the bag or

If the information was **accidentally** passed to Ron who then **unknowingly** let the cat out of the bag.

Either way, it is an indisputable fact that information from our conversation on Monday has been passed to Ron before I have had a chance to vet it.

Regards

Andrew

From: kwatkins@kirkleescollege.com

Sent:18 June 11:46

To: asmithy@kirkleescpllege.com

Cc: jdavis@kirkleescollege.ac.uk

Subject: Management Investigation

Dear Andrew,

The role of the investigating team is to establish facts, and I can assure you that we did not say to Ron or anyone that you have said this or that, but general questions were posed to Ron regarding training arrangements that he had made for yourself.

I hope this clarifies the matter, however, please do not hesitate to contact me if you have any further questions.

Regards

Karen

Hi Karen,

It is clear that very specific points have been passed on to Ron before they have been vetted. We were all assured this would not happen.

I know you need to check the facts. Before the checking of facts must surely come the checking of accuracy of witness statements by those witnesses.

You ask if I have further questions. I do not. The issue is the same. Why was detailed information passed to Ron before it was checked for accuracy?

Regards

Andrew

Subject: Management investigation

Dear Andrew,

Just to clarify that the investigating team's role is to establish facts, and we do that by asking general questions. I would advise anyone against making assumptions with regards to who said what, as quite often, several people give us the same information / facts.

I hope this helps – if you would like to discuss any of these issues further, I would suggest that a face to face meeting may be more productive.

Best Regards

Karen

Karen knows she has been caught out but won't admit it. Andrew didn't waste any more time on her and instead emailed the Director of HR (Jill Lampson) the following day:

From: asmithy@kirkleescollege.com

Sent 19 June 2012 08:24

To: jlampson@kirkleescollege.com

Subject: Management Investigation

Hi Jill,

Could you please confirm that college procedures have been followed in this instance?

Thank you in anticipation

Regards

Andrew

Well the Director of HR knows what's going on now, but will she care – or will she stick with the rest of management?

30/6/12

After all those emails I still haven't received my investigation notes – never mind my conclusion! It's over two months since I initiated Stage 2. I did expect to be treated better now it is being dealt with by Directors of the college. I just can't understand it. I am going to the free legal advice center this week again to see if they can advise me.

4/7/12

I went to the free legal advice center again. I saw a different solicitor to last time, but she looked through my 'file' so was 'up to speed' with it. I told her how I had now been kept waiting for over two months for Stage 2 of Grievance and showed her the emails regarding the un-confidential investigation nightmare. I told her that neither I nor my colleagues had received our interview notes back (and showed her the letter from Karen promising me that I should have received them the week after the investigation meeting).

She assured me that I was doing everything right. That I was following procedure and was filing all documentation/emails from college. She said that she couldn't understand why a large college, that had a HR department, wasn't following its Grievance Procedure.

She suggested that I check my home insurance policy to see if I had Legal Insurance with them. She said that if I did, I should contact them and get advice from them also.

When I got home, I got our home insurance policy out and we do have Legal cover, so I may telephone them for advice.

<u>6/7/12</u>

I had another doctor's appointment this morning. Doctor Mattins seemed surprised that Stage 2 hadn't been concluded. I told him about the lack of confidentiality throughout the investigation, that I hadn't even received my interview notes back and about my colleague's (Andrew's) emails. I showed him the paperwork and told him that I had been seeking free legal advice. I told him I was due to go on holiday in two weeks, that it was pre-booked and that I would be informing college. Doctor Mattins said that a holiday would do me good and that I should try to enjoy it and not think about work. He gave me another sicknote.

I scanned my sicknote and sent it as an attachment in an email to HR. I then took the sicknote down to the post office and sent it to college recorded delivery. I have been doing this for the last couple of months. I just don't trust them and wonder if they will start saying that I haven't sent them my sicknotes if I don't have evidence to show that I have. I wouldn't put anything past them after how they are behaving.

I bet Ron and Dale are expecting me to come back to work this month as my wage will go down to half pay now that I have been off for six months. I remember when Ron had undermined an ex plumbing colleague so badly that his health had seriously suffered (about two years previously). They had laughed when he came back when his wage went down by 50%. Unfortunately, his return to work didn't last long before he couldn't take anymore and left his employment with the college.

I'm too ill to work, so I can't go back yet even if my wage goes down to zero. Luckily Robert's working and we have savings for a rainy day (and is this a rainy day!) so we'll manage. I can't believe I haven't worked for six months! I don't think I've had six days off before now and I've worked for twenty-six years.

10/7/12

I still haven't received my investigation notes back. I keep asking myself if I'm going mad? Is this happening? Surely College wouldn't treat me this way after eleven and a half years?

11/7/12

John Forrest telephoned me in a bit of a panic this morning, to say that everyone in the electrical and plumbing department has been sent an email, saying that they needed to attend a meeting the following day to discuss concerns regarding the individual and overall performance of the team!

Jack Booth had immediately gone to find a Union representative, only to find that the Union was now closed over the summer and that there was no one to represent them at such short notice. Surely HR should be aware of this and take it into account when planning their meetings?

Everyone in the section was concerned and worried as present at the meeting were going to be Ron Atler, Dale Rolland and Jill Lampson – who is the Director of HR)!!!!!

Andrew Smithy telephoned me in the afternoon; luckily, he is in a different Union and they are going to be present to represent him.

<u>12/7/12</u>

John Forrest and Andrew Smithy telephoned me after their meetings. They said that the meetings were intimidating and that Jill Lampson was stating that she was there as an impartial person, but that from her comments it was clear that she was on the side of her fellow management. Jill Lampson said to everyone at their separate meetings that these meetings were nothing to do with my Grievance and that the meetings were being held as management was concerned about the performance of individuals, and the team.

Andrew Smithy said that he questioned that the meetings were nothing to do with my grievance/investigation. The people who had said the most negative things about Ron Atler in the investigation meetings seemed to have the toughest performance meetings, with comments such as 'they must shape up or ship out'.

Steve Clay was told this and was also told that there were plenty of people queuing up to do his job and that they would do it for £20,000! Steve was also told that if he didn't have certain tasks in place by September, he would be receiving a disciplinary!

It seemed too much of a coincidence for these performance meetings not to be related to the investigation meetings.

I can't see me getting a positive result from my Grievance after this!

16/7/12

I am due to go on holiday tomorrow for a week. It has been booked for months and I should be looking forward to it (5-star Thompson hotel – adults only), but I'm not excited in the slightest. Just depressed, stressed and exhausted!

I sent HR an email to let them know that I am going on my annual pre-booked weeks holiday (and that I will be uncontactable in case they want to contact me – doubtful?)

17/7/12

I went on holiday still not knowing my Grievance outcome. The hotel was the nicest I've ever stayed at. I managed to feel quite relaxed during the day (I felt free somehow), but I still couldn't sleep on a night for thinking about Ron Atler, Dale Rolland and Kirklees College in general.

24/7/12

I got home from holiday to find two letters from Kirklees College.

One was my investigation notes. Sent out 18/7/12 (5 weeks after the investigation!?!?). They weren't even accurate!

The other letter was my conclusion to Stage 2:

20th July 2012

Strictly private and confidential

Dear Janette

Following your appeal hearing in line with Stage 2 of the college's grievance procedure, which was held on 18th May 2012, a full management investigation was commissioned, into allegations made regarding your line manager displaying bullying, undermining and intimidating behaviour. Also, the panel has sought clarification regarding the timescales, following the submission of your original grievance.

The College does endeavor to deal with grievances on time however the process can be prolonged if further information is to be sought from various sources. The panel does acknowledge that there was a delay in you receiving an outcome of the Stage 1 grievance you submitted and that any delay, as a result of having to obtain all necessary information should have been communicated to you.

The management investigation has now concluded, and the panel reconvened to hear the findings of the investigation on Wednesday 18th July 2012. Therefore, I am now in a position to confirm the panel's decision based on the findings present.

The panel is satisfied that a thorough investigation was concluded in line with the College's investigation procedure. The panel is confident that the necessary personnel was interviewed within the correct setting and that the questions asked during the investigation were relevant, to abstract information regarding the allegations made and to enable conclusions to be drawn from the evidence gathered.

Management style not conducive to a happy working environment/Communication

The panel upholds the allegation, as evidence from the investigation shows your Line Manager can be ineffective in terms of his methods of communication. Evidence suggests that regular team meetings are infrequent and the use of email is often used as a tool for communicating. Also, results from the investigation show that your line manager's management style can be construed as challenging and un-conducive to a happy working atmosphere.

Bullying, undermining and intimidating behaviour

Based on the balance of probabilities on the evidence presented, the panel does not uphold this allegation on the counts of bullying and undermining; but do uphold the allegation on the count of your line manager displaying intimidating behaviour. The evidence presented suggests that your line manager needs to make changes to his behaviour to effectively manage and lead the team.

Lack of maintaining confidentiality

The panel does not uphold this allegation in terms of personal information divulged. The evidence presented shows that where any personal information has been disclosed this has remained confidential. However, the panel upholds this allegation, based on work-related issues. Evidence provided, suggests that on occasions inappropriate discussions regarding work-related issues have taken place.

Treating everyone the same

The panel upholds this allegation as the evidence presented indicates that your line manager is not consistent in his approach to all members of the team and there is a feeling of favouritism amongst the team.

In addition to the findings highlighted above, the investigation has also found:

- *A failed responsibility on the college's behalf to provide support to your line manager*
- *An embedded culture within the team, with evidence suggesting a reluctance amongst the team to be managed*
- *A general negative approach and attitude amongst the team, where examples of underperformance are evident*
- *A reluctance from the team to adapt to new working practices*
- *Falsifying completion dates on students tracking documents, including the recording of student's completion on strike days and where students weren't in college*
- *Staff internally verifying their own work which contravenes all college procedures*
- *A feeling of frustration from your line manager with dealing with the challenges of a negative team, which in some instances has manifested in displays of inappropriate behaviour*

Further Action

I would like to reassure you that the college takes these issues seriously and we acknowledge changes need to be made in terms of your line manager's style and approach to dealing with difficult situations. However, this investigation has highlighted wider issues amongst the team which we feel have been a significant contributing factor, therefore the panel's decision based on the evidence provided is that no formal action will be taken against your line manager.

The panel has made the following decisions:

- *A programme of support to be put in place to enable your line manager to:*

- *Develop their leadership skills*
- *Develop strategies to enable effective communication*
- *Develop strategies to ensure a consistent approach to managing the team*

The support programme identified will be regularly reviewed as, there has to be a period of time, to measure if the support put in place has been successful.

Examples of underperformance and falsifying of college documents to be addressed with individual members of the team and any appropriate action taken

Discussions and training to be provided to all team members, to ensure a clear understanding from the team at all levels relating to teaching and learning standards and individual performances, in line with these standards and expectations,

I trust you feel that your grievance has been thoroughly dealt with fairly and objectively. However, as per College Grievance Procedure, if you do not agree with this outcome, please progress to Stage 3 of the procedure, by notifying the Vice Principal, in writing, within 10 working days of receipt of this letter.

Finally, we are aware you are currently absent from work, and we need to arrange a meeting, to look at planning a successful return to work. Therefore, I have scheduled a meeting following my return to work from annual leave on Wednesday 15th August at 9:00 in F063. If for any reason this is inconvenient, please contact SMT support on ext 7014.

I understand that this has been a difficult time for you and would like to assure you that the college will endeavour to provide any necessary support to ensure you can effectively return to your role and to ensure that the relationship between you and your line manager works effectively for both of you.

Yours Sincerely

Jean Turrand

Director of HE, Development & Innovation

c.c.Alan Wiley, Linda Anison

I felt physically sick after I read this – and felt sick for three days. I just couldn't believe what I had read. I felt like giving up and leaving college!

The false accusations shocked me to the core!

- Underperforming
- Falsifying completion dates on student trackers
- Internally verifying own work
- Inappropriate behaviour

Utter lies! How could they turn it all around and into an assassination of me and my character?

Ron is intimidating, but not a bully? – and is still my line manager!

I brought this grievance. This grievance is about me – but they are discussing the 'team' – not just me personally – which parts are relating to me??

Then the threat that 'appropriate action will be taken'

And then an invite to a 'back to work' meeting!

So, I either return to work or I leave (and I think that's the option that would suit them down to the ground). I have dared to question them, so now they make an example of me and punish me – or I leave.

A win-win situation for them.

They state in the letter that they reconvened on 18th July to make their decision. My investigation notes are dated 18th July also. These notes were supposed to be sent out, signed and then sent back – then the panels' decision made after reading the witness statements.

I telephoned Amy, Tanya, Andrew, John, Steve, Kay and, Judith to check if they had received their interview notes back. None had except Amy and Kay (who had received them – but after the 18th of July)

After three days of feeling sick and distraught, I started trying to 'pick myself back up'.

I must have read and re-read the letter many times. The letter was nonsense, contradictory and proved in black and white that the procedure had not been followed again:

- Timescale – should have been completed in 15 working days – it took 3 months!
- Investigation procedure – not followed – investigation notes not sent out to be checked and signed, only then should the panel reconvene to make their decision
- Investigation not confidential

30/7/12

As for me signing and sending my interview notes back (as Karen has requested me to do). That's not going to happen. I emailed her to that effect:

From: janettecastle@hotmail.co.uk

Sent 30 July 2012 08:54:38

To: kwatkins@kirkleescollege.com

Subject: Interview notes

Hi Karen,

You sent me the interview notes out on 18/7/12 whilst I was on holiday.

I do not understand why it took you over five weeks to type up these notes and send them to me. In the meeting on 11/6/12, you stated that I might have to wait a week for my notes. Judith Hamilton (my representative at the meeting) took notes at the meeting in shorthand and managed to furnish me with a comprehensive, accurate account of the meeting within 48 hours.

After reading your notes on the meeting I find them to be:

1. *Very brief*
2. *Inaccurate in places*

Something else that I find confusing is that in the meeting I was told (and everyone else interviewed also) would receive copies of their interviews for accuracy. Everyone would then sign their interview notes and return them to you. You would then give all the interview notes to The Panel, who would read the notes and then make their decision about Stage 2 of my Grievance.

The interview notes were sent to me by yourself on 18/7/12 and the conclusion to Stage 2 of my Grievance was sent to me by Jean Turrand on 20/7/18 (stating that the panel made their decision on 18/7/12).

The investigation procedure was not followed!

Regards

Janette Castle

From: kwatkins@kirkleescollege.com

Sent: 30 July 2012 09:45:55

To: janettecastle@hotmail.co.uk

Subject: Investigation notes

Dear Janette,

Thank you for your email. I understand that the reason why you were not able to sign and return the notes which were sent to you on 18th July was due to you being away from 20 July until 27 July.

I look forward to receiving the notes once you've had a chance to sign them. Please do note that the notes from the interviews are not meant to be verbatim but are designed to capture key issues discussed in the interview. If for some reason you feel that the notes do not reflect accurately our meeting and that these inaccuracies would have had a bearing on the panel's decision, I'd be happy for you to contact me to discuss this with me.

I can only apologise with regards to the timescale that it took to be written up and assure you that these have been done as soon as it was possible, particularly given the investigating team conducting more than 15 interviews.

Best Regards

Karen

She has ignored the fact that I have pointed out that the investigation procedure was not followed, and still thinks that I am going to sign and send back her inaccurate notes. What would be the point of that?

From: janettecastle@hotmail.co.uk

Sent 30 July 10:16:30

To: kwatkins@kirkleescollege.com

Subject: Interview notes

To Karen,

Thank you for your reply.

As I have already received the conclusion to Stage 2 of my Grievance, I do not see that there is any point in signing your incorrect notes and returning them to you at this time.

Regards

Janette

CHAPTER 4

Stage 3 of Grievance Procedure

<u>31/7/12</u>

I made the decision not to accept what Kirklees College was doing to me.

This meant one of two things:

Option 1 – Leave Kirklees College

Option 2 – Carry on fighting

I decided on Option 2

The Grievance procedure states that I should contact a Vice-Principal of the college to initiate Stage 3 of my Grievance. There are two Vice Principals, so here goes...

From: janettecastle@hotmail.co.uk

Sent: 31 July 2012 07:53:08

To: amitchell@kirkleescollege.com
mrook@kirkleescollege.com

Subject: Stage 3 of the Grievance Procedure

Dear Anthea/Mandy,

My name is Janette Castle and I have been a lecturer in the electrical section for eleven and a half years.

I have been off work due to Work-Related Stress for most of this year. My illness was caused because of the behaviour of my line manager Ron Atler.

I put in a formal grievance about Ron Atler, and I am currently going through the college's Grievance Procedure. I have recently received the outcome of Stage 2.

I am not satisfied with the outcome of Stage 2, and therefore I am writing to inform you that I would like to proceed to Stage 3.

Kind Regards

Janette

I pressed the send button and got the feeling of immense stress and sickness again. I have already gone through 'two rounds and have been knocked down' - now I must go through it all again, but this time with a Vice Principal of Kirklees College.

Andrew Smithy telephoned me to tell me he had just handed his notice in!!!!

He said he had had enough, and that he'd managed to get a job with another college (our nearest rival). He is leaving at the end of August and can't wait to see the back of Ron Atler.

I told him that I had just begun Stage 3 of the Grievance and Andrew said that he would be happy to be my witness. This pleased me, as after what has happened to John, Steve, Jack, etc (threats from management), I don't want to put Judith in a difficult position – so I wasn't going to ask her for Stage 3 (and thought I might have to go alone).

Andrew said that it was such a good feeling, to know that he was leaving the toxic environment that the electrical/plumbing section has become.

3/8/12

I had another Doctor's appointment. I showed Doctor Mattins my Stage 2 conclusion letter with the false accusations, and that they wanted me back at work to take appropriate action!

I told him how I had felt like giving up and walking away, but that I had decided to keep on fighting, and had initiated Stage 3 of the Grievance.

Doctor Mattins couldn't believe how long college had 'strung out' Stage 2, that they had stated that Ron Atler was intimidating, but not a bully and he advised that I took legal advice if I could. He was very sympathetic and gave me another sick note.

I drove over to College after my doctor's appointment. I felt nervous, but I had to pick up my evidence folder that I had handed in at Stage 2 of the grievance as I want to add to it before handing it over again at Stage 3. I went to the HR department. My legs felt like jelly and my breathing felt laboured, but I tried to appear OK when an HR person came to the reception desk. I asked for my evidence folder and Joan Horncastle (the HR manager) must have overheard. She came out and handed me my folder. I walked out and was relieved to get to my car without seeing anyone else from college.

When I got home, I flicked through the folder and noticed that some of my evidence was missing! Someone had removed three pieces of evidence!

What they have failed to realise is that I have a master file of all my evidence, so they may have removed documents of evidence – but I still have another copy.

<u>5/8/12</u>

I received a letter from Anthea Mitchell dated 31st July 2012

Anthea Mitchell, Vice Principal, Curriculum and Quality

31st July 2012

Strictly Private and Confidential

Dear Janette,

Thank you for your email of today's date notifying me that you wish to appeal against the outcome of your grievance which was heard by Alan Wiley and Jean Turrand under Stage 2 of the college's procedure.

A grievance hearing has therefore been set up at Stage 3 and will be heard by myself and Joan Horncastle, HR Manager at 2 pm on Thursday 16th August in room F066.

In advance of the meeting, you will need to forward me:

1. *Your reasoning behind your appeal*
2. *Any new evidence since the earlier decision*

You are, of course, entitled to be accompanied at your Stage 3 hearing by either your trade union representative or a colleague of your choice.

Yours Sincerely

Anthea Mitchell

Vice Principal, Curriculum and Quality

Cc Joan Horncastle

After reading the letter I checked the Grievance Procedure - 4.4.2 of the grievance procedure states that the hearing for Stage 3 should be within 10 working days of college being informed. The date for the hearing has been set for the 16th of August, so it's just slightly over 10 working days – but at least she has informed me straight away.

I started writing the response that I needed to send to Anthea before the meeting. This took me ages as I knew that I was now dealing with someone of considerable intelligence and experience. I kept writing it, adding/altering it until I felt I had got it just right.

Once I was confident that I had covered everything I typed it up and attached it to an email:

From: janettecastle@hotmail.co.uk

Sent: 06 August 2012 17:29:31

To: amitchell@kirkleescollege.com

Subject: My Stage 3 Grievance

1 attachment

Hi Anthea,

In response to your letter dated 31/7/12, I have attached the reasoning behind my appeal and new evidence since the earlier decision.

Kind Regards

Janette

The attachment read:

Dear Anthea,

The reasons behind my appeal against the decision of Stage 2 of my grievance are as follows:

The decision of the grievance was made from evidence gathered at interviews of myself and my colleagues. Having been contacted by several of my colleagues it appears that these interview notes:

- *Have not been sent back to the majority of my colleagues to check and sign that they are true statements of what was discussed in their interviews*
- *The few interviewees who did receive their interview notes back found them to be brief, random, incorrect or 'out of context'*
- *Of the minority of the interviewees who did receive their interview notes back, all received them AFTER the panel reconvened and made their decision on Wednesday 18th July 2012*

This means that the decision that was made did not follow the College's investigation procedure and was made from incomplete, inaccurate, and un-verified sources.

Also, my grievance has not been addressed:

The panel has not upheld bullying – but has upheld the allegation that my line manager displays intimidating behaviour.

I have shown a solicitor my Stage 2 grievance outcome letter, and the solicitor has informed me that bullying and intimidation are the same things, so the bullying allegation should also have been upheld.

I am also told that bullying is still taking place in the plumbing and electrical section.

All the lecturers were given just 24 hours' notice that they needed to attend a meeting on 12th July with Ron Atler, Dale Rolland and Jill Lampson.

I was informed that at these meetings, certain colleagues were told "Either shape up or ship out", "If you think the grass is greener elsewhere then leave" and "We have plenty of people queuing up to do your job and we could pay them £20,000"

These types of comments seem threatening and unprofessional.

All interviewees were told that the meetings were about underperformance issues within the team and nothing to do with my grievance and the comments they had made against Ron Atler in their grievance interviews. That said, it appears that the people who stated the most negative comments against Ron Atler had the most difficult meetings.

Surely if there had been any underperformance issues within the section, these would have surfaced and been addressed during the academic year and not the first week of the summer holidays and just after the grievance interview meetings.

These meetings were called when the union had 'shut down' for the summer period (was this planned?)

Since these very unsettling meetings, some of my colleagues have been threatened with disciplinary action.

I would also like to address the following:

This was my Stage 2 grievance. My grievance was against my line manager. As such, I would have expected the conclusion to address me (and my line manager) only.

Serious allegations have been made against the team, and the letter states that 'appropriate action will be taken against individual members of the team'.

As part of that team, I expect to receive written confirmation if any of these allegations are being made against me.

If any of the allegations are being made against me, I need to know which one(s) and what proof there is to substantiate these claims.

Finally, the College's Grievance Procedure has not been followed at Stage 1 and Stage 2, this means that Kirklees College is in Breach of Contract.

I will discuss my concerns further with you at my Stage 3 hearing on 16th August. My witness on that day will be Andrew Smithy.

Yours Sincerely

Janette Castle

My email is clear and shows that I mean business. I may be down – but I'm not out (yet). Let's see if this Anthea Mitchell woman will take me and my allegations seriously.

<u>7/8/12</u>

I have checked through my evidence folder. I replaced the evidence sheets that whoever from Kirklees College felt they needed to 'destroy'. I also added the conclusion letter I received from Jean Turrand and her 'incompetent crew'.

As I have now completely lost trust in management and HR, I wrapped up the evidence folder in a bin bag and securely tightened it with parcel tape. I stuck a label on the front stating that the only person to open this was Anthea Mitchell.

I then printed out a sheet of paper that I am going to get the person who takes the evidence folder to sign to say that they have received it:

I...have received Janette Castle's evidence folder and will ensure it is safely stored in the Human Resources office and then given to Anthea Mitchell on her return to work Monday 13/8/12

Signed.....................................

Date.......................................

No more trusting Miss Nice Lady from me! I do NOT trust them. They have proved that they are not to be trusted on any level.

I didn't feel comfortable going into College today, so I sent my dad in with the folder.

I then sent an email so that Anthea Mitchell would understand why I had felt the need to seal my evidence folder.

I also think that I need to get everything that happens documented. I have no idea where this 'thing' is going and I want evidence of every underhand trick the College has undertaken.

From: janettecastle@hotmail.com

Sent:07 August 2012 15:38:52

To: amitchell@kirkleescollege.com

Subject: Folder of Evidence

Hi Anthea,

My father has taken my folder of evidence into the Human Resources Department for me this afternoon. Sarah Hume has signed for the folder and is storing it for you until you return from your holidays.

I have sealed the folder in plastic, binding it tightly with parcel tape and affixed a notice to it stating that only you are to open it.

The reason why I felt I had to go to this trouble was that when I checked the folder after retrieving it last week from college, I found that 3 pieces of evidence had been removed from the folder. These items were:

- *Sheet numbered 1 – which consisted of reasons why I was putting in a formal complaint about Ron Atler*
- *Sheet numbered 4 – Titled 'January 2011 Issues regarding my A Unit qualification'*
- *Sheet titled '23rd March 2012 – 'Meeting with Dale Rolland at Brunel House' – this sheet explains how Dale Rolland tried to apologise and make excuses for Ron Atler's behaviour. He then initiated trying to sort the problem out between us. I refused and told him I wanted a written conclusion to my grievance. Dale told me he would email me the conclusion by dinnertime the same day, but this never happened (and I ended up having to wait until16th April)*

These items were removed either during or after the Stage 2 Grievance. I have photocopied the three sheets from my master file and have put them in my folder.

Regards

Janette

8/8/12

I spent today and the next few days preparing for my Stage 3 grievance hearing. I find that I have to do everything in writing, then change and alter things until I have everything in the right order. I then re-write it in the correct order and finally type it up; so, it takes ages – but the one thing I have right now is time. I must get this right. I don't imagine Anthea Mitchell will be unintelligent if she's managed to work her way up to the position of Vice-Principal.

Seven months now of not sleeping, so it makes it all harder. I walk into rooms not knowing what the hell I've gone in there for. My head 'is a shed' - 'full of cotton wool.' I am zombie-like at times, so it's hard to prepare for something as important as this, but it's the most important thing in my life at present, so I need to carry on and do the best I can.

<u>11/8/12</u>

I need to go to a "back to work meeting' in a few days. More stress. Not sure how it will go, or what they are going to do/say to get me back under their control? I can't wait for this week to be over. Two stressful meetings to attend.

<u>14/8/12</u>

Joan Horncastle (HR Manager) telephoned me this afternoon. She said that she had just returned from holiday, found out about the meeting, and decided that there is no point having a back to work meeting the day before my Stage 3 hearing. So, she said it is postponed and asked if this was OK. My reply to this was, "Yes, that's fine but as the meeting is scheduled for tomorrow if you're going to cancel the meeting, can you put it in an email to me this afternoon please?". Joan replied that she would.

There is NO WAY that I am NOT going to attend a meeting that has been arranged unless I get it in writing that it is canceled. I don't trust any of them. The way I feel now she could be tricking me into not going to the meeting. I will not rely on a telephone call that I can't prove has happened.

I checked my emails about an hour later:

From: <u>jhorncastle@kirkleescollege.com</u>

Sent: 14 August 2012 14:28:45

Subject: Meeting on 15th August

Hi Janette,

Further to our telephone conversation today. I confirm that I have come back from annual leave to find 2 meetings in my diary with yourself, one tomorrow (15th) with Jean Turrand and myself and one on 16th to hear your grievance under stage 3 of the procedure with Anthea Mitchell.

I have been told that the meeting arranged for tomorrow was to discuss and plan your return to work as a result of your grievance being concluded under Stage 2. Since the meeting was arranged you have appealed and requested that it be taken to the next level, and hence the second meeting being arranged. The timing of the two is purely coincidental.

However, as we discussed on the telephone, I do not see any benefit in having the back to work discussions tomorrow and feel that it would be best to hear your grievance on Thursday first and postpone the return to work discussion planning meeting until we have exhausted the grievance procedure.

At your agreement, we have therefore decided that we will hear your grievance on Thursday and then plan a return to work meeting after that.

Kind Regards

Joan

I printed the email off and put it in my master folder. They can't pretend that I have missed a meeting now that I have it in black and white that the meeting is cancelled.

I feel slightly relieved that I only need to concentrate on one meeting now this week.

<u>16/8/12</u>

I drove to college and met Andrew Smithy in the car park before we went into my Stage 3 hearing. The meeting was chaired by Anthea Mitchell (Vice Principle) and Joan Horncastle (HR manager).

Anthea Mitchell conducted the meeting very professionally and she appeared neutral and supportive towards me.

Once Anthea had introduced herself and stated her aims for the meeting, I read through my prepared statement which is as follows:

My original complaint was about my manager Ron Atler. I informed HR and Dale Rolland that I wished to make a formal complaint about Ron Atler on 31st January 2012.

Since this date, my Grievance has not been dealt with in line with Kirklees College's Grievance Procedure.

So now, not only do I have an issue with Ron Atler, but also with the management and Human Resources of Kirklees College as their combined incompetence has had a detrimental effect on my health.

Stage 2 officially began 18th May 2012 – this was four weeks after I notified Jean Turrand that I wished to move to Stage 2 of Grievance. Kirklees College's grievance procedure states that a panel should be convened to hear the grievance within ten working days of receipt of the grievance form. Jean Turrand received my grievance form 18th April 2012.

At the stage 2 hearing I complained about the length of time Stage 1 had taken (ten and a half weeks), and the fact that HR had not kept track of the investigation and kept me up to date throughout which I found very stressful.

After the Stage 2 hearing, I received a letter dated 18th May from Linda Anison in HR stating, 'I will ensure you are kept up to date in terms of timescales of the investigation'. After this, I heard nothing during the nine weeks it took for the investigation to be completed!

I had an investigation meeting with Jane Davis and Karen Watkins on the 11th of June. I was told at this interview that I may need to wait one week to receive my interview notes – I would then check them for accuracy, sign and return them.

All interviewees would do the same. These interview notes would then go to the panel and the panel would decide the outcome of my grievance.

My interview notes were sent out to me on the 18th of July, as were Amy Lambs. Kay Ramsden received hers on 20th July. Judith Hamilton, Tanya Brown and the lecturers in plumbing and electrical have not received theirs back.

My notes were very brief and had many inaccuracies, as were Amy Lambs and Kay Ramsdens.

I received the conclusion to Stage 2 from Jean Turrand – letter dated 20th July – but stating that the panel convened on 18th July and decided the outcome – HOW IS THIS POSSIBLE?

Stage 2 decision:

'The panel is confident that the necessary personnel were interviewed…..to enable conclusions to be drawn from the evidence gathered' – AS WE KNOW, THIS 'EVIDENCE' IS FLAWED

'The panel does acknowledge that there was a delay in you receiving an outcome to Stage 1 grievance you submitted and that any delay, as a result of having to obtain all necessary information should have been communicated to you'

This is untrue as Dale Rolland finished interviewing all staff on Monday 5th March (John Forrest). All the other staff was interviewed on Monday 27th February.

Dale Rolland sent me an email on 20th March stating 'I have completed the investigation with staff, is it possible for you to meet with me at Brunel House to discuss it on Friday 23rd March'.

At the meeting, Dale Rolland showed me a report of interviews with my colleagues where the majority had made very negative comments about Ron Atler's management style. Dale then started making excuses for Ron Atler's behaviour (eg he had come off some tablets and it 'hadn't done him any good'). Dale tried to get me to help him 'sweep my grievance under the carpet'. When I refused and said I wanted him to give me my conclusion in writing the goalposts were moved and I was kept waiting until Monday 16th April for the conclusion.

Findings are the same as Stage 1 – Bullying should have been upheld.

This is my grievance – I understand that my colleagues needed to be interviewed – but the reply to my grievance should have been to me alone.

As stated in my letter to you Anthea, I require written confirmation about the following:

The findings of the investigation have cast serious allegations about the team (five allegations)

Are any of these allegations against me personally? If so, which ones?

Further action

- *No formal action will be taken against my line manager*
- *Appropriate action will be taken against the team*
- *Discussions and training will be provided to ALL team members, to ensure that a clear understanding for the team at all levels relating to teaching and learning standards and individual performances...*

In Summary

The reason for me going to Stage 3 of the grievance procedure is:

*That my grievance has not been addressed – Bullying was **NOT** upheld, and bullying is still going on in the section.*

*Kirklees College's grievance procedure has **NOT** been followed throughout my grievance – **Kirklees College is in breach of contract!***

At my Stage 2 hearing, I also discussed and included copies of:

- *ACAS's definition of Employer's Duty of Care which I feel Kirklees College is contravening*
- *Kirklees College's Values and Behaviours Policy – Both of which seem to have been ignored!*

*Also, on the College portal Strategic **Objective no 6 states** 'To attract, nurture and retain highly skilled and professional workforce who work collectively to deliver the college mission and values'*

Our Values no 2 *states 'Integrity, transparency, fairness and honesty in our management and communication'*

Our Values no 4 *states 'Respectful and supportive behaviour towards each other'*

Our Values no 5 *states 'Care: Playing our part to provide an environment that is safe, healthy and supportive'*

I feel I have been seriously let down by this college:

I have always done over and above what is expected of me

I have always proved myself to be an honest, conscientious and hardworking member of staff who has given over eleven and a half years of unblemished service.

I have been made ill by the management of Kirklees College, and I am seeking a fair, honest solution to this mess.

Andrew was a good witness. He backed my claims up by telling them that he had not received his investigation notes back for him to verify.

He informed them that the investigation was NOT confidential and that Ron Atler had been intimidating him as he had found out what Andrew had said about him during the investigation interviews. Joan started to dispute this, but Andrew cut her short – telling her that he would forward her some emails to prove this and that he had informed HR, but that he had been 'dismissed' by them.

Andrew finished by telling them that he was leaving the college as he couldn't work in the section any longer.

Anthea Mitchell assured me that she would complete my Stage 3 Grievance ASAP and that she would write to me very soon with the result.

After the meeting Andrew and I talked in the car park about how he thought the meeting had gone, and if he thought that Anthea Mitchell might do something about the situation and Ron Atler.

I drove home with mixed emotions and my mind spinning. Anthea Mitchell had seemed like she wanted the outcome to be positive for me. She had commented in the meeting about me being a Grade 1 Lecturer and the length of time I had worked for the College. One half of me thinks 'why would they want to lose me?' I know I can only go back to college if Ron Atler is no longer my boss – BUT will she sack or demote him?

17/8/12

Andrew Smithy copied me in on a reply to an email he had received from Joan Horncastle:

From: jhorncastle@kirkleescollege.com

Sent: 17 August 2012 08:49

To: asmithy@kirkleescollege.com

Subject: Grievance

Hello Andrew,

Thanks for attending the hearing yesterday with your colleague. Anthea is planning to speak to Janette today.

We were concerned to hear from you that details of your confidential interview had got back to your line manager, and your line manager had taken issue with you over this. I need to take this further and investigate exactly what happened.

I wonder if you would be kind enough to put together a written statement for me outlining the details of what you said yesterday...And would you be willing to come in and have a chat with me about it, so I can get a clear picture of what has taken place.

Kind Regards

Joan

From: asmithy@kirklescollege.com

To:jhorncastle@kirkleescollege.com
amitchell@kirkleescollege.com

Cc: janettecastle@hotmail.co.uk

Subject: Grievance

Hi Joan,

I am pleased that your department has finally taken an interest in this issue but very surprised that you do not already know all about it. I am about to forward you a sequence of emails that tell the whole story. If you look at the addresses, you will see how many people in your department have been aware of this for a while.

All the denials and the college's complete disregard for the procedure at Stage 2 (after Jane Davis had assured us about the rigour of this process), can only have contributed to Janette's feeling that she was up against the whole college, and not just her line management.

I was not the only member of staff whose comments found their way back to Ron before they have been checked. I don't know by what route this (unverified) information travelled, but it had made the journey...and very quickly.

Regards

Andrew

Andrew had then forwarded Joan the **many** emails he had sent to Karen Watkins (HR and copied to Jane Davis) – and the replies he had received back.

Reading the email response from Andrew improved my mood. It feels good to have someone on my side when I feel like I've been fighting this alone for eight months. Andrew has given them the facts and he copied Anthea Mitchell in, so she knows the score – and the controversy that I (and the rest of the section have been put through). It's just a shame that Andrew is leaving at the end of August.

21/8/12

I received the outcome letter from Anthea Mitchell dated 20/8/12:

Anthea Mitchell, Vice Principal Curriculum and Quality

Ref: JH/AM

20th August 2012

Dear Janette,

I am writing to confirm the outcome of the Stage 3 Grievance Hearing yesterday at which you were accompanied by Andrew Smithy. The Panel consisted of myself and Joan Horncastle, HR Manager.

We carefully considered the information you presented at the hearing and have now come to the following conclusions:

1. We uphold your complaint that the grievance process to date would appear to have taken far longer than would have been expected. There are lengthy gaps between interviews being concluded and feedback being given and delays in your grievance being heard between Stage 1 and Stage 2. I have asked Joan Horncastle to undertake an investigation to look at timelines and establish the cause of the delays. Also, she will investigate if you were kept informed and notified of how investigations were progressing.

2. We uphold your complaint that the typed investigation notes were not sent out to the interviewees for checking and amending in a timely fashion and therefore that the notes presented to the Stage 2 panel may not have been completely accurate or a true account of the meetings. Again, Joan Horncastle will contact all of the people interviewed, to ask them to amend their notes if they so wish and send back so we can determine whether any of the content would significantly change.

3. We uphold your complaint that although 3 out of 5 allegations against your manager were upheld at

Stage 2, no formal action was deemed necessary. Formal action will be taken to ensure that his behaviour towards you and your colleagues does change and that he develops a management style more conducive to a supportive, motivated and productive team.

4. *We uphold your complaint that the letter detailing the outcome of Stage 2 acknowledges a failed responsibility on the College's behalf to support your manager but does not acknowledge a failed responsibility to yourself. Clearly, as you feel your manager's actions have caused you to be unwell and be off work for such a lengthy period the College does have to take some responsibility for this.*

5. *We uphold your complaint that the letter detailing the outcome of Stage 2 is worded inappropriately in terms of allegations of underperformance and falsifying of documents without being clear what the allegations against you are specifically. Joan Horncastle is going to speak to Dale Rolland and find out specifically what the allegations are against yourself, and how the management team intends to take this forward once you return to work.*

6. *Joan and I were very disappointed to hear Andrew's evidence that details of his confidential interview had got back to his line manager and his line manager had taken issue with him about it. This would appear to be a breach of confidentiality. I have asked Joan to investigate this fully and she will be contacting Andrew for a written statement.*

We took your grievance extremely seriously and we are recommending several actions to be implemented, which Jean Turrand will personally monitor.

MANAGEMENT ACTION

- *Formal action to be taken to ensure improvements are made and these will be formally monitored to ensure progress is made within a set timescale. This will be managed by Jean Turrand, Director*
- *Mentoring and coaching to be offered to all management team – overseen and monitored by Jean Turrand, Director.*
- *Values and Behaviours refresher training for all management teams.*

ACTION FOR JANETTE

- *Janette to be given a mentor within the HR team – someone to meet with regularly to make sure things are going well and that you don't feel threatened or intimidated*
- *Janette to be informed asap what allegations are being made against her (if any) in terms of underperformance and how it is going to be addressed*
- *Any 1:1 meeting's with line manager will have a third person present for an agreed timescale – possibly the mentor allocated to your line manager who will also be a CTL with good management skills*
- *An offer for Janette to undertake counselling sessions through our occupational health provider, financed by the College.*
- *Some team building activities for the whole team*

I do acknowledge Janette the contribution that you have made to the Section and the College and as a Grade 1 teacher, you are extremely valued.

I hope that you will now feel able to come back to work and allows to put in place the things we have identified and support you back into your role.

Your relationship with your manager will be closely monitored to ensure that you are not made to feel uncomfortable or unsafe.

If you have any questions about anything contained in this letter, please do not hesitate to contact either myself or Joan Horncastle. Hopefully, we can soon be in a position where you can arrange to come back into College to meet with HR and your managers to agree and plan a 'return to work' schedule.

If you are not satisfied with the outcome of Stage 3 you do have the right to appeal. If you wish to do so you must appeal in writing, to the Principle within 10 working days of receipt of my decision.

Yours Sincerely

Anthea Mitchell

Vice Principal of Curriculum and Quality

Anthea Mitchell is upholding quite a few points that the 'clown' Panel at Stage 2 dismissed. She is agreeing that I have been kept waiting far too long throughout the grievance procedure and **she thinks that I require counselling!!!**

The fact that she thinks I require counselling – and that she is happy for Kirklees College to pay for said counselling proves that Kirklees College has been negligent in its Duty of Care towards me.

She has stated that Ron Atler will have formal action taken against him, that he will receive training, <u>BUT</u> he will still be my boss!!!

The main accusation made by me (bullying) has been ignored! I kept re-reading the letter to double-check – but no, bullying was NOT mentioned anywhere!

Anthea Mitchell is an intelligent woman. I feel that she has tried to appease me; but that she has put Kirklees College first. She has ignored my bullying allegation (as clearly this would be a sackable offense) and must be hoping that I will be appeased enough to accept her findings, return to college and 'toe the line'.

The end bit is all about me coming back to college. She has stated that I will have a third-party present at all one to one meetings with Ron Atler, I will have meetings with HR, to make sure I don't feel threatened and intimidated (which she knows I will feel!!).

Also discussing allegations and how they will be addressed!

No way am I returning to work with Ron Atler as my boss! That is not going to happen. He would do everything in his power to destroy me and my career for daring to challenge him!

Robert said months ago that he thought management would stick together rather than sort out the problem for me (the innocent victim). I was hoping he would be wrong - but unfortunately, so far, he has called it correctly.

<u>22/8/12</u>

I got out of bed, had breakfast and then took Indie for a walk. As I walked through the woods, I kept thinking 'What the hell am I supposed to do now? It's still not over eight months in!'

I spent today and the next day thinking through all the stress and anguish I had been through and trying to decide what I should/could do. I've worked so hard to get to where I am professionally. It's my livelihood. I've done nothing wrong. Why am I being so badly treated when all I've done is work hard and behave professionally?

Once again it has come down to options:

Option 1 - Go back to work with Ron Atler as my boss – NOT GONNA HAPPEN!

Option 2 – Leave College

Option 3 – Go to the final stage of the Grievance procedure with the Principal of the College

I chose Option 3......

<u>23/8/12</u>

I spent time preparing for what I wanted to put in my email to Paul McKant (the Principal of Kirklees College as he is the person who will deal with my Stage 4 Appeal). The last and final stage of this debacle.

CHAPTER 5

Stage 4 Appeal

<u>24/8/12</u>

I sent the email to Paul McKant:

From: <u>janettecastle@hotmail.co.uk</u>

To: <u>pmckant@kirkleescollege.com</u>

Sent: 24 August 2012 09:32:32

Subject: Stage 4 of the grievance procedure

Hi Paul,

My name is Janette Castle and I am a lecturer in the Electrical Installation section. Unfortunately, I have been off work ill for the majority of this year due to Work-Related Stress. My illness was caused by my line manager Ron Atler and has been compounded by the incompetence of certain managers and human resources personnel at college. I am currently going through the College's grievance procedure and met last week with Anthea Mitchell for a Stage 3 hearing.

At the Stage 3 hearing, I informed Anthea (and Joan Horncastle) that I had shown my Stage 2 outcome letter to a solicitor, and that the solicitor told me that my accusation of bullying should have been upheld as the College had upheld my allegation of intimidation. The solicitor stated that bullying and intimidation are the same things.

Anthea and Joan told me that they had looked up the definition of 'bullying' and 'intimidation'. I informed them that I wanted my allegation of bullying to be upheld.

I have received my outcome for Stage 3 from Anthea. My accusation of bullying has been ignored and so, therefore, I wish to proceed to Stage 4 of the grievance procedure.

At the Stage 3 hearing, I complained that the college grievance procedure had not been followed and that this was a breach of my contract. I also informed Anthea that the College's investigation procedure had not been adhered to.

Anthea has upheld both of these complaints, which proves that Kirklees College has been negligent.

Also, at the Stage 3 hearing, I discussed serious allegations that had been made against me in my Stage 2 outcome letter. These complaints included:

- *A negative attitude and approach where evidence of underperformance is evident*
- *Falsifying of college documents and completion dates on student tracking sheets*
- *Internally verifying own work*
- *A reluctance to adapt to new working practices*

I told Anthea that I needed written clarification and proof, to substantiate if any of these serious allegations were directed to me personally as the letter also stated that 'appropriate action would be taken'.

These allegations have now been drastically amended to 'there is still an issue with tracking sheets and that all staff needs to agree to use the identified standard sheet'. This more minor allegation is still false, and I have written evidence to prove this.

The above allegations are more evidence that I have been subjected to bullying and intimidation by managers of Kirklees College.

Anthea has offered me counselling sessions to be paid for by the college. This proves that Kirklees College has failed in its 'Duty of Care' to me as an employee.

This process has now dragged on for over seven and a half months. I have hardly slept during this time. I am on medication and feel exhausted both physically and mentally. I have lost confidence in the college and wonder if I will ever feel well enough to resume my post.

I look forward to hearing your reply about moving to Stage 4 of the grievance procedure.

Yours Faithfully

Janette Castle

Again, the feeling of dread and sickness in the pit of my stomach as I press the send button.

Here we go again! More stress to put myself through – but the last part of the procedure, so hopefully I should be near the end of this horrible journey. Who knows how this will end?

Just under an hour later I receive a reply:

From: kmarsden@kirkleescollege.com

To: janettecastle@hotmail.co.uk

Sent: 24 August 2012 10:22:12

Subject: Stage 4 of the grievance procedure

Dear Janette,

I acknowledge receipt of your e-mail to Paul McKant and will respond in due course as outlined in the Grievance Procedure.

Regards

Kay Marsden

Executive Assistant to the Principal

Well, that was short and 'sweet'. Let's see if the Principal of Kirklees College can adhere to the grievance procedure – 4.5 Right of appeal….

4.5.1 States 'the Principal will arrange a hearing…..within 20 working days of receipt of the request'

So, my Stage 4 appeal hearing should be no later than 20th September.

I now need to prepare all over again for my final battle. Up against the Principal of Kirklees College!!!! I would never have predicted this in a million years.

28/8/12

No correspondence from College – so no date yet. I started making notes of everything I want to bring up at my Stage 4 Appeal Hearing.

<u>1/9/12</u>

A week has now passed and still nothing. I just want a date for the Appeal Hearing so that I can plan and try to get a witness. I have been speaking to Tanya Brown, and bless her – she says she will be my witness if she can (but I need a date to give her, to make sure she can get cover for any classes if it falls on a workday (she teaches part-time).

<u>8/9/12</u>

This is getting ridiculous! No correspondence! No date! Surely after I informed the Principle about the detrimental effect this is having to my health, he would not keep making me waiting like this???

<u>13/9/12</u>

I received an email from the Director of HR:

From: jlampson@kirkleescollege.com

To: janettecastle@hotmail.co.uk

Cc: mrook@kirkleescollege.com
jhorncastle@kirkleescollege.com
pmckant@kirkleescollege.com jturrand@kirkleescollege.com
amitchell@kirkleescollege.com

Date: 13 September 2012

Subject: Appeal Hearing

Hi Janette,

I am sending a letter inviting you to an appeal hearing in tonight's post.

Kind Regards

Jill Lampson

Director of Human Resources

15/9/12

No letter in the post. If I don't get anything tomorrow, I need to email her back.

17/9/12

Still no letter! I sent an email to Jill Lampson:

From: janettecastle@hotmail.co.uk

To: jlampson@kirkleescollege.com

Sent: 17 September 2012 14:01:45

Subject: Appeal Hearing

Hi Jill,

I have not yet received the letter that you stated would be sent on Thursday evening's post inviting me to an appeal hearing.

I need to know the date, so I can arrange for a colleague to accompany me as a witness.

Could you please confirm if Paul McKant and Mandy Rook will be the only people present at the hearing?

Thank you

Janette

18/9/12

Received a letter in the post from Jill Lampson:

13th September 2012

Strictly Private and Confidential

Dear Janette

The appeal against your recent grievance hearing at Stage 3

Further to your email on 24th August, notifying the Principle that you wish to appeal against the outcome of your grievance which was heard by Anthea Mitchell under Stage 3 of the college's procedure.

An appeal hearing has now been set up and will be heard by Paul McKant and Mandy Rook at 2 pm on 19th September in F066.

I would like to apologise for the short notice of the hearing. We have been trying to find a suitable diary slot for both Paul and Mandy's diary, and an available slot became available today due to a cancellation. If you feel it is too short notice, then please let me know and I will re-arrange. It would appear from Paul and Mandy's diaries that the next available date after 19th September will be 5th October 2012.

You are, of course, entitled to be accompanied at the hearing by either your trade union representative or a colleague of your choice.

Yours Sincerely

Jill Lampson

Director of Human Resources

May be too short notice! You don't say!

The letter may be dated 13th September, but the postmark on the envelope proved it had been sent 17/9/12 (after my email reminder I suspect). How can they be so incompetent – to let me receive a letter on 18th for a meeting the following day!

I think they must be trying to make it difficult for me to get a witness to accompany me – and I will need a witness as they are being so underhand and unprofessional.

The Director of Human Resources (who is rumoured to be paid a salary of around £65K) can't even post a letter on time, whilst I, (ultra-competent employee) am being driven out of the college. It doesn't make sense?

No way can I ring Tanya Brown and ask her to drop everything and get cover for her class tomorrow!

They have given me another possible date of 5th October. So, Paul McKant and Mandy Rook can't re-arrange their diaries for anything earlier. I think this shows how seriously they are taking me and how much they care about the stress I'm going through!

Here we go again. I notified Paul McKant that I wished to appeal on 24th August and I have had to wait until 5th October!

Anyone would think I was making it up. I sometimes think I must be dreaming about it. I informed Paul McKant that the grievance procedure was not followed at Stage 1 and Stage 2. I have been off work for almost nine months with Work-Related Stress – and he makes me wait another six weeks!!

I rang Tanya to see if she still felt able to be my witness and gave her the date. She said 'Yes' (what a star). Luckily Tanya is in another section of the college, so she shouldn't be victimised like the rest of my section is being.

I'm really glad that Tanya has agreed to be my witness; but anxious about being in front of another Vice-Principal and the Principal of Kirklees College.

21/9/12

I had another doctor's appointment today. I took my letter in to show him and I think he was surprised that even the Principal was dragging it out for me and doing nothing to help an employee of his college. Doctor Mattins was sympathetic as always and checked I was attending the meeting with a witness. He then gave me another sick note.

25/9/12

I looked through the notes I had prepared for my appeal hearing and started typing them up in the order I want to go through them on the day.

5/10/12

I met Tanya outside college and we went to HR. I had taken pens and two notepads and asked Tanya if she could write down what was said during the meeting.

Appeal Hearing

Present: Paul McKant, Mandy Rook, Carol Wood (HR), Joan Horncastle (HR manager – first 20 minutes only), Janette Castle, Tanya Brown (witness).

Paul started the meeting by informing me that he had asked Joan Horncastle to attend the beginning of the meeting to update me on what had happened since my Stage 3 grievance hearing.

Joan started reading through Anthea Mitchell's Stage 3 outcome letter to me. Joan said that the investigation notes (from Stage 2) had been sent out to my colleagues, but that they had not sent them back.

I disagreed with this and told her that Amy Lamb, Kay Ramsden and I had received our notes back but that they were received after the Stage 2 decision had been made (and that the notes had been inaccurate). I told the panel that all the other interviewees had NOT received their notes back. Joan tried to reassure me that they had been sent out; she implied that my colleagues will not have wanted to make changes to the content, so will not have sent them back to college.

I replied "The notes have not been sent out. Tanya here, received an email from Joan (Horncastle) in August asking her if she would like to alter any of the content of her interview notes and send the interview notes back. Tanya emailed back to say that she had never received any interview notes. Tanya has not received a reply to that email and that was six weeks ago!"

The Panel (except Joan) all looked at Tanya and she confirmed that what I said was true. Paul and Mandy then looked at Joan and said that this would need looking into. Joan was looking very uncomfortable and had a rash all over her neck and chest (which pleased me enormously).

Joan tried to compose herself and said that I had been angry that Jean Turrand had asked me to go to an informal meeting to introduce herself to me before moving to Stage 2 of the grievance procedure.

I replied that I had not been angry – I had been very upset and 'at the end of my tether'. I stated that I'd had to find out about the grievance procedure, that I had read the grievance procedure and that I had followed the grievance procedure throughout. I then said that if the College had gone to the trouble of writing a grievance procedure, that I would expect that the managers of the college would follow the procedure.

Joan Horncastle left the meeting (with her tail firmly beneath her legs).

Paul McKant said that Ron Atler was engaged and more than happy to do what is required to change his style of management.

I replied that Ron Atler would say what was required to the management above him, but that it wouldn't be the truth and 'that a leopard cannot change its spots'. I said that Ron was in his 50's and that his bullying was habitual and that he couldn't change. I told them to ask my colleagues if they thought he had changed. I added that perhaps now my colleagues may not dare to answer any more questions, as they had been interviewed twice and knew that nothing had been confidential and that Ron would find out what had been said.

I told them that Ron Atler had not changed and that a colleague of mine (Judith – but I didn't name her for fear of reprisals against her), had heard Ron shouting at Andrew Smithy about what he had said to HR about him during Stage 2 grievance, and that my colleague (Judith) was extremely shocked that everyone's right to confidentiality (and repeated assurances of that confidentiality) had been breached, leaving employees exposed to reprisals. She felt that Andrew should not have been the subject of such anger and unprofessionalism. She felt she should inform someone but who could anyone inform? All staff within the Section were now well aware that no-one in management or HR was upholding the rights of the employees or following any of the procedures designed to safeguard their staff. Ron seemed to behave however he wanted – even after an investigation into his behaviour'.

Paul and Mandy asked me if I could work with Ron Atler and I replied, "No, and he will never have any control over my life again after making me so ill!"

They began suggesting that I could teach functional skills so that I could work in another area of the college. I replied that that was not my job. Mandy asked me what I did before working for the college. I replied that I was an electrician. Mandy said that I could perhaps work in the college's 'Building and Estates' department whilst my grievance was resolved!

I then read through my prepared statement:

My outcome to Stage 3 dated 20th August 2012 states:

- *Anthea upholds the grievance process has taken far longer than expected. I have asked Joan Horncastle to undertake an investigation to look at timelines and establish the cause of the delays. Also, she will investigate if I was kept informed and notified of how investigations were progressing.*

Has this happened?

- *Anthea upholds that typed investigation notes were not sent out to the interviewees for checking and amending in a timely fashion. Joan will contact all people interviewed to ask them to amend their notes if they so wish and send them back so that we can determine whether any of the content would significantly change.*

I paused, looked up at Paul and Mandy and said, "We know that this has not happened!" I paused before continuing.

- *Joan and I were disappointed to hear Andrew's evidence that details of his confidential interview had got back to his line manager and his line manager had taken issue with it. This would appear to be a breach of confidentiality. I have asked Joan to investigate this fully and she will be contacting Andrew for a written statement.*

Has this been investigated?

Management action (to be implemented and monitored by Jean Turrand)

- *Formal action to be taken and formally monitored*
- *Mentoring and coaching to be offered to all management team*

Jean Turrand was the Director in charge of the Stage 2 grievance. Most of her decisions were overruled by Anthea Mitchell at Stage 3, and she is the person who sent me the intimidating and bullying Stage 2 outcome letter which made serious allegations against me and told me that 'appropriate action would be taken'. The allegations were fictitious – did she even try to verify their accuracy? I have no confidence in her what so ever!!!

<u>Actions for Janette</u>

- *Janette to be given a mentor within the HR team – someone to meet with regularly to make sure things are going well and that you don't feel <u>threatened or intimidated!</u>*

I will feel threatened and intimidated if Ron Atler is still my line manager as he is a bully, and so far, I have found HR to be incompetent!

- *Your relationship with your line manager will be closely monitored to ensure that you are not made to feel uncomfortable or <u>unsafe</u>*

This seems to show that Anthea knows I will not feel comfortable and safe working with Ron Atler because he is a bully.

I cannot understand why this college will not admit that Ron Atler is a bully and remove him from his post.

When I asked why bullying had not been upheld at Stage 2 when there was enough to prove that he was Anthea replied that '<u>they had worked on the law of averages</u> and that only four people said that he was a bully'.

The law of averages may be used to work out a mathematical equation but would not be used to decide if someone was a bully or not.

I have not received an apology from anyone in this college!!! No one has said sorry and I don't feel that anyone is bothered about what I have been through.

<u>Stage 1</u> - was dealt with incompetently and the outcome was full of contradictions

Stage 2 – the outcome was an absolute disgrace with the blame turned around onto me, with false accusations and threats of 'appropriate action being taken' against me which was trying to intimidate me. **Also, 3 pieces of evidence were removed from my evidence folder at Stage 2!**

Stage 3 – I feel Anthea tried to appease me by upholding some of my accusations but ignored bullying and stated that things would happen (like investigating certain matters) which have NOT happened.

Summary:

- *The way I have been treated by Kirklees College is criminal*

- *I have been bullied and intimidated by the management of this college. The bullying has made me ill and I feel that my teaching career has been stolen away from me.*

- *I will not rest until I get justice, I will pursue this at all costs until I get the justice that I deserve*

- *Under the Freedom of Information Act, I, Janette Castle request that any information regarding me from January the 5th 2012 until October the 5th 2012 (including all emails, minutes of meetings and any other correspondence) shall be forwarded to me in paper format as soon as possible from all the following employees of Kirklees College: Ron Atler, Dale Rolland, Jean Turrand, Alan Wiley, Jane Davis, Anthea Mitchell, Jen Walden, Linda Anison, Karen Watkins, Joan Horncastle, Mandy Rook, Jill Lampson and, Paul McKant*

- *Under the Freedom of Information Act, I would like to be given the name(s) of the person(s) who made the allegations against me in the Stage 2 grievance letter dated 20th July 2012*

I broke down in tears whilst reading out the summary part of my statement. I wondered if they knew (or cared) how stressful it was to go through this process?

Paul McKant asked me to email him my request under the Freedom of Information Act. I agreed.

Mandy Rook said to me that I had been within my rights to bring problems to the attention of management and that she was sure that senior managers would do everything they could to support me back to work.

I asked, "Do you class Dale Rolland as senior management?" Mandy replied "Yes." And I just shook my head in disbelief.

Paul McKant said, "I can't second guess the outcome. What could happen that would make you return to teaching?"

I replied, "Bullying is gross misconduct and as such Ron Atler should be sacked. If the grievance procedure had been followed as it should have been done months ago, I would have been back at work".

Paul replied, "From what I've read – is it bullying or poor management? Was it intentional, intimidatory behaviour?" Paul then went on to say, "It sounds to me that unless Ron is sacked soon there isn't a way back for you. I'm always sorry to lose a good teacher – but I think the only way back is if Ron Atler is sacked from college".

I replied, "I will come back if he is sacked".

Paul replied, "I can't prejudge. I have to follow the process, read through and reflect on what has gone on" He then asked, "Do you expect Ron to be sacked?"

I replied, "I did months ago during the investigation, but it's been going for on so long I doubt that it will happen now".

Mandy Rook then asked, "What has your family thought about what's happened?"

I replied, "They have been very unhappy about the way I have been treated and my partner has been very worried about my health and that he too has been surprised how badly I have been treated".

The meeting ended with Paul telling me he would inform me of his decision as soon as possible.

Tanya and I walked out and had a chat and a hug in the carpark. Tanya said that I had done very well and that she had felt very nervous, so she couldn't imagine how I had felt! She also said that I sounded very professional and was impressed, particularly when I requested information under the Freedom of Information Act.

I was so glad that Tanya had accompanied me as my witness, as when Joan Horncastle had tried to make out that the interview notes had been sent out Tanya corrected her and which (in my opinion) made Joan look incompetent, and it proved yet again that Kirklees College can't follow Procedures!

I didn't know what to think when I got out of the meeting. Would they sack Ron Atler after all this time? I felt drained after the hearing; but so glad it's over. This is the final stage!

I drove home wondering if Paul McKant will follow the grievance procedure and give me the outcome within ten working days?

When I got home, I emailed Paul McKant my request under the Freedom of Information Act:

From: janettecastle@hotmail.co.uk

To: pmckant@kirkleescollege.com

Sent: 05 October 2012 15:12:22

Subject: Re: Freedom of Information Act

Hi Paul,

As discussed in this afternoon's meeting:

Under the Freedom of Information Act, I, Janette Castle request that any information regarding me from January 5th, 2012 until October 5th, 2012 (including all emails, minutes of meetings and any other correspondence), shall be forwarded to me, in paper format, as soon as possible from all the following employees of Kirklees College:

Ron Atler
Dale Rolland
Jean Turrand
Alan Wiley
Jane Davis

Anthea Mitchell
Jan Weldon
Linda Anison
Karen Watkins
Joan Horncastle
Mandy Rook
Jill Lampson
Paul McKant

Also, under the Freedom of Information Act, I would like to be given the name(s) of the person(s) who made allegations against me in the Stage 2 outcome letter dated 20th July 2012.

Thank you

Janette Castle

I received a reply email from Paul McKant soon afterward:

From: pmckant@kirkleescollege.com

To: janettecastle@hotmail.co.uk

Cc: mrook@kirkleescollege.com

Sent: 05 October 2012 03:12:35

Subject: Re-Freedom of Information Act

Hi Janette,

Thank you.

I have forwarded your request to Mandy (Rook) who will progress as appropriate.

I will send an initial response to today's appeal hearing early next week, but a more detailed, outcome will be subject to further investigation over a longer period.

Regards

Paul

That sounds to me like he's in no rush to get his conclusion to me (surprise, surprise).

8/10/12

Tanya copied me into the email:

From: tbrown@kirkleescollege.com

Sent: 08 October 2012 09:42:25

To: pmckant@kirkleescollege.com mrook@kirkleescollege.com cwood@kirkleescollege.com

Cc: janettecastle@hotmail.co.uk

Subject: FW: Grievance – Janette Castle Meeting 5.10.12

Hi all,

With regards to the meeting with Janette Castle/Paul/Mandy/Carol 5/10/12, please see below the email that was sent to me from Joan with regards to the investigation notes.

Thanks

Tanya

Hi Joan,

Sorry, I've been away but just to let you know, I never received any!

Thanks

Tanya

Hello

You have recently been interviewed as part of the grievance investigation, Jane Davis was the investigating officer.

When we came to hear the grievance the member of staff concerned raised an issue about the notes taken during the investigation meetings. Comments made indicate that:

1. *In some case',s the notes were far too brief and missed out elements of the discussion*
2. *In some case's, the notes were in some instances inaccurate*
3. *There was a delay in sending the notes out for checking and amending.*

Therefore, I would be grateful if you could let me know if you are satisfied that the notes you have been sent accurately reflect the discussion that took place and if not, please advise me what changes you wish to make. You can either do this via email or if you feel a meeting would be useful, I am happy to meet with you.

It is very important that notes taken at investigation meetings do accurately reflect the discussions as these are used as evidence and are key to any action or decisions taken by the panel.

Kind Regards

Joan

Well, there's no escaping the truth. It's there in black and white. It proves yet again that I have been speaking the truth, and that Joan and the rest of HR cannot follow the procedure!

I would like to be a fly on the wall to see/hear how Joan Horncastle will get out of that one – being told that the interview notes had NOT been sent out – and then doing nothing about it – and then stating AGAIN that they HAD been sent out – and in front of the Principal and Vice-Principal!

10/10/12

Happy birthday me – NOT! Nothing to celebrate, unfortunately, better luck next year hopefully?

12/10/12

I had another doctor's appointment. I told Doctor Mattins about my appeal meeting and that they were discussing me being redeployed rather than Ron Atler being sacked. He gave me another sicknote whilst I waited for my conclusion

13/10/12

I received a letter in the post from Paul McKant dated 12/10/12:

12 October 2012

Dear Janette

Grievance Appeal

Thank you for taking the time to outline your concerns about the process and outcome of the Stage 3 Grievance.

First and foremost, I would like to apologise to you for the impact that the protracted nature of this case has had on your wellbeing and would like to reiterate the College's wish to support you back into the workplace, or redeployment if you do not feel able to return to your existing position as a lecturer within the plumbing and electrical team.

I have asked Anthea Mitchell, Vice Principal: Curriculum and Quality, to follow up on her initial investigation and to find out if the changes that the College has introduced have had a positive impact on members of the team within the department, and to take further action as appropriate.

As you seemed to be unaware of the inadequate student success rates in the plumbing and electrical area, I have attached data from ProAchieve for student performance over the past 4 years. As stated on Friday this performance was failing our students, but significant improvement has occurred in 2011/12.

Going forward please can you clarify the information you require about yourself held by the College so that I can respond to your request within College procedures.

I would also like to suggest a formal follow-up meeting with you in the next 4-week period with ACAS in attendance, to help us to explore a process of support that would enable you to return to work. Please can you consider if you wish to take up this offer and let me know?

I hope that your recovery is progressing, and I will contact you again once I have received Anthea Mitchell's feedback on her progress review.

Yours Sincerely

Paul McKant

Principal and Chief Executive

ACAS! Not right now – not happening until I get a conclusion that I am happy with.

Paul McKant is just trying to get me back to work and trying to make it look like this is for my benefit – What ten months later – after all the mental torture I have been through!!!

I am not being bullied into a meeting with ACAS (within four weeks??? How's that following the grievance procedure? – and he wants the meeting before he sees fit to give me my appeal outcome. It hardly follows the ten working days stated in THEIR grievance procedure - and after all the complaints I have made about Kirklees College NOT following their grievance procedure?

And student's success rates being inadequate; the attachment he sent just showed the results of the day release students. The day release students are about 10% of our students. He did not show the success rates for the JTL apprentices that I teach which are the other 90% of students in the electrical section – the rates are above the benchmark (which means higher than at other colleges and so very good).

Just another example of the management of Kirklees College trying to turn things around and generally try to make me out to be part of an unprofessional, unsuccessful department!

And as for him asking me to clarify the information that I require? I made that crystal clear in my email to him on 5th October. Is he just trying to wind me up?

I now need to work out how I respond to Paul McKant's letter. I will not let him force me into a corner and force me into a meeting which is for his benefit (not mine) when he seems unwilling to do what he is supposed to be doing – **following the grievance procedure and giving me my outcome!**

15/10/12

I responded to Paul McKant's letter with an email:

From: janettecastle@hotmail.co.uk

Sent: 15 October 2012 07:24:35

To: pmckant@kirkleescollege.com

Subject: Grievance

Hi Paul,

Thank you for your letter.

To clarify the information that I require about myself held by the college I have attached the email I sent you on October 5th, 2012.

I will wait for your written outcome of my appeal. If I agree with your conclusion to my grievance, I will be happy to come to a follow-up meeting with ACAS in attendance.

Kind Regards

Janette

(Below this email was the email I had sent him on 5/10/12 which clearly states what information I required under the Freedom of Information Act).

Clear and succinct – and letting him know that I don't intend to be manipulated by him at this late stage in the proceedings!

19/10/12

No outcome – so even the Principal of Kirklees College cannot follow the Grievance Procedure!

Tanya and others from college have been texting me to see if I have got my conclusion letter yet. Told them all 'No'.

John Forrest rang me and said that Ron Atler is as cocky as ever. That Ron and Dale Rolland sit in his office (Ron's) laughing and joking (rather than working). John said that he was at the end of his tether. He has lost two stone in weight and has been having tests. He has been panicking (thinking it's something bad, like cancer). The tests have revealed nothing, so his doctor is saying it must all be down to stress (no surprise there). John says he can't take anymore and is looking for work elsewhere.

Poor John; another excellent lecturer feeling that he needs to leave College for the sake of his health.

It doesn't bode well for me if Ron Atler is behaving without a care in the world. This seems to mean that Paul McKant can't have been reading him the riot act, therefore he can't be thinking about sacking him any time soon?

25/10/12

Still no outcome from Paul McKant! He's just prolonging the agony like all the rest of them have!

27/10/12

I received my outcome letter from Paul McKant in the post, dated 26th October:

Strictly Private and Confidential

26 October 2012

Dear Janette

Further to our appeal meeting of October 5th and my subsequent letter of October 10th Anthea (Mitchell) has now concluded her follow up discussion as to the improvements in the team working, and Joan (Horncastle) regarding the college internal process, involving Ron Atler.

Anthea's finding concluded that since the move to Brunel House, the team, on the whole, are much happier, being with the rest of the department and that the development programme put in place for the manager is impacting positively. Joan Horncastle has also informed me that the college investigation process involving Ron Atler is ongoing, but Ron has been engaging with the peer mentorship and training programme wholeheartedly, to improve his management of the staff team.

As indicated in my previous letter, the impact on student performance has already been achieved with the improved student success rates of college students in plumbing and electrical in 2011/12. In light of these updates, I have to report to you, that your expressed wish for Ron Atler to be dismissed has not been the conclusion of the college process.

The above notwithstanding I endorse the findings made my Anthea Mitchell in her Stage 3 appeal letter of August 20th that the college process has taken far longer than it should in the early stages and this impacted upon you. That said the college process has been followed and is now concluded.

As indicated in my previous letter I would hope that when the time is right for you, the college can assist you back into work on a phased basis either working back in the construction department or through consideration of retraining/redeployment into another area. If you felt that an external arbitrator such as ACAS could assist you in the process of return, the college will arrange for this.

I am sorry that this is not the outcome that you would wish, and I am also saddened that you are still unable to return to work. I know that your contribution is valued by the management of the college and I trust the college HR Department will provide you with any support we can to assist your return to work.

The information regarding e-mails that you requested under the Freedom of Information Act is being researched by the HR and MIS departments and will be the subject of separate communication from Joan Horncastle or Jill Lampson.

Yours Sincerely

Paul McKant

Principal and Chief Executive

So:

- Things are a lot better and the rest of the team are happy (that's not what they're telling me!)
- Ron is staying in his position!
- I, on the other hand, can either go back to work under Ron! Or get redeployed somewhere else in the college

So – the Grievance Procedure which should have been completed within about 2 months maximum was stretched out, and I was made to wait <u>8 months and 27 days!</u>

I am an innocent victim. I have been put through hell – and then the outcome is derisory!

I bet Ron Atler and Dale Rolland are laughing their socks off!

I read through the letter a few times, then I telephoned Robert to let him know.

I don't even know if I'm at all surprised by the outcome – or if I expected it??? I have done all I could have done, BUT it hasn't done me any good.

Because I believe very much in right and wrong, I'm not a happy bunny, but I realise I can't do anything more. I have come to the end of the procedure and they seem to have won. Not fair – but life isn't always fair is it?

So, it's back to options again:

Option 1 – Go back to work under Ron Atler (NEVER GONNA HAPPEN)!

Option 2 – Be redeployed somewhere else in the college (why should I have to move when I've done nothing wrong?)

Option 3 – Leave college

I only have one option as far as I'm concerned and that's option 3.

How unfair is that?

A grade 1 conscientious lecturer is forced to leave the College whilst the intimidating, bullying manager can stay.

I have gone through this fight, battered from all sides of college management and so far, I have failed. I may have decided that my only option now is to leave – but that does NOT mean that it is right. I am not prepared to just leave quietly and 'let them off'.

I will go to an employment tribunal and hopefully prove that Kirklees College is a college that treats its staff with total disregard, makes them ill, and that it also disregards Employment Law.

I have been forced to leave and that is Constructive Dismissal. I aim to prove that. I just don't know what cost it will have for my health, as I don't know how much more stress I can take.

When Robert comes home, we discuss the letter and Robert accepts that I need to leave college. I have been forced into it which is disgusting, but I think he's relieved in some ways as he has seen the 'mess' that I have become.

28/10/12

I rang the Legal team from our home insurance policy for advice. The man I spoke to, told me a few phrases that he advised I put in my resignation letter and he told me what information I would have to send their law department, so that they could check my case, to see if they were willing to represent me at an employment tribunal. I made copious notes and then spent the rest of the afternoon researching employment tribunals/constructive dismissal on the internet. I made notes as I went and printed out information also.

29/10/12

I started drafting out my resignation letter. This took me quite some time as I wanted to get it just right.

I will not send my resignation letter in the post. I am going to go into college and hand a resignation letter to Paul McKant, then a copy to HR and then a final copy to Dale Rolland. I want to look them in the eye as I hand my resignation letter to them, and I want them to know that it's not over yet.

Its October half term so I will have to wait until next Monday to hand it in. I also want to pick up my teaching files (all the work I have produced over the past twelve years in case I decide to teach again somewhere else, at a later date – although the way I feel now, the last thing I can imagine myself doing is teaching again).

I typed up my resignation letter and dated it 5th November - so it matches Monday when I plan to go to College (for the very last time) and hand it in.

My resignation letter:

5/11/12

Dear Paul,

I am very disappointed in your decision and that you are not taking appropriate steps to deal with bullying from a member of your management team (letter dated 26th October 2012). You seem to be siding with the bully as you state that I can undertake to retrain so that I can be redeployed into another area. This is not acceptable as it is punishing me (the victim) and affectively ending any progression I might have had at the college.

This is a breach of my contract and my statutory rights. It leaves me with no choice but to hand in my notice. This leaves me in a situation where I have been constructively, automatically, unfairly dismissed and in due course, I will be taking advice on going to an employment tribunal.

Another issue I am taking advice on is the vicarious liability in respect of Kirklees College for the losses caused to me, by the unlawful acts of harassment, by Ron Atler during his employment. I will be taking advice on pursuing a claim for such harassment for the civil liability the college has under Section 3 of the Protection of Harassment Act 1997.

I hereby give you two months' notice. As such, my official leaving date will be 5th January 2013. The bullying and harassment I have been subjected to have caused my illness, and as such my doctor has given me a sick note to cover the first month of my notice period. I have given this to Human Resources.

Yours Sincerely

Janette Castle

That should make it clear that it's not over yet and that they will be seeing me again!

I have a college laptop which I will have to return. Normally you would give it to your line manager, but I am not prepared to do this (and have Ron possibly deny I have brought it back). I have decided that I will hand it in, to HR and make them sign for it.

2/11/12

I received a letter in the post from the Director of Human Resources dated 1/11/12.

1 November 2012

Private and Confidential

Dear Janette

Further to Paul McKant's letter of 26 October and your email of 31 October, the information you have requested under the Freedom of Information Act is in the process of being collated.

However, as your request involves personal information about yourself, the request is being dealt with under the Data Protection Act 1998, as a Subject Access Request, which has resulted in delays in getting permission from other individuals it relates to.

Due to this being handled under the Data Protection Act 1998 and that these requests usually result in a wider search for information, the Act states that we have 40 calendar days to respond to your query, therefore the information will be provided to you by Tuesday 13 November.

Yours Sincerely

Jill Lampson

Director of Human resources

More delaying tactics. Surprise, surprise.

5/11/12

I drove over to college with my laptop and my three resignation letters. I felt apprehensive and conspicuous when I got there. I decided that I wanted to collect my teaching files first, so I went into J Block. I knew that the electrical and plumbing section had moved down to the construction building (Brunel House), so I didn't feel too bad walking into the empty staff room.

Some of my stuff was still there on my shelves (but my filing cabinets had been removed). I collected my teaching files and put them in the boot of my car.

I then nipped into the exams office and said a quick 'goodbye' to the girls in there, then I walked round to the Principal's office.

I felt a bit weird as I was nervous, but I also felt the need to see the Principal, and to personally hand him my resignation.

As I walked along the corridor towards Paul McKant's office he stepped outside and started walking towards me. I stopped in front of him and said, "Hi Paul. I have come to hand in my resignation letter".

He looked at me and I could tell that he didn't know who I was! He couldn't remember me!!!

I handed my resignation letter to him and walked back down the corridor and up the staircase to the HR office.

I went into the HR reception and rang the bell. A young HR girl came out. I informed her that I wanted to hand my resignation letter to the HR manager. I told her that I was handing back my college laptop and that I needed her to sign my sheet of paper to acknowledge receipt of it. The HR girl started telling me that I needed to hand my laptop over to my line manager. I replied, "I have issues with my line manager. I am leaving college because of him and I will not hand my laptop back to him as I don't trust him".

I repeated that I was leaving my laptop with her and that I needed her to sign for it. I put my laptop on the reception desk and handed across the acknowledgement sheet that I had prepared. She reluctantly signed it.

Joan Horncastle (HR manager) came out. I handed her another copy of my resignation letter and told her that I wanted my evidence folder back. Joan replied that she would try to find it for me. I told her I would take my parking barrier card back to finance and would then return for it.

When I returned to the HR office Joan had found my evidence folder. She gave it to me and I was polite as I had decided that I would leave with respect, and my head held high.

As I walked down the stairs to the main entrance Paul McKant was walking along the corridor below. He looked up and gave me a dirty, filthy look of distaste. I just returned his stare. Now you know who I am I thought….and now you know I intend to take this further.

I then drove down to Brunel House. I went into reception and asked the receptionist if I could see Dale Rolland.

As I walked into his office he was 'all smiles and friendly'. I said "Hi. I've just come in to give you my resignation letter".

Dale replied, "Oh… Aren't you coming back?" He seemed genuinely surprised.

I gave a bit of a snort, shook my head and said "No". I put my duplicate resignation letter on his desk, then asked if I could go to the electrical staffroom to collect my belongings.

Dale replied that "Yes, that was fine and that he would take me there". We walked there, chatting amicably. I had decided that it would be far more effective for me to be polite and professional (as this would just compound what they already knew – that I was a professional, competent teacher, and that they now needed to replace me).

I didn't see any point in behaving rudely, being cocky or sulky. They knew I had an unblemished career, that they had put me through hell – and here I was, standing with Dale Rolland, conducting myself in a dignified manner, head held high (but after letting him know that I wasn't letting it go – and that I was taking them to an Employment Tribunal). Dale Rolland had given me a Grade 1 when he had observed me teaching. He knew I could teach, that I was organised and that I had kept the electrical section going at times in the past. Now he knew that I was leaving!

When we got to the staffroom Steve and Eddie (the plumbers) were in there on a free period. Both were happy to see me and were asking me how I was. I explained that I had just come to collect my stuff. James Tebb was also in the staffroom but I completely ignored him. We couldn't find a key for my filing cabinets, so I asked Dale if it was OK to go and ask Jack (Booth who was teaching) where the keys were. Dale said "Yes" and walked me to his classroom. Jack came out and Dale left us. I had a quick word with Jack and asked him if it would be Ok to say a quick 'goodbye' to the class he was teaching (as I had been their course tutor). I was very professional and just informed them that I was leaving, but that I couldn't tell them why. I apologised for being off work and wished them well for the future.

I went back to the staffroom and started putting my belongings into bags. John Forrest came in and gave me a massive hug, then Judith Hamilton came in and did the same thing.

After a quick chat I left and as I was walking towards the exit door, I noticed Ron Atler and Scott Shard (another manager) stood talking by the door, (I imagine Dale Rolland had told him that I was in the building and so he had stood there purposely). I just kept my head held high, walked past and said "Bye" to Scott and completely ignored Ron.

I drove home and felt a little bit 'free' on one hand (that they couldn't punish me further), but also weird that in two months I would be officially unemployed! This was a massive thing for me. I had worked for twenty-six years since leaving school at sixteen. What was I going to do now?

I was glad that I had handed my resignation to Dale Rolland, as I knew that he would inform his mate Ron Atler that I was threatening to take them to a tribunal. Would Ron scoff at this, or would it worry him (if College management gave him grief about it)?

6/11/12

John Forrest telephoned me to tell me that he had handed in his notice. He has managed to get a job at Manchester college, which will be further for him to travel, but said that he just couldn't stay working for Kirklees College any longer. Steve Clay (another plumbing lecturer) is off sick because of stress (which means because of Ron Atler).

There were only seven lecturers in the plumbing and electrical section. Andrew Smithy left in August and then I handed in my notice yesterday. John handed his notice in today, and Steve is off sick due to stress (all due to Ron Atler).

I worked there for 12 years, John for 7 and a half and Steve has worked there for 11 years. So, Kirklees College will lose

30 years of experienced teachers (if Steve ends up leaving) – and all because they decided to stick with Ron Atler the bully boy!

CHAPTER 6

I know I have a lot to do, but I don't know how to go about doing it. I got back in touch with the legal cover of our home insurance policy. I informed them that I had now handed in my notice and that I needed to know how to go about taking Kirklees College to an employment tribunal.

I was told that I would need to send my evidence to one of their solicitors to see if they thought that I had a case – and if so, they would represent me.

So once again I have lots of preparation to do. I prepared my folder of evidence and sent it recorded delivery to the lawyers' firm.

I spent the rest of the week researching employment tribunals, constructive dismissal, etc.

8/11/12

I decided it would be a good idea to email staff in the electrical and plumbing department to ask if they had received their investigation notes back to check and sign and send back at Stage 2 of my grievance (I already knew the answer to this – but I wanted written proof to use as evidence at my tribunal) to prove that the investigation procedure hadn't been followed.

From: janettecastle@hotmail.co.uk

Sent: 08 November 2012

To: jbooth@kirkleescollege.com

Subject: Investigation notes

Hi Jack,

Can you please confirm whether you did, or did not, receive your interview notes back from your investigation meeting with Jane Davis and Karen (HR) in May/June that was part of my Stage 2 grievance process.

Thank you

Janette

I sent the same email to Paul Schofield, John Forrest and, Judith Hamilton

9/11/12

I received replies to my emails:

From: jbooth@kirkleescollege.com

Sent: 09 November 2012 12:30:01

To: janettecastle@hotmail.co.uk

Subject: Investigation notes

Janette.

I did not, and I emailed them to that effect!

Regards

Jack

From: jhamilton@kirkleescollege.com

Sent: 09 November 2012

To: janettecastle@hotmail.co.uk

Subject: Investigation notes

Hi Janette,

I can confirm I have not received them yet!

I did get an email from Joan Horncastle on 17 August stressing their importance and replied on 28 August that I had not yet got them despite my interview taking place at the end of May; I heard nothing more...

Kind Regards

Judith Hamilton

From: pschofield@kirkleescollege.com

Sent 09 November 2012

To: janettecastle@hotmail.co.uk

Subject: Investigation notes

Hi Janette,

No, I have never received any notes back from my interview.

Cheers

Paul

From: jforrest@kirkleescollege.com

Sent: 09 November 2012

To: janettecastle@hotmail.co.uk

Subject: Investigation notes

Hi Janette,

No, I didn't receive any notes from that meeting.

Regards

John

Proof in black and white that the investigation procedure was not followed. I printed the emails off and put them in my evidence folder (with the emails from Tanya Brown and Andrew Smithy regarding them not receiving their investigation notes back).

13/11/12

I received a letter in the post from Kirklees College dated 12th November

12 November 2012

Dear Janette,

I write regarding your formal request on 5 October 2012.

Please find attached a range of documents that have been pulled together from key members of staff who have been involved in your grievance investigations. However, there are several documents which the college has decided to

refuse you access to for the following reasons in line with the Data Protection Act:

1. Some of these documents, in particular, the meeting notes with other members of staff contain information about other individuals and those individuals have not permitted its release to a third party. In this case, neither the author of the email nor the recipient of the email has given their permission for this to be released. The College does not believe it is reasonable in this situation to release this information without their permission.

2. Sharing the information with a third party (ie yourself) would be a breach of confidence owed to the other employees of the college due to the sensitive and confidential content.

3. The documents that we are withholding from you were not addressed to yourself, and the information within it is not classed as personal information about you.

I trust you will see the appropriateness of this response and I hope that the information supplied is satisfactory to your requirements.

Yours Sincerely

Paul McKant

Principal and Chief Executive

They are refusing me access to information about **me** as it would be a breach of confidence owed to other employees of the college – those other employees being the bullying, manipulative management who have stolen my career!!!!

Well, the truth 'will out' as Macbeth said (at the tribunal).

I looked through the pages of information Paul McKant had deemed fit to send me. Most of it was what I had already, such as letters college had sent me at different stages of my grievance.

Some slightly interesting pages were emails where I was discussed:

From: pmckant@kirkleescollege.com

Sent: 16 October 2012

To: mrook@kirkleescollege.com cwood@kirkleescollege.com jhorncastle@kirkleescollege.com jlampson@kirkleescollege.com amitchell@kirkleescollege.com jturrand@kirkleescollege.com

Subject: Janette Castle Appeal – 5 October

Dear All,

Following the appeal hearing can I request:

1. *Joan to find out what happened to the e-mails which HR sent out and which Janette and Tanya said were not received*
2. *Mandy to discuss possible reinvestigation with Anthea and Joan*
3. *Joan to consider FOIA request for e-mails*
4. *The accusation which JC refers to, at Stage II – were they verbal or written? Are they recorded?*
5. *PM to review with MR and Joan*

OK?

Paul

So, Paul wants to know whether the accusation (false accusations against me) are written and recorded. I bet he does!

Well Paul, they are, and they are in my evidence folder!

From: drolland@kirkleescollege.com

Sent: 23 March 2012

To: jturrand@kirkleescollege.com

Subject: Investigation

Hi Jean,

I've just met with Janette Castle.

I talked to her about the interviews with the staff that I have done. She was wanting the conclusion to it, which I haven't done yet. She will probably want to take it to the next level after the conclusion.

Could you give me a little time with it? Need it quite urgently though.

Thanks

Dale

So, Dale thought I would take it to the next stage. This must be because he knew that he had conducted Stage 1 in a poor manner!

From: jweldon@kirkleescollege.com

Sent: 08 May 2012

To: jturrand@kirkleescollege.com

Subject: Grievance procedure

Hi Jean,

My feeling is that she is fairly adamant about progressing to Stage 2, so I am going to start arranging the Stage 2 hearing.

I'll contact Charlotte for your availability over the next week or so.

Thanks

Jan

I told Jean Turrand on 18th April that I wished to move to Stage 2 - so why would Jan think (3 weeks later) that I was adamant about progressing to Stage 2?

The only reason I can think is that she and Jean tried very hard to dissuade me progressing (and failed!)

From: lanison@kirkleescollege.com

Sent: 20 July 2012

To: jhorncastle@kirkleescollege.com

Subject: Janette Castle

Attachments: Stage 2 Grievance Outcome letter

Hi,

I've attached the letter I did for her outlining the outcome of the Stage 2 grievance.

If I'm honest, I think she will take the grievance to Stage 3.

Thanks

Linda

It seems that at each stage HR and management thought I would go to the next stage of the grievance. Why is this?

They knew that I wasn't being represented by the Union, I had never been an employee who had caused problems in the past?

They must have known that either I was very determined; or that they had dealt with each stage in an incompetent manner?

8/12/12

I received an email from the lawyer in London informing me that she had evaluated my case and she had found that she couldn't proceed as she didn't believe it was over 50% conclusive that the case could be won (as she felt she hadn't enough proof)!!!!!

I just felt shell shocked!

I telephoned the lawyer as I couldn't take it in that I had been dismissed yet again! The lawyer told me that to win a constructive dismissal case was very difficult (much harder than a wrongful dismissal claim). She went on to inform me that to win a constructive dismissal claim you had to prove either:

- Breach of Contract
- Loss of Mutual Trust and Confidence

I can't understand why she doesn't think I have enough evidence to prove my case????

The solicitor at the free legal advice center had assured me that intimidation and bullying were the same things (and Kirklees College had admitted that Ron Atler was intimidating). Kirklees College hadn't followed the Grievance procedure or investigation procedure. They had stretched out the grievance procedure to 8 months and 27 days – how could there not be a loss of mutual trust and confidence (on my part)?

So, yet another smack in the face. I just felt sick and full of despair! I rang the home insurance legal department again for advice, but the advice was all negative. (They wouldn't take my case and represent me).

I just cried all afternoon. I feel like the whole world is against me. If a lawyer is telling me I don't have a case – are they right? They have experience. I've never had anything like this happen to me before. I know I'm in the right – but is that enough?

I spoke to Robert when he got home. I have looked up telephone numbers for local solicitors, so we discussed that I will ring a few of them tomorrow for advice, and the cost of being represented by them at the tribunal.

Robert has a mate called Mick Clark who is retired now, but he used to work for a union. He was 'high up' and used to travel all over the world with his job. Robert gave me his telephone number, so I will ring him for advice tomorrow too.

9/12/12

I telephoned a few local solicitor's firms to ask how much it would cost me for them to represent me at my employment tribunal.

I was astounded to find out that their fees would be between £7,500 - £10,000 per day!

I was also informed that even if I won the case, I would have to pay the legal fees! I had assumed it would be like normal courts, where the side that loses the case pays the legal costs.

One of the companies said that as it was a constructive dismissal case against a large organisation, he thought the length of the tribunal would be three days?

So, it would cost me between £22,500 - £30,000 to be represented AND I would have to pay these fees whether I won or lost!

I know I am 100% in the right – but I am soon to be officially unemployed. How can I spend £22,500 - £30,000 on a case that a professional lawyer has told me that she thought couldn't be proved?

I feel sick and feel I like I'm 'up against the world'. It feels like everywhere I turn there is someone who wants to beat me down!!!

After tea, I decided I'd ring Mick Clark. I had previously met with him briefly (around Stage 3 of my grievance) and shown him my Stage 1 and Stage 2 grievance outcome letters and had told him the length of time the grievance had taken. Mick had pointed out at the time that the Stage 1 outcome was all wrong, (they hadn't informed me of my right to appeal at Stage 1 and they had admitted that Ron Atler was intimidating (so he was a bully)). Mick had told me that he thought I had a case against them.

When Mick answered the phone, I updated him that I had handed in my notice and that I wanted to take Kirklees College to an employment tribunal. I told him my home insurance legal department wasn't willing to represent me and that the fees of other solicitors were extortionate.

Mick informed me that I could represent myself at no cost. As soon as he said this, I felt like a massive weight had been lifted off my shoulders. I know what I've been through. I've lived it, I know every fact – so I'm probably the best person to represent me.

When I got off the phone, I told Robert that Mick had told me that I could represent myself. I told Robert that this was what I wanted to do.

My grit and determination came back to me. I will NOT give in. I will represent myself and take Kirklees College to a tribunal. I have nothing to lose (as I've already lost it). I'm sure it will be as scary as hell. I have no idea what I will have to do, or how I'm going to do it, but I will do my homework, be prepared and do my best.

The way I see it is that if I end up losing, at least I will know that I have done everything in my power – and I'll know that I didn't give in and let them win without a fight.

I spent the rest of the week on the internet researching representing yourself at employment tribunals/constructive dismissal cases etc

1/1/13

Thank goodness 2012 is over – but what will 2013 bring?

CHAPTER 7

<u>6/1/13</u>

I am now officially unemployed as my notice period has ended. I can't believe it. Unemployed!!!

You need to inform an Employment Tribunal that you wish to bring a case against your former employer within three months of leaving the company.

I don't see any point in waiting – I have now officially left, so I will do it now without delay. My thinking is that the earlier I start proceedings, the faster it will end, and then hopefully I will get my life back.

I went on the internet and started to fill out the employment tribunals ET1 form. The form took me a long time to fill out – hopefully, I did it correctly.

I made a copy of the electronic document, so I could print it out for my file. I then pressed 'SEND' and felt mixed emotions:

- Glad that I have begun the process as I'm determined not to give up.
- The stress of the unknown. I have to do battle again – and have no idea how to go about it!

I need to go back to the free legal advice service and get whatever advice I can from them, about how I go about representing myself. They are only held once a fortnight, so I will have to check when the next session is.

<u>11/1/13</u>

I received a letter from the employment tribunal:

EMPLOYMENT TRIBUNALS

Date: 10 January 2013

Case Number 1800254/2013

Claimant   Respondent

Miss J Castle   V   Kirklees College

NOTICE OF A CLAIM

NOTICE OF HEARING on Thursday, 23 May 2013 at 10:00 am

The Claim

The Employment Tribunal has accepted a claim against the above respondent(s). It has been given the above Case Number, which should be quoted in any communication relating to this case. A copy of the case is enclosed for the respondent(s).

The Response

To submit a response, a prescribed form must be used. Alternatively, you may respond on-line at www.justice.gov It must be received by this office by **07/02/2013**. If a response is not given by then, and no extension of time has been applied for and given, the claim will proceed undefended, or a default judgement may be made.

The Hearing

The claim will be heard by an Employment Judge and members at **Employment Tribunal, 4th Floor, City Exchange, 11 Albion Street, LS1 5ES, on Thursday**

*23rd **May at 10:00 am** or as soon thereafter on that day as the Tribunal can hear it. **1 day** has been allocated to hear the evidence and decide the claim. If you think that this is not long enough, you must give your reasons in writing, and your time estimate.*

You may submit written representations for consideration at the hearing. If so, they must be sent to the Tribunal and all other parties not less than 7 days before the hearing. You should ensure that any relevant witnesses attend the hearing and that you bring sufficient copies of any relevant documents.

Case Management Orders

The parties shall comply with the following Case Management Orders and timetable.

By no later than	The following shall be done
7 February 2013	*The claimant shall set out in writing what remedy the Tribunal is being asked to award. The claimant shall send a copy to the respondent. The claimant shall include any evidence and documentation supporting what is claimed and how it is calculated. The claimant shall also include information about what steps the claimant has taken to reduce any loss (including any earnings or benefits received from new employment).*
21 February 2013	*The claimant and the respondent shall send each other a list of any documents that they wish to refer to at the hearing or which are relevant to the case. They shall send each other a copy of these documents if requested to do so.*
7 March 2013	*The respondent shall then prepare sufficient*

	copies of the documents for the hearing. The documents shall be fastened together in a file to open flat. The file of documents shall be indexed. The documents shall be in a logical order. All pages shall be numbered consecutively. The respondent shall provide the other parties with a copy of the file. Four copies of the file shall be provided to the Tribunal at the hearing (and not before)
21 March 2013	The claimant and the respondent shall prepare full written statements of the evidence they and their witnesses intend to give at the hearing. No additional witness evidence may be allowed at the hearing without permission of the Tribunal. The written statements shall have numbered paragraphs. The claimant and the respondent shall send the written statements of their witnesses to each other. Four copies of each written statement shall be provided for use by the Tribunal at the hearing (and not before)
16 May 2013	Where the claimant and the respondent are both professionally represented, the professional representatives shall prepare a draft statement of issues or questions that are to be decided by the Tribunal at the hearing. The draft statement of issues shall be subject to the Tribunals agreement at the commencement of the hearing

These Orders are made under rule 10 of the Employment Tribunals Rules of Procedure 2004. The timetable above is part of the Orders and it must be complied with. A claimant or a respondent who fails to comply with these Orders may be liable to have the *whole or any part of its case struck out and/or to costs and/or (in case of failure to disclose a document) to a fine not exceeding £1,000.*

Signed Martin Maynard

For the Secretary of Employment Tribunals

Dated 10 January 2013

Cc Acas

The tribunal has accepted my claim. Fantastic news! I have a case number and I have a hearing date of Thursday 23rd May 2013.

Positive news for a change. And, it should all be over in just over four months. Halleluiah!

Kirklees College will have received a copy of the letter too, so they will know that I mean business.

Miss J Castle V Kirklees College. Sounds good to me.

I wonder if they are surprised/shocked or if they aren't bothered in the slightest?

I hope Ron Atler and Dale Rolland find out imminently – so that they know that I haven't disappeared and gone away to lick my wounds. Hopefully, it will refocus some stress back onto them – and that their behaviour is back under the spotlight of their managers.

I must have read the 'Case Management Orders' that came with the letter about ten times and highlighted parts so that I know what I need to do, by what date.

I need to set out what Remedy the Tribunal is asked to award by the 7th of February, so I need to find out how to do this.

I telephoned Robert at work to let him know the news and then I texted Tanya, Judith, Kay, Andrew, John, etc to let them know also.

<u>14/1/13</u>

I drove to the free legal advice service in Beeston. I made sure I got there for about 5.40 pm so that I was the first one waiting when the session began at 6 pm.

I was dealt with by a very nice female solicitor. I showed her the documents from college (outcome letters from grievance etc) and told her I was representing myself at the tribunal and that I needed to know how to complete my 'remedy'.

She took my email address and said that she would email me a copy of a Remedy form to fill out. She assured me that intimidation was the same thing as bullying and that the length of time the grievance procedure had taken was far too long, (which gave me confidence in my case).

She told me that I would benefit from attending the tribunal, to sit in on other cases, so that I would understand the format of what went on at a tribunal, and gain experience from that. This seemed like a brilliant idea.

<u>16/1/13</u>

I telephoned the tribunal to ask what I needed to do to attend a tribunal hearing. I was told that there was a hearing starting on Monday at 10 am for an unfair dismissal case where a solicitor was representing a client.

They said that I was welcome to sit at the back and watch the hearing.

I will go and watch this tribunal and see what the solicitor does, to try and find out what I will need to do to attempt to represent myself.

I received an email from the solicitor from free advice service with the attached Remedy form – so I will try to fathom out how to fill it out.

<u>19/1/13</u>

I drove to Leeds and found where the tribunal building was. I went up to the 4th floor and waited in reception.

Today was very worthwhile. Simple things like knowing where the building was, what floor the tribunals were held on, where the toilets were, procedure for keeping claimants and respondents away from one another, etc, - The court stewards go and get both parties (claimants and respondents) from their respective waiting rooms, and then they all walk down together to their courtroom.

I walked down behind everyone and sat down at the back of the room with my note pad and pen. It was interesting to see how the Hearing began, where the Judge, claimant, respondent, lawyer and, witnesses sat.

The claimant was claiming unfair dismissal from her job as a carer for a disabled lady. Evidence was heard and both the claimant and the respondent gave evidence, but the lawyers represented their clients for the rest of the hearing.

I listened intently and wrote down any words that I didn't understand (so that I could 'google them' when I got home).

I wasn't very impressed by the claimant's lawyer and the whole case fell apart at the end as the Judge ruled in favour of the respondent as the claimant hadn't lodged her claim for unfair dismissal within three months of being sacked. I think she was only over by 1 – 2 days, but the Judge agreed with the respondent's lawyer (that this invalidated the claim).

I found it a really good experience. I went home and googled 'fundamental breach of contract' that the respondent's lawyer had said during the hearing and wrote down the meaning in my notebook. I intend to attend more tribunal hearings. I want to go to a mixture of ones represented by lawyers, and ones where the claimants are representing themselves.

<u>26/1/13</u>

I went to another tribunal hearing. The claimant was represented by a lawyer, but the respondent (a small businessman) represented himself.

It was a very strange case; the claimant claimed that she had been unfairly dismissed and that it was due to her son being in prison for murder (you just couldn't make it up!). Anyway, the claimant seemed pretty unintelligent, and in the wrong (to me) whilst the respondent came across as an intelligent, decent boss who had tried to accommodate the claimant whilst she had been his employee.

BUT...the claimant won her case as the respondent hadn't followed the correct procedure when he had finally dismissed the claimant.

I felt sorry for the respondent BUT, by this second case, I was beginning to realise that facts and procedure were everything – and that they won cases.

This gave me a bit of confidence as I have many facts about procedures NOT being followed by Kirklees College.

<u>27/1/13</u>

I sent a letter to Paul McKant at Kirklees College:

Employment Tribunals – Case Number: 1800254/2013

Miss J Castle V Kirklees College

Dear Mr. McKant,

In compliance with the Case Management Orders, I have listed the documents that I plan to use as evidence at the hearing. The documents are as follows:

- *My contract of employment from Kirklees College (formerly Huddersfield Technical College)*
- *Kirklees College's Grievance Procedure*
- *Kirklees College's Values and Behaviours Policy*
- *The folder of evidence (that Kirklees College management has seen previously during my grievance against Ron Atler) which contains various letters and emails between myself and college*
- *A letter from my doctor stating the illness caused to me was due to Work-Related Stress whilst employed by Kirklees College*
- *Internal classroom observations conducted by the management of Kirklees College during my employment*
- *A character reference from my previous line manager (of 9 years) at Kirklees College*
- *A character reference from the lead training officer of JTL (Joint Training Limited) who I worked closely with during my employment at Kirklees College*
- *Witness testimonies from various ex-employees and present employees at Kirklees College*

- *ACAS' Guidance for employees – Bullying and Harassment at work booklet*

Yours Sincerely

Janette Castle

I have received all my witness testimonies from my ex-work colleagues and need to print them out and put them in my evidence folder.

2/2/13

I received a letter from Paul McKant dated 31st January:

31 January 2013

Dear Miss Castle,

Thank you for your letter dated 27 January 2013. The College will forward the details to our solicitor who is dealing with the case on behalf of the College.

Yours Sincerely

Paul McKant

Principle and Chief Executive

Bloody hell – that was a quick response. A shame they didn't respond to me so quickly 12 months ago, then we may not be in the position that we are now.

4/2/13

I filled out my remedy form. It took ages, and I'm not sure I have done it correctly? I will just have to send it off and hope for the best.

8/2/13

I received a letter from Kirklees College's solicitors:

SY Law Solicitors Ltd

Ref: 1800254/2013

Regional Secretary
Leeds Employment Tribunal

Dear Sir/Madam,

Claimant	:	**Miss Janette Castle**
Respondent	:	**Kirklees College**
Tribunal Number	:	**1800254/2013**

We are instructed to act on behalf of the named Respondents in this action namely Kirklees College.

We enclose ET3 on behalf of the named Respondent together with attached Grounds of Resistance.

We look forward to hearing from you further.

Yours Faithfully

Stephanie Path

Senior Employment Litigator

SY Law

I read through the attached Grounds of Resistance (and quickly renamed it 'Grounds of Nonsense')

Nonsense such as:

- *The Electrical and Plumbing curriculum area was performing poorly, and student outcomes / successes were low*
- *It is contended that the grievance was dealt with in line with the Respondents grievance procedure!!!*

The only bit of truth within the 39 paragraphs of lies stated *'The Respondent did acknowledge that Ron Atler's management style was at times inappropriate...'*

It's just full of nonsense. Well, I aim to prove that it's all nonsense at the Tribunal.

<u>18/2/13</u>

Kirklees College has got all my documents for the tribunal and I should have theirs in three days. I can't wait to see them. They can't have any negative or incriminating evidence against me (unless they have fabricated it), as I was the perfect employee.

<u>21/2/13</u>

I haven't received any documents from Kirklees College. Surely, they are not going to disregard the tribunal's Case Management Orders????

<u>22/2/13</u>

I telephoned the tribunal to inform them that Kirklees College solicitors hadn't followed the Case Management

Orders, as I hadn't received any documents that they planned to use at the tribunal. The person I spoke to said that they would 'note it down' on the case notes, but didn't give any indication that they would do anything about it?

25/2/13

I received a telephone call from ACAS this morning. ACAS must have spoken to Kirklees College. The woman from ACAS told me that she had been asked (by Kirklees College) to offer me £1000 to drop my case against them!

I laughed and said, "The answer is 'No', and tell them that I laughed when you offered me £1000".

She replied, "I won't say that you laughed, I will say that you thought it was a derisory amount". She told me that Kirklees College was not admitting fault, but was making the offer for commercial reasons.

I told her that they were at fault and that I aimed to prove it. She replied, "Their solicitor says that you won't win the case".

I replied (with sarcasm), "Then they have nothing to worry about then" and the conversation was over.

£1000 for what they've put me through! I don't think so!

28/2/13

I still haven't received any documents from Kirklees College, but I did receive a letter from the tribunal dated 26/2/13:

EMPLOYMENT TRIBUNALS

Date 26 February 2013

Case Number: 1800254/2013

Claimant   **Respondent**
Miss J Castle   V   **Kirklees College**

REQUEST FROM TRIBUNAL
Employment Tribunals Rules of Procedure 2004

Dear Sir/Madam,

Employment Judge Knight has asked for the parties to give their views about the length of Hearing currently listed on 23rd May 2013.

Please reply within 7 days of the date in this letter.

Yours Faithfully

Ella Smithy

For the Secretary of Employment Tribunals

Cc Acas

Length of hearing? I thought it had already been decided that one day was enough?

I wrote a reply letter back to Judge Knight:

Case Number: 180254/2013
Miss J Castle V Kirklees College

Dear Judge Knight,

I have never been to an employment tribunal before, so I have no idea what to expect, but I would think that one day should be sufficient for the Hearing on the 23rd of May 2013.

Yours Faithfully

Janette Castle

<u>7/3/13</u>

I was supposed to receive a file today which contained my documents (which Kirklees College has) and their documents (which they haven't sent me). That means they have not followed the tribunal's Case Management Orders again. How can they get away with it, and how the hell am I supposed to prepare for my tribunal without any documents!!!!!

<u>8/3/13</u>

I checked my emails first thing this morning and I had received nothing from Kirklees College's lawyers, so I decided to write to the Tribunal.

8/3/13

Case Number 1800254/2013

Miss J Castle V Kirklees College

Dear Sir/Madam,

I am writing to inform you that Kirklees College has missed another date for the Case Management Orders.

Yesterday (7/3/13) I should have received a file containing the documents for the hearing. I have not received one.

Kirklees College also missed the previous deadline of 21ˢᵗ February when they should have provided me with a list of the documents they wish to refer to at the hearing. I informed you about this by telephone and in an email on the 25ᵗʰ of February. I received back from you an automatic email; but I have not yet received any information as to when, or if, I will receive a list of their documents.

I feel that this is putting me at a disadvantage. I am representing myself, which is daunting. I have provided them with a list of documents that I plan to use and feel that it is only fair that they should have done the same, as stated in the Employment Tribunals Rules of Procedures.

Yours Sincerely

Janette Castle

<u>12/3/13</u>

I still haven't received documents from Kirklees College, so I telephoned the tribunal and spoke to Julian again. I informed him that I hadn't received any documents. Julian looked at our case notes and then told me that I must have received the documents from them as Kirklees College's lawyer had sent the tribunal information and had stated that they had sent me copies of everything!

I denied this and reiterated that I hadn't received anything through the post or via email. I could tell Julian didn't believe me as he said, 'It shows here that she has copied you into this correspondence.'

Then it suddenly clicked…. I asked, "Can you tell me what email address she supposedly sent it to?"

Julian replied, "janetcastle@hotmail.com"

"That's not my email address" I replied, "Its janettecastle@hotmail.co.uk. A solicitor would not make that many mistakes with one email address!"

Julian said that he would check what email address I had put on my ET1 form. When he returned he said that it was very clearly written as janettecastle@hotmail.co.uk and that it did seem suspicious that a solicitor would miss off two letters and then alter.co.uk to .com. Julian told me that he would make a note of this issue in the case file and that he would forward me a copy of the email (from the solicitor) to my correct email address.

Email from Julian with attachment (email dated 6th March from the solicitor which they sent to 'wrong' email address:

Your reference: 1800254/2013
Regional Secretary
Leeds Employment Tribunal

6th March 2013

Dear Sir/Madam,

Claimant:	*Miss Janette Castle*
Respondent:	*Kirklees College*
Tribunal Number:	*1800254/2013*

We refer to your separate correspondence on 26th February 2013.

With apologies for the delay in responding, which was occasioned by the sickness of the relevant fee earner in this matter, we respond as follows:

In respect of the disclosure, which was due on 21 February, we have today provided the Claimant with a complete list of all the documents on which the Respondent intends to rely. We have also invited the Claimant to request copies of any documents that she wishes to inspect.

Whereas we regret that disclosure of the list did not take place on 21 February 2013 as Ordered, it is submitted that the delay of 12 days does not cause the Claimant any prejudice as a complete copy of the hearing bundle shall be provided to the Claimant. Further, it is also submitted that the delay was occasioned by the diligence of those instructed in that we are seeking to ensure that copies of the documents that are now included in the list of disclosure were of a quality that is legible and satisfactory for the use of both parties and the tribunal.

In respect of the hearing, due to the complexity of the narrative in this matter, it is submitted that the single day for which the matter is currently listed is insufficient. We therefore respectfully suggest that the matter be vacated and re-listed for 3 days according to Employment Tribunal (Constitution and Rules of Procedure) Regulations 2004 rule 10 (2) (m).

We confirm that we have sent a copy of this correspondence to the Claimant.

Yours Faithfully

SY Law

Stephanie Path

It seemed to me to be another example of underhand behaviour! I knew Kirklees College had behaved appallingly, but I didn't expect lawyers to behave like this???

And one day for the tribunal is insufficient (due to the complexity of the narrative – I assume that means 'case' to normal people). It doesn't seem complex to me – I am in the right and have done no wrong, whilst Kirklees College is completely in the wrong – SIMPLE.

It seemed obvious to me that this was intentional; an attempt to 'grind me down' and hope that I would give up – but can I prove it?

I attended another session at the free legal advice service this evening to gain advice about Kirklees College's solicitor's behaviour and to see if there is anything that I can do about it.

The solicitor I spoke to tonight advised me to write to the tribunal and ask for an '**Unless Order**'. This means that if the respondents don't conform to Case Management Orders and meet deadlines, then they can be 'struck out' – the tribunal would still go ahead but they wouldn't be able to represent themselves, so the Judges would listen to my case and decide the outcome.

These free legal advice sessions are invaluable. Knowledge is power. I will prepare a letter for the tribunal, asking for an Unless Order.

I am also concerned that I have another deadline coming up (21/3/13 - prepare my written statement – which I can't do without the documents from Kirklees College). So, I will write a letter about that too:

14/3/13

Tribunal number 1800254/2013

Miss Janette Castle V Kirklees College

Dear Judge Knight,

I am writing to you about my concerns about the case so far.

I telephoned the tribunal and emailed them on the 25th of February to inform them that Kirklees College had missed their deadline of 21st February to send me their list of documents to be used at the hearing.

I then telephoned and sent a letter to the tribunal on the 8th of March to inform them that Kirklees College had missed their 7th of March deadline to send me their file of documents.

After receiving no response by the 14th of March, I telephoned the tribunal and spoke to Julian. I discussed my concerns about the deadline I have for 21st March and asked what action could be taken.

Julian looked at the case notes and said that Kirklees College's solicitors had sent a letter to the tribunal dated 6th March and had sent me a copy via email. When I replied that I hadn't received an email Julian checked the email address and found out that it was not my email address.

Firstly, I do not believe that a solicitor would make such a mistake.

My email address is janettecastle@hotmail.co.uk

The address they sent it to is janetcastle@hotmail.com

One mistake in an address may be believable, but two mistakes lead me to believe that this could have been intentional.

Julian kindly emailed me the solicitor's letter so that I could read it. When I read it, I telephoned Julian to discuss the inaccuracies. The inaccuracies are as follows:

It states that they have provided me with a complete list of all documents that they intend to rely on and that they have invited me to request any copies that I would like to inspect. This is not true.

It states that a complete copy of the hearing bundle shall be provided to the claimant. This was supposed to happen by 7th March but has not.

It then states that they think one day for the tribunal is insufficient and that they wish for the matter to be vacated and relisted for three days. I believe that this is just delay tactics and their way of trying to wear me down further.

They were notified on the 10th of January that one day had been allocated for the hearing. I would have thought that a solicitor would have been able to make their judgement of the timescale required before now.

Because of my experience of Kirklees College's lack of being able to keep to procedures and deadlines during my grievance with them in 2012 and the fact that they have not followed the Orders under rule 10 of the Employment Tribunals Rules of Procedures 2004, I wish to request that an Unless Order is made against Kirklees College.

Yours Sincerely

Janette Castle

I then wrote another letter to the tribunal for advice (and so that they had a record to put on my file before the tribunal):

14/3/13

Tribunal number: 1800254/2013

Miss Janette Castle V Kirklees College

Dear Tribunal,

After speaking to Julian today about my concerns about being able to meet my deadline of 21st of March to prepare my full written statement of evidence due to Kirklees College not following the Case Management Orders, I wonder if I could have written clarification about where I would stand if I was unable to meet my deadline.

My deadline for the 21st of March is now only a week away. I have kept up with the Case Management Orders so far and met my 7th of February and 21st of February deadlines. I have also prepared my folder of evidence ready for the 21st of March deadline but am unable to prepare my full written statement due to my not having Kirklees College's documents.

I await your advice on this matter

Yours Sincerely

Janette Castle

Right, let's see if that does the trick. No doubt the solicitor Stephanie Path (or 'Psychopath' as I prefer to call her - due to her name being S Path and her annoying me greatly), will be annoyed that I've informed the tribunal of the situation but hopefully, the Unless Order will be brought against Kirklees College.

I need to find out ASAP what is going to happen about my deadline on the 21st. Robert and I get married on the 22nd. I shouldn't have to be chasing documents, causing additional stress. If I can follow the Case Management Orders and I'm a lay-person, then a lawyer should be able to follow them!

I then sent another letter regarding my wedding next week:

14/3/13

Tribunal number: 1800254/2013

Miss Janette Castle V Kirklees College

Copies sent to both tribunal and Kirklees College

Dear Tribunal/Paul McKant,

I am writing to inform you that I am getting married on the 22nd of March 2013, which means that on that date my name will change to Janette Hirst.

I intend to keep my email address in my maiden name until after the tribunal hearing to avoid any confusion.

I will also use my maiden name on all other correspondence between the tribunal and college unless the tribunal suggests otherwise in writing.

Yours Sincerely

Janette Castle

<u>19/3/13</u>

I received a copy of the letter sent from tribunal to 'Psychopath' dated 18th of March:

EMPLOYMENT TRIBUNALS

To: Stephanie Path

SY Law Solicitors

Date 18 March 2013

Case number: 1800254/2013

Claimant		**Respondent**
Miss J Castle	**V**	**Kirklees College**

REQUEST FROM TRIBUNAL
Employment Tribunals Rules of Procedure 2004

Dear Madam,

An Employment Judge has asked for your comments on the enclosed letter from the claimant.

Please reply by return.

Yours Faithfully

Ella Smithy

For the Secretary of Employment Tribunals

Cc Miss J Castle

Cc ACAS

So, they are doing something about it. This will be interesting. I bet 'Psycho' won't like it one bit - Let her have some stress for a change, instead of me!

20/3/13

I received a letter from the tribunal dated 19/3/13:

EMPLOYMENT TRIBUNALS

Case number 1800254/2013

Claimant		*Respondent*
Miss J Castle	*V*	**Kirklees College**

ACKNOWLEDGEMENT OF CORRESPONDENCE

Employment Tribunals Rules of Procedure 2004

Dear Madam,

I refer to your letter dated 14th March 2013, which has been placed on file.

An Employment Judge asks that if you require an extension of time to the deadline of the 21st of March then please clarify until when.

Yours Faithfully,

Ella Smithy

For the Secretary of Employment Tribunals

Cc Stephanie Path

Cc ACAS

I telephoned the tribunal to discuss my not being able to make the deadline and they don't seem to understand that it is Kirklees College's fault and not mine!

I just started crying on the phone. I don't know how much more I can take. I am asking for advice from the tribunal, and they are not helping or giving any advice. I ended up asking for an extension to the deadline. This had better not go against me when it is Kirklees College and 'Psycho's' fault!

Anyway, I replied to the letter by email:

From: janettecastle@hotmail.co.uk

To: esmithyleedset@hmtcs.gov

Sent: 20 March 2013

Subject: Case number 1800254/2013

To Ella,

I am responding to your letter where you state that the Employment Judge wants to know how long I require my extension of the 21st of March deadline to be.

I request a 2-week extension for Kirklees College to supply me with the relevant documents and folder that they should have supplied me by their deadline of the 21st of February and 7th of March respectively.

I have stated in a letter and telephone conversations to Julian and yourself that I have prepared my folder of evidence (including signed witness statements) and that I just need to write my statements of evidence (for which I require the information from Kirklees College).

The fact that I am unable to meet my 21st of March deadline because of matters beyond my control is making me feel physically unwell and I have been unable to sleep. I have telephoned the tribunal numerous times and sent letters informing the tribunal of the problems I have encountered so far.

I am attempting to represent myself in as professional a manner as any layperson could, and would like it to be put on my notes that I have chased this issue and tried to resolve it before the deadline.

Just to sum up – I have requested a 2-week extension, but I can only keep to that 2-week extension if Kirklees College furnishes me with their documents before this new deadline ends.

Please keep me informed about any response from Kirklees College and/or if any action is taken by the tribunal.

Regards

Janette Castle

The solicitor 'sent me' 7 documents attached to an email at 2.40 pm this afternoon:

From: spath@sylaw.co.uk

To: leedset@hmcts.gov

Cc: janettecastle@hotmail.co.uk

Subject: 1800254/2013

20th March 2013

Dear Sir/Madam,

Claimant: Miss Janette Castle

Respondent: Kirklees College

Tribunal number: 1800254/2013

We write further to the correspondence received from the claimant today.

For the avoidance of doubt, notwithstanding, that our contact details are included in the ET3 form, we have not received any correspondence from the Claimant concerning this matter. Further, we note that the Claimant has sent recent correspondence directly to the Respondent.

As indicated to the Tribunal by the Claimant, a response to the tribunal's correspondence was sent to the tribunal and the Claimant on 6th March 2013.

Whereas it is accepted that the email address used for the Claimant was incorrect, it is submitted that any such error was a genuine and honest mistake on the part of the person entering the email address. It is further utterly denied that there was any intention behind the error.

For the avoidance of doubt, having mistakenly entered the email address once, it remained incorrect on the email system and therefore the error was duplicated in the absence of any knowledge. Had the Claimant attempted to contact us at any point the mistake would have come to light much earlier than today and the case management directions would have been complied with more readily.

The Claimants contention that it is not true that we have provided documents and asked her to provide copies of hers is mistaken. The copies of documents were sent to the email above. Therefore, the error in this regard exacerbated the situation. Therefore, on the basis that we did not receive the Claimants documents, the bundle has yet to be finalised.

In any event, notwithstanding that the Claimant was not prevented from sending copies of her disclosure documents to us at any time, she failed to do so.

Having not received any documents from the Claimant we once again requested copies of the same on 14th March 2013. Regrettably, once more the email was sent to the email address which had been incorrectly entered on the first occasion. However, we did attach a delivery receipt to this email which was returned as successful. It was, therefore, our reasonable belief that the correspondence had been received.

For the assistance of the tribunal, and the Claimant, copies of all relevant emails are attached.

In respect of the length of the hearing, the Respondent remains of the view that the matter should be listed for 3 days. As our submissions in this regard were in response to a direct request from the tribunal, it is submitted that the Claimants contentions in respect of when the assessment of the length of the hearing should have been made are without vexatious and merit. The Respondent is entitled to indicate its assessment of the length of the hearing, and any submissions that they are trying to wear the Claimant down are denied.

On the basis that this email, together with all relevant emails and documents are being sent to the Claimant at the address that she has quoted, it is respectfully submitted that there is no necessity for an Unless Order.

It is also further requested that the Claimant corresponds with SY Law Solicitors as the Respondent's solicitors.

Yours Faithfully

Stephanie Path

Senior Employment Litigator

Utter nonsense! A mistake that they sent it to the wrong email address – Surely the tribunal won't believe them? I sent my documents to Kirklees College as I thought that was the correct thing to do. How is a non-legal person supposed to know what to do, if no one tells them?

When I tried to open the documents, some were blocked and wouldn't open, and some were pointless and not the documents I had been waiting for since 7/3/13!!!

I was so upset and frustrated. The solicitors aren't behaving professionally at all. I have no idea what I'm supposed to do.

When Robert got in from work, he found me crying uncontrollably. Robert tried talking to me and tried to calm me down. When he couldn't he said, "I think you are going to have to give up and walk away from this, as it's making you ill again". This is the second time he has told me that I need to give up.

I couldn't stop crying, but managed to reply, "I'm not going to give up!"

I just cried all night and felt sick. All I could think about was the fifteen to sixteen months of hell I'd already been through and that I am supposed to be getting married in two days – and that if I didn't manage to 'pull myself together' then my wedding would be spoilt also!!!

21/3/13

I got up and after having my breakfast and taking Indie out for a walk I decided that I would email the solicitor and copy in the tribunal:

From: janettecastle@hotmail.co.uk

Sent: 21 March 2013 10:00:20

To: spathclaims@sylaw.co.uk leedset@hmcts.gov

Subject: Case number 1800254/2013

1 attachment

Dear Mrs. Path,

I am responding to the email you copied me into yesterday afternoon, hours before my deadline.

Firstly, the email had 7attachments:

- *The first 2 attachments are the same document*
- *The third is a letter*
- *The last 4 have been blocked by you so I am unable to open them*

Could you please resend me the attachments in a format that I can open and download.

In the email copied to me yesterday, you attached an email dated 6th March (previously sent to incorrect email address) which asks me to send you all my documents. I have all my documents prepared ready, but due to the lateness of you sending me the email and the fact that I am getting married tomorrow and having a short honeymoon, I will be unable to now send you my documents until I return from honeymoon towards the end of next week.

*Could you please send me all your documents in **paper format** to my home address next week?*

*After you have received my documents, could you please send me the complete bundle **again in paper format** to my home address ASAP.*

From the date I receive the completed bundle I estimate that due to me being a 'layperson', that I will need two weeks to then check all my evidence is in the bundle, and then to write up my written statement to evidence and cross-reference with the page numbers.

I have also attached a letter dated 7th of March that I sent to Paul McKant requesting his permission to let two staff members of Kirklees College be my witnesses. As yet I have received no response. As Paul McKants solicitor, could you please look into this matter and respond to me.

Yours Sincerely

Janette Castle

I received a reply soon after:

From: spathclaims@sylaw.co.uk

Sent: 21 March 2013 10:09:00

To: janettecastle@hotmail.co.uk

Subject: Case number 1800254/2013

Dear Miss Castle,

Copies of the documents enclosed in the relevant emails shall be sent to you in the post.

We shall also send you copies of our client's documents by post as requested.

Whilst I will discuss the issue of witnesses with my client, for the avoidance of doubt, you are not prevented from contacting witnesses directly yourself.

Kind Regards

Stephanie Path

I then decided that I needed to contact Ella from the tribunal:

From: janettecastle@hotmail.co.uk

Sent: 21 March 2013 10:21:54

To: esmithyleedset@hmtcs.gov

Subject: Case number 1800254/2013 Miss Castle V Kirklees College

Dear Ella/Tribunal,

I am writing about the email I sent you yesterday in response to your email asking me what extension I would like to my 21st March deadline.

I was extremely upset and stressed yesterday as I wrote my response to your email (as I was concerned about not meeting my deadline).

I asked for a 2-week extension, then I worried about it all night because I get married tomorrow, then have a short honeymoon. When I return from my honeymoon it is the Easter holidays when people will not be contactable and places like the post office will be closed.

I realised last night that my 2-week request had been naïve particularly due to my being a 'layperson'.

Also, after sending the email yesterday I received an email that the respondent's solicitor sent to you. I have responded to the solicitor this morning (and have copied you into it) explaining that I will need two weeks after I receive the bundle from the solicitors to then prepare my written statement and cross-reference it with the bundle.

I have asked the solicitor to furnish me with the bundle ASAP, but I do not expect it to be possible for the solicitors to send me the bundle until approximately 2 weeks from now so, therefore, I imagine that I really will need a 4-week extension to my 21st of March deadline.

This request for a 4-week extension is depending on me receiving the bundle within 2 weeks of this date.

I thank you kindly for your time and apologise for any inconvenience this may have caused.

Kind Regards

Janette Castle

I spent the rest of the day trying to remain calm and hoping that my mood would lift, in the hope I would feel better by tomorrow, and hopefully enjoy my wedding. I took Indie out a few times and spent lots of time cuddling her for comfort.

On the evening news, it gave out a weather forecast for heavy snow tomorrow! Robert seems to think that our area should be OK?

22/3/13

I woke up and looked out of the window to check the weather. Everything was white, and it was snowing heavily. "Robert, it's snowing!" I shouted.

I had breakfast and we took Indie out for a walk. The snow was falling thick and fast and cars were struggling on the roads. Unbelievable!

The weather forecaster was saying that it was the worse snow in March for fifty years! Well why wouldn't it be – it's my wedding day after all.

I took Indie out for another short walk after dinner. I was talking to other dog walkers and laughing saying, "I'm getting married in two and a half hours".

"You're joking!" came the replies.

The snow for some reason made me feel OK. It meant that I could do nothing to control the day – what was going to happen, was going to happen. The snow amused me and made me laugh, and I felt so much better than the previous depressing two days.

I took Indie back home and jumped in the shower and started getting ready. Robert and I have been together for twenty years. Perhaps the fact that we've waited twenty years to get married has made it snow!!

Our friends from Durham had set off for the wedding, but they had to turn back due to the snow. Two of our other guests were struggling, but our mate (and fellow guest) Jimmy managed to pick them up in his Land Rover.

We managed to get to the registry office for 3 pm (and it was still open, thankfully). The day was fun and very informal (just what the doctor ordered). We went to 'The White Bear' for a meal, then a coach I had ordered took us to Leeds for a night out.

On Sunday we went to Seahouses for three days. I have never been so cold (even though I had appropriate clothes for the weather)!

<u>27/3/13</u>

I arrived back from my short honeymoon to find that I still hadn't received the documents from the solicitors which had been promised to me by 21/3/13!

I went down to the Post Office and sent my documents to the solicitors. I made sure I sent them registered post (so they couldn't say that they hadn't received them!)

I did receive a letter from the tribunal:

EMPLOYMENT TRIBUNALS

To: Miss J Castle

To: Mrs. Stephanie Path

Case Number 1800254/2013

Claimant		Respondent
Miss J Castle	*V*	*Kirklees College*

AMENDED

NOTICE OF CASE MANAGEMENT DISCUSSION
(By Telephone)
Employment Tribunals Rules of Procedure 2004

A Case Management Discussion ('CMD') will be conducted by an Employment Judge by telephone commencing on Monday 8 April 2013 at 10:00 am. It has been given an allocated time of 30 minutes.

To take part you should telephone 0845 302 3035 on time and, when prompted, enter the access code 28712.

The date and/or time of the CDM may be altered if both parties agree and consult the Tribunal in good time beforehand.

You must be able to discuss:

To agree a time estimate

Signed,

Ella Smithy

For the Secretary of Employment Tribunals

Cc Acas

I don't know why we need to have a telephone discussion about time estimate?????? Just something else to worry about.

28/3/13

I still haven't received Kirklees College's documents from the solicitor! I decided to write an email to solicitors and copy in the tribunal so that they knew I was still being messed about.

From: janettecastle@hotmail.co.uk

Sent: 28 March 2013 13:54:19

To: spathclaims@sylaw.co.uk leedset@hhtsc.gov

Subject: Case number 1800254/2013 Miss J Castle V Kirklees College

1 attachment

Dear Mrs. Path,

I sent you a folder in yesterday's post that contained all my documents as promised. I paid an extra fee to ensure that the documents would be in your possession before the close of business today.

The documents are in a folder in 12 separate sections (eg Stage 1 of grievance, Stage 2 of grievance, Stage 3 of grievance and so on...)

The documents are in a logical order that will be easy for the tribunal to follow. I would appreciate it if when you make up the bundle you could place Kirklees College's documents either in front of or behind my documents.

I have attached a list of documents above and have also placed one at the front of the said folder.

I have not yet received copies of your client's documents that you promised to send to me on 21/3/13. Please could you look into this as a matter of urgency?

Regards

Janette

Shortly after sending the email 'Psychopath' telephoned me at home (so I had made her sit up and take notice by copying in the tribunal). She told me that the documents had been sent out and that they must have been lost in the post????

Thirty minutes later a different female from her solicitor's firm rang my mobile to apologise, to tell me it was her fault and that she would send me their documents today.

30/3/13

I received a letter (dated 22nd March) and documents from 'Psycho':

PRIVATE AND CONFIDENTIAL

22nd March 2013

Dear Miss Castle

**Janette Castle V Kirklees College
Case number: 1800254/2013**

Please find enclosed herewith a hard copy of our correspondence to the tribunal of 20 March 2013 together with all relevant attachments. (NB: the documents are presented in chronological order).

Also enclosed is a complete set of the Respondent's disclosure. We look forward to receiving a complete copy of yours by return. Thereafter we shall proceed to compile the joint hearing bundle.

Yours Faithfully

Stephanie Path

Senior Employment Litigator

I may not be a solicitor, but I am not thick – and I don't expect to be treated as such!

<u>1/4/13</u>

I sent an email to 'Psycho' and copied in the tribunal (so they have all the facts in black and white)

From: janettecastle@hotmail.co.uk

Sent: 01 April 2013 10:52:07

To: spathclaims@sylaw.co.uk leedset@hmtcs.gov

Subject: Case number: 1800254/2013 Miss J Castle V Kirklees College

1 attachment

Dear Mrs. Path,

I received your documents on Saturday 30th March.

I would just like to clarify a few points:

The letter you enclosed in the document wallet is dated 22nd March which is not when the documents were sent out. I informed you in the email attached below on the 28th of March that I had not received your client's documents.

Instead of responding to me by email, you telephoned me at home and told me that they had been sent out and that they must have been lost in the post???

About thirty minutes later a female member of your staff telephoned my mobile to inform me that it was her fault that the documents had not been sent out, that she would send them out that day, and that I would receive them on Saturday.

The letter also states that you 'look forward to receiving a complete copy of my documents by return'. Again, to clarify, you received my documents on the 28th of March by recorded delivery.

I look forward to receiving the joint hearing bundle.

Kind Regards

Janette Castle

(Below this email was the email I sent them 28/3/13 which proved everything I was stating was true).

No response to this email.

I have made my point and shown her that I will not take this lying down, and will challenge her - so let's see if she starts treating me with some respect from now on.

2/4/13

I received an email from 'Psycho':

From: spathclaims@sylaw.co.uk

Sent: 02 April 2013 16:52:28

To: janettecastle@hotmail.co.uk

1 attachment

Dear Miss Castle

Please find attached a proposed hearing bundle in this matter.

The documents have been placed in chronological order for ease of use by all parties and the tribunal. We shall now proceed to paginate the bundle which shall be sent to you directly upon completion.

Kind Regards

Short and not so sweet!

5/4/13

Still no bundle. I waited until the post arrived (or rather didn't arrive) and then decided to email the solicitor:

From: janettecastle@hotmail.co.uk

Sent: 05 April 2013 14:38:23

To: spathclaims@sylaw.co.uk   leedset@hmtcs.gov

Subject: Case Number 1800254/2013 Miss J castle V Kirklees College – The Bundle

Dear Mrs. Path,

I am concerned that I have not yet received the bundle.

You have now been in receipt of my documents for eight days. I have completed my written statement (including my closing statement) but require the bundle in order, to reference my statement as to where the evidence can be found in the bundle.

Please can you look into this as a matter of urgency, so that we can both prepare fully in time for our tribunal hearing next month?

Kind Regards

Janette Castle

I received a reply shortly afterward:

From: spathclaims@sylaw.co.uk

Sent: 05 April 2013 14:47:15

To: janettecastle@hotmail.co.uk

Subject: Case Number 1800254/2013 Miss J Castle V Kirklees College – The Bundle

Dear Miss Castle,

This matter is subject to Case Management Discussion on Monday at which time Case Management Orders will set out in relation to the hearing date and preparation for the hearing.

Kind Regards

It does seem that I am a mushroom again, in the dark and not knowing what's going on??

Or is she following procedure that I don't understand?

<u>7/4/13</u>

I need to ring the Tribunal at 10 am tomorrow and have a Case Management Discussion (where seemingly I will be speaking to one of the tribunal Judges and Kirklees College's solicitor ('Psychopath')).

I don't know what this will entail, so therefore I can't prepare for it and feel very nervous about it.

CHAPTER 8

<u>8/4/13</u>

Absolute nightmare!

I feel sick again and cannot believe that I have been kicked in the teeth yet again!

The Case Management Discussion was to discuss the length of time that the tribunal would take.

Kirklees College's solicitor ('Psychopath') stated that because of the complexities of the case it would need more than one day. She asked that the proposed tribunal on 23rd May was postponed – and that we would need a three-day hearing!

I tried to argue against this but was so upset that I just started crying and could hardly speak.

The Judge agreed with 'Psychopath' and when he looked through the tribunal diary for the next three-day slot he told us it would now be sometime in December!

I was crying so hard I couldn't make myself understood. The Judge told me that December would be better for me as I had more time to prepare and would hopefully be calmer and less emotional by then!

I just cried and cried when I put the phone down. I felt so sick and depressed. There I was thinking that I had to only go through another six weeks before it would all be over – and now I must go through another eight months of torture!

When I'd got myself together enough, I telephoned Robert to tell him and then my mum and dad. Mum and dad ended up coming down to my house as they could tell how distraught I was.

I spent the rest of the week feeling depressed and despondent. The only comfort I feel is cuddling and talking to Indie. She is my companion, who is always by my side when Robert is at work during the day.

Kirklees College (Ron Atler and Dale Rolland especially) will be laughing their socks off now that the tribunal has been postponed. They will probably think that I'll give up and walk away.

Kirklees College's solicitor will be thinking that I'm a 'wet lettuce' – crying uncontrollably down phone whilst she was creeping around the Judge and calling him 'Your Honour'. She'll be thinking that I'll give up now (or that if I do make it to the tribunal, that she will be able to easily eliminate me) as she will think me a seriously weak female!!!

I am beginning to feel worried about how dangerously depressed I feel. I am starting to think that it would be easier if I was dead!

I don't want to commit suicide – but I feel that death would be a way out (problems solved).

I keep this knowledge to myself as I don't want to put any more stress on Robert, and I certainly won't tell Doctor Mattins as he already wants me to try antidepressants (which is a road I don't want to go down).

I just can't see a way forward. I have no idea what my future holds. I know I'm not well, mentally and emotionally, and that my confidence has been shattered.

All I can think is 'how will I earn money in the future?' I can't imagine teaching again and the thought of having a boss petrifies me.

I think in the future I will have to work for myself (so no one has any power or control over me). But what would I do that got me a guaranteed income of over £31,000 per year?

18/4/13

I received a letter from solicitors dated 17th April:

PRIVATE AND CONFIDENTIAL

Dear Sirs

Miss Janette Castle V Kirklees College
Case no: 1800254/2013
Further to the order of the tribunal, please find enclosed herewith a paginated copy of the joint bundle hearing.

Yours Faithfully

Stephanie Path

Senior Employment Litigator

So now I have the bundle – it contains all my evidence, and all of Kirklees College's evidence that we wish to rely on, at the tribunal.

I spent the rest of the day reading through it. Because of my impeccable work record and how conscientious I had been throughout my twelve years at Kirklees College, I knew beforehand that Kirklees College 'didn't have anything on me'.

I thought there may be some fabrications and lies somewhere in the bundle…..

But no - I was rather confused after reading through the bundle as most of the evidence was from me (which had lots of incriminating evidence in it). The 'evidence' from Kirklees College was mainly correspondence from them to me (which incriminated them).

They seem to be 'clutching at straws'.

Before reading the bundle, I felt that I had enough evidence to prove that I was in the right – and now I was confused (in a good way) as to why Kirklees College had put certain documents in the bundle – as it painted them in an even a worse light (and gave me extra evidence to use against them).

I read through the bundle and thought 'Are you dim or what?'

I painstakingly went through the bundle again and highlighted all sections that I felt I could use to prove that I was constructively dismissed. I also put 'markers' on the side of each page that I had highlighted information on.

I was completely astounded when I read through Jane Davis' Investigation Report into Ron Atler, which was undertaken at Stage 2 of the grievance procedure.

It goes through the evidence given by all staff in the plumbing and electrical section during their interviews. All, (except Ron's mate James Tebb) back up what I have said.

Page 10 of the document summarises how my ex-colleagues described Ron Atler's management style:

I quote:

- *Forceful, dominating, all guns blazing, Hitler, like Jekyll and Hyde (2 people stated)*
- *Unapproachable*
- *When Ron is under pressure 'it's like attack'*
- *Takes own stress out on staff*
- *It's like walking on eggshells*
- *Intimidating – like a bull in a china shop*
- *Ron holds a grudge (3 people stated)*
- *No consistency in his personality*
- *Very defensive*
- *Forceful – rules with an iron rod*
- *Flies off the handle*
- *Slags staff off behind their backs (x 2 people interviewed)*
- *He's like a dog with a bone – if somethings not to his liking, he'll carry it on forever*

It then goes on to say….

*'As shown in (see Appendix 6) there is cause for concern regarding Ron's behaviour in the form of **intimidation** as over half of the staff interviewed felt Ron was **intimidating**, a third of staff felt Ron was **unprofessional**, a quarter felt Ron was **undermining and was a bully** and a staggering 10 out of 12 people felt that staff were not treated equally or the same'.*

At the end of her report, Jane writes that *'Ron's management style is **inappropriate** and that he could **step down** (her suggestion).*

She then went on to state *that college **MUST**:*

- ***Ensure staff can access counseling or cognitive behaviour therapy ASAP***

So, the Directors of Kirklees College received this report from their investigative officer, read it, and then did nothing about it!!!!!

They kept Ron Atler (who is an intimidating bully) in his position as manager and sent me (the innocent victim) an outcome letter that stated false accusations against me, informed me that appropriate action would be taken against ME! – and that I could go back to work under HIM!

Why have they given me this evidence when it works against them? Are they completely daft or just arrogant???

They have also given me copies of internal emails in which they admit that they took too long with my grievance and an internal letter from Joan Horncastle (HR Manager) states:

'Follow Up from Stage 3 of Grievance Procedure' where she finishes by writing...

'I do however find that Janette could have been kept better informed throughout the process as we need to appreciate how stressful such a process is for a member of staff. HR will review procedures to ensure that any member of staff going through a grievance process will be regularly updated on progress and the reason for any minor/major delays'

In black and white the HR Manager of Kirklees College has stated that they need to review their procedures and an admittance that I could have been kept better informed.

You don't say!

26/4/13

I need to pick myself up somehow. I know that my tribunal hearing is months away. I can't do anything about that. It is out of my control. I need to try to move forward, and as the tribunal is months away, I am going to change my email address to my married name:

From: janettehirst@hotmail.com

Sent 26 April 2013 13:35:37

To: spathclaims@sylaw.co.uk   leedset@hmtcs.gov

Subject: J Castle V Kirklees College Case no 1800254/2013

Dear Mrs. Path,

As the tribunal is now delayed for some considerable time, I have changed my email address to my married name. I will still put my maiden name in the subject box of further emails to avoid confusion.

Could you please reply to this email to confirm that you have received my new email address?

Thank you in anticipation

Janette

Shortly afterward she replied:

From: spathclaims@sylaw.co.uk

Date 26 April 2013 14:02:22

To: janettehirst@hotmail.com

Subject: J Castle V Kirklees College Case no: 1800254/2013

Dear Mrs. Hirst,

Thank you for your update, I can confirm receipt.

Kind Regards

I needed to copy the tribunal and make sure I got a reply confirming my new email address from 'Psycho' so that she can't be underhand again and 'accidentally' send important information to my old email address (or another made up one).

I may not have legal training, but I know how to dot the 'i's' and cross the 't's'.

14/5/13

I decided that I needed to check through the bundle again – to check it against my evidence folder to make sure all the evidence of mine that I had sent them has been put in the bundle. This took me a few hours, as the bundle was 464 pages, and in a different order to the order of my evidence file.

It was worth the time and effort as I found that they had left out three of my pieces of evidence.

One of the documents was Acas' 'Defining of Employer's Duty of Care' which states:

Employers have a 'Duty of Care' to their employees, which means they should take **all steps which are reasonably possible to ensure their health, safety and, wellbeing.**

Legally, employers must abide by relevant health and safety and employment law, as well as the common law duty of *care. They also have a moral and ethical duty not to cause, or fail to prevent physical or psychological injury and must fulfill their responsibilities concerning personal injury, and negligence claims.*

Requirements under an employer's duty of care are wide-ranging and may manifest themselves in many different ways such as:

- *Clearly defining jobs and undertaking risk assessments*
- ***Ensuring a safe working environment***
- *Providing adequate training and feedback on performance*
- *Ensuring that staff do not work excessive hours*
- *Providing areas for rest and relaxation*
- ***Protecting staff from bullying and harassment***, *from either colleagues or third parties*
- *Protecting staff from discrimination*
- ***Providing communication channels for employees to raise concerns***
- *Consulting employees on issues which concern them*

An employer can be deemed to have breached their duty of care by failing to do everything reasonable in the circumstances to keep the employee safe from harm. *Employees also have responsibilities for their health and wellbeing at work – for example, they are entitled by law to refuse to undertake work that isn't safe without fear of disciplinary action.*

Very strange that the solicitor has 'accidentally' forgotten to put this document in.

Another document left out of the bundle was from an ex-colleague of mine called Derek at Kirklees College who was made ill and 'forced out' of the college (by Ron Atler), before me leaving. I had contacted him to ask him for a witness testimony.

His testimony was short but very clear:

Hi Janette,

Sorry to hear about what has happened, which does not surprise me. I would have liked to help but when I took voluntary redundancy, I had to sign an agreement with a solicitor appointed by the college, which they paid for, to say that in the future I would not say anything derogatory about the college.

So, I am unable to help. Good luck with your case.

Kind Regards

Derek

So, proof that College felt the need to make Derek sign a 'gagging order'. And this document was also mysteriously 'lost'.

Well, I am not going to accept this!

From: janettehirst@hotmail.com

Sent: 14 May 2013 12:45:02

To: spathclaims@sylaw.co.uk leedset@hmcts.gov

Subject: Case number 1800254/2013 Miss Castle V Kirklees College

Attachment

Dear Mrs. Path,

So far, I have found that three of the documents that I sent you to use as evidence have not been put into the bundle. I have scanned the missing documents and attached them to this email. I have numbered two of the documents 465 and 466 so that they can be easily be placed at the back of the bundle. The other missing document I have numbered 111A. This needs to be placed in the bundle directly after the page numbered 111 as it is the second page to the email that I sent on 4/1/12 (which you numbered 111).

Kind Regards

Janette

Caught out again! – She needs to put all my documents in the bundle and stop trying to catch me out!

I may lack legal expertise, but I am seriously organised – and I double-check everything!

I received a reply shortly afterward:

From: spathclaims@sylaw.co.uk

Sent: 14 May 13:05:56

To: janettehirst@hotmail.com

Subject: Case number 1800254/2013 Miss Castle V Kirklees College

Dear Mrs. Hirst,

Contrary to your insinuations, we believe that all documents received were included in the bundle. Should any relevant documents have been omitted it is a matter of error on behalf of one or other of the parties. The additional documents shall be included forthwith.

Yours Sincerely,

SY Law

Well, I have the proof for 'Psycho' and more importantly the Tribunal:

From: janettehirst@hotmail.co.uk

Sent: 13:45:27

To: spathclaims@sylaw.co.uk leedset@hmcts.gov

Subject: Case Number 1800254/2013 Miss Castle V Kirklees College

Dear Mrs. Path,

You state you believe all the documents received from me were included in the bundle. Just to clarify this point and to prove that I am not sending you anything extra please refer to my 5-page list of documents that I sent you with the said documents.

Page 1 under 'Documents to refer to':

7th item on the list described as 'Undated – Witness Statement declined by Derek Hanson'

11th item on the list described as 'Undated – Acas' definition of employer's duty of care'

Page 1 under 'Issues/documents/emails in the run-up to the claimant's illness and time off work

14th item on the list described as '4/1/12 Email from the claimant to Ron Atler'. (You have included the first page of this email, but not the second).

Kind Regards

Janette

You can't argue with facts

From: spathclaims@sylaw.co.uk

Sent: 14 May 2013 14:15:34

To: janettehirst@hotmail.com

Subject: Case number 1800254/2013 Miss Castle V Kirklees College

For the avoidance of doubt, we shall refrain from wasting costs by corresponding with you further unless required as part of the case preparation.

We reserve the right to make representations in respect of the 'evidence' you have submitted at the hearing.

Kind Regards

So now she is not going to correspond with me further. I don't think she likes being 'outsmarted' by a common 'layperson'. I have a factual paper trail of evidence. She cannot argue with that.

30/5/13

I sent my witness statements to Kirklees College's solicitors months ago, but they still haven't sent me theirs! I can't work on my case without them. I thought you trained to become a solicitor so that you could uphold the law? This one seems as dodgy and underhand as can be.

21/6/13

Received a letter from 'Psycho' dated 20th June which was copied to the tribunal also:

Dear Sir/Madam,

Claimant	:	***Miss Janette Castle***
Respondent	:	***Kirklees College***
Tribunal Number	:	***1800254/2013***

We write further to the Order of the tribunal of 8 April 2013.

Amongst other matters, the tribunal ordered that witness statements be exchanged in this matter no later than 4 pm on 28 June 2013.

Whereas the respondent's witnesses have been working towards this date, one of its witnesses, Dale Rolland, is currently absent from work due to sickness and is therefore unable to complete his statement. We therefore respectfully request, pursuant to Employment Tribunals (Constitution and Rules of Procedure) Regulations 2004 rule 10 (2) (n) that the Order is varied in respect of witness statements for the exchange on 26 July 2013.

On the basis that the hearing is not due to commence until the 10th of December it is averred that the Claimant will not be prejudiced by the granting of this variation.

Further, it is also averred that the granting of this application will be in line with the overriding objective in that it will ensure that the parties are on an equal footing as they will be able to rely on all witness evidence. The matter will then be dealt with fairly. This application has been sent to the tribunal within 7 days of receipt and copied to us.

We confirm that we have complied with the Employment Tribunal (Constitution and Rules of Procedure) Regulations 2004 rule 11(4) in that a copy of this application has been sent to the Claimant who is duly advised that any objections to the same, must be sent to the tribunal within 7 days of receipt and copied to us.

Yours Faithfully

Stephanie Path

Senior Employment Litigator

SY Law

So, of course, I sent an objection straight away:

Tribunal number: 1800254/2013

Miss J Castle V Kirklees College

Dear Sir / Madam,

I am writing in response to the respondent's correspondence of 20/6/13.

I wish to object to the respondent's request that the exchange of witness statements be postponed until 26th July 2013.

During the CDM on 8th April 2013, the Judge informed both the respondent and myself that the witness statements needed to be exchanged no later than 4 pm on Friday 28th June 2013.

In the Judge's CDM follow up letter (dated 18th April 2013) he wrote **'there is ample time for that to occur'** referring to the witness statements before the preparation time of the exchange date of Friday 28th June.

I would have expected the respondent's witness statements to have already been completed before Dale Rolland's illness due to the original Case Management Orders (dated 10th January 2013) stated that witness statements were to be exchanged on 21st March 2013.

I sent the respondents my five written statements (and just excluded my statement) when I sent them my full written evidence on 28th March 2013. Therefore, the respondents have been in receipt of five of my six written statements for almost three months already.

The respondent cannot determine the length of Dale Rolland's illness, nor can they assume that he will return to work before their proposed date of the 26th of July. Therefore, I would like to keep to the original date of 28th June 2013 for the exchange of witness statements.

When making your decision on this matter I would ask that you take into account that the respondents did NOT comply with the deadlines of the original Case Management Orders *(dated 10ᵗʰ January 2013) and also please refer to my letter dated to the tribunal 14/3/13.*

Yours Sincerely

Janette Castle

I posted my letter to the tribunal and sent a copy to the solicitors.

I am pig sick of this. I am the innocent victim here. I'm ill, have no legal experience and I don't really know what I'm doing – and yet I'm the one who is following all procedures and deadlines, whilst the qualified solicitor and a large College cannot seem to follow any rules what so ever. Where is the fairness in this!?!?

30/6/13

Still no response from the tribunal!

Yet again, I followed the rules by submitting my objection within 7 days – and still, I get ignored!

The tribunal seems to be favouring the solicitor and Kirklees College at every step. If this is the case at the tribunal hearing, then it seems that I have no chance. All I want is to be treated fairly!

26/7/13

Today is the day that the 'Psycho solicitor' had asked the tribunal for the extension date, for finally giving me their witness statements, but I haven't received them.

I'm sick of waiting for things that never happen. There is no point in me contacting the tribunal, seen as I never received a response from my objection of 20/6/13.

2/8/13

I have received Kirklees College's witness statements!

I spent hours going through the seven Kirklees College witness statements (or 'lies' as it would more accurately describe them).

Again, I am surprised at how pathetically weak the statements are. I know they don't have 'any dirt' on me, but I would have expected them to attempt to make, (fabricate) a better case against me with their statements.

Some of the witness statements even acknowledge incompetence from Kirklees College and that it affected me!

I quote (from Anthea Mitchell):

- *'We upheld the claimant that the grievance procedure did seem to take an inordinately long period of time. I requested that the HR Manager investigate the timescales to establish the cause of the delays*
- *We did feel that some acknowledgement needed to be made that the claimant had been unwell and off work for a lengthy period and that the cause of this was in part due to the situation at work'*

This can only help my case – Not theirs!

I quote (from Paul McKant):

- *'I agreed with the claimant that the grievance procedure had taken far longer than it should have been concluded in the early stages and acknowledged that this may have had an impact on her'*

So, more acknowledgment that they didn't follow procedure – and that it affected me!

I quote (from Jean Turrand):

'*Based on the balance of probabilities on the findings of the investigation the panel did not uphold the allegation of bullying and intimidating behaviour. However, the panel upheld the allegation of the claimant's line manager displaying intimidating behaviour*'

Admitting intimidating behaviour - which is Bullying!!!

Another interesting lie that Jean Turrand (and Alan Wiley and Jen Walden) put in their witness statements was…

I quote:

'*Following communication of the above findings, the claimant was asked to attend a meeting on Wednesday 15th August 2012 with myself. The claimant did not attend this meeting*'.

Well, that lie is easy to disprove as I have the email on page 327 of the bundle:

From: jhorncastle@kirklescollege.com

Sent: 14 August 2012

To: janettecastle@hotmail.co.uk

Subject: Meeting on 15th August

Hi Janette,

*Further to our telephone conversation today, I confirm that I have come back from annual leave to find 2 meetings in my diary with yourself, **one tomorrow (15th)** with Jean Turrand and myself and one on 16th to hear your grievance under Stage 3 of the procedure with Anthea Mitchell.*

I have been told that the meeting arranged for tomorrow was to discuss and plan your return to work as a result of your grievance being concluded under Stage 2. Since the meeting was arranged you have appealed and requested that it be taken to the next stage hence the second meeting being arranged. The timing of the two meetings is purely coincidental.

***However, as we discussed on the telephone, I do not see any benefit in having the return to work discussions tomorrow** and feel that it would be best to hear your grievance on Thursday first and postpone the return to work meeting until after we have exhausted the grievance procedure.*

At your agreement, we have therefore decided that we will hear your grievance on Thursday and then plan a return to work meeting after that.

Kind Regards

Joan

Facts in black and white – don't these managers/HR talk to one another???

The most negative witness statement against me was from Ron Atler. He has tried to paint me in a bad light. There

were many lies in his statement about me (and the section).
I went through his statement and highlighted all the lies.

I quote (from Ron Atler):

- *'There were no schemes of work or lesson plans in place (which are fundamental documents when teaching FE)*
- *No lesson observations had been undertaken within the Electrical Department under the previous manager*
- *Allowing her to set and work to her own timetable and working pattern. This included taking Wednesdays off to allow her to spend time with her dog*
- *Not asking her to do anything over and above her teaching and general admin duties or to work what may be considered unsocial hours*
- *I (Rob Atler) personally covered all open evenings and recruitment events myself so that staff could be at home with their families'*

I was quite amused after reading Ron Atler's statement as it gave me loads of 'evidence' that I can easily disprove and show that he has lied.

Ron Atler doesn't know that every week that I handed in my timesheet, I took a photocopy of it and kept it for my records (as I didn't trust him). So, I have timesheets for every week that I worked since he took over the section and introduced them. So, that covers about sixteen months, until I was off sick.

My timesheets prove that I worked between 47- 49 hours each week (instead of the 37 hours I was contracted to and paid a salary for).

My timesheets also prove that:

- I worked every day and did NOT take Wednesdays off!!
- That I covered open evenings and recruitment events (which covers unsocial hours and things above general teaching)

I went into the attic and brought down the folder where I kept all copies of my timesheets. In the folder, I also found my lesson observation forms (going back to 2002).

I looked through my lesson observation forms and highlighted parts which disproved Ron Atler's lies like:

'Well organised schemes of work and lesson plans'

I also found the last Performance Development Review that Ron Atler did for me. In black and white I have what Rob Atler wrote about me:

Under 'Summary of Strengths' he wrote *'Committed to learner success and wellbeing. Excellent organisational abilities. Good Work ethic'.*

Under 'Areas for Development' were left blank

And under 'Any Issues Arising' he wrote *'Recognise sometimes when you need to share your workload'*

So, in summary – before I was off work with stress, I was a good teacher with a good work ethic – and that I did too much work, (and should have shared my workload).

I need to photocopy these documents and get them to put them into the 'bundle' to use as evidence at my tribunal!

<u>7/9/13</u>

I emailed the solicitor:

To: spathclaims@sylaw.co.uk

Sent: 07 August 2013 13:33:45

From: janettehirst@hotmail.com

Subject: Janette Castle V Kirklees College Case number: 1800254/2013

Dear Mrs. Path,

I have read through the respondent's witness statements.

I have some more documents that I wish to rely on at the tribunal in December. I am planning to send these to you recorded delivery sometime over the next two weeks so that you can put them in the bundle.

Kind Regards

Janette Hirst

From: spathclaims@sylaw.co.uk

Sent: 07 August 13:50:20

To: janettehirst@hotmail.com

Subject: Janette Castle V Kirklees College Case number: 1800254/2013

Dear Mrs. Hirst,

I await receipt of the documents.

Kind Regards

Stephanie Path

<u>11/8/13</u>

I started photocopying my extra documents of evidence. I then prepared a list of the new documents that I planned to send the solicitor.

<u>14/8/13</u>

I went to the post office and sent the extra documents to the solicitor's recorded delivery (so that they can't get 'lost in the post').

<u>16/8/18</u>

I received an email from the solicitor:

From: spathclaims@sylaw.co.uk

Sent: 16 August 2013 11:03:44

To: janettehirst@hotmail.com

Subject: Castle V Kirklees College

1 attachment scanned documents for the bundle

Dear Mrs. Hirst,

I can confirm that we have received your documents as attached. The documents will be reviewed and, subject to any issues regarding relevance or admissibility, the bundle will be amended accordingly.

Kind Regards

Stephanie Path

When I looked through my documents that she had scanned and sent as an attachment to me she had removed one of my documents and put a rogue document in.

Well, I am not standing for this!

From: janettehirst@hotmail.com

Sent 16 August 2013 16:53:21

To: spathclaims@sylaw.co.uk   leedset@hmtcs.gov

Subject: Castle V Kirklees College Case no: 1800254/2013

1 attachment

Dear Mrs. Path,

Thank you for confirming the receipt of my documents.

I would not have sent these extra documents had I not thought that they were relevant to my case. Please decide as quickly as possible if you intend to leave any of these documents out of the bundle. I will then have time to correspond with the Judge and explain the relevance of said document(s) and they will then be able to make their decision on the matter.

Also, I have checked through the copies you attached to this email of the documents that I sent you. Two mistakes have been made. There are still 67 pages of documents but:

*Document 28 titled 'Self Analysis Matrix – Leadership and Management' was **not** sent to you by me. If you look at the list of extra documents sheets that I sent you it is under the description of '4/4/11 Claimants Performance Development Review Meeting with Ron Atler'. As you can see, I wrote 4 pages for this document, so I have no idea where this 'page no 5' has come from?*

One of the pages I sent is missing. The document is described on the same sheet as: with the other activity planner timesheets.

'6th Sept '10' Claimants activity Planner timesheet'. I have scanned this document and attached above for you to include

Kind Regards

Janette Hirst (formerly Janette Castle)

<u>23/8/13</u>

I received an email from the solicitor trying to be clever:

From: spathclaims@sylaw.co.uk

Sent: 23 August 2013 14:06:22

To: janettehirst@hotmail.co.uk

Subject: Castle V Kirklees College Case no:1800254/2013

Dear Mrs. Hirst,

When you refer to document 28, I would be grateful if you would explain what you are referring to. There is nothing in the bundle index that refers to a 'self-analysis matrix'. Further, the document you have now sent has never been received from you before. Whereas we shall now include it, any liability for its omission to this point is denied.

We shall revert to you with the amended index shortly.

Kind Regards

Stephanie Path

From: janettehirst@hotmail.com

Sent: 23 August 2013 14:27:32

To: spathclaims@sylaw.co.uk leedset@hmcts.gov

Subject: Castle V Kirklees College Case no: 1800254/2013

Dear Mrs. Path,

I have referred to the rogue document as document 28, as that is what you named it in the SCAN Documents folder you attached to the email you sent me on 16/8/13.

The reason that there is nothing in the bundle index that refers to a 'self-analysis matrix' is because I did not send this document to you.

*You have made it look like it is the 5th page of the document I described as **4/4/11 – Claimants Performance and Development Review Meeting with Ron Atler (<u>4 pages</u>)**.*

You state that the document I have 'now' sent you was not previously sent by myself – as I explained in my previous email, it is described on my evidence description sheet as '6th Sept '10' Claimants Activity Planner Time Sheet'.

Also, I sent you 67 pages of documents. I have copies of them all here. You sent me a document file consisting of 67 documents?????

Regards

Janette Hirst (formerly Janette Castle)

I copied the tribunal into this email again to keep them informed.

From: spathclaims@sylaw.co.uk

Sent: 23 August 2013 15:20:12

To: janettehirst@hotmail.co.uk

Subject: Castle V Kirklees College Case no: 1800254/2013

Dear Mrs. Hirst,

We shall amend the bundle as stated and send it to you. There is nothing to be gained by entering further correspondence with you.

Further, please note that the inclusion of the documents in the bundle does not constitute out client's agreement to the inclusion of the same. We, therefore, reserve our client's position in this regard.

Kind Regards

Stephanie Path

Nasty! Nasty! She doesn't want to correspond further with me.

I thought I'd send her one last email just to annoy her before the weekend:

From: janettehirst@hotmail.com

Sent: 23 August 2013 16:38:51

To: spathclaims@sylaw.co.uk   leedset@hmtcs.gov

Subject: Castle V Kirklees College Case no:1800254/2013

Dear Mrs. Path,

I would have thought that you would have spoken to your client about this matter during the week that has passed since I made my request for clarification.

Please ask for your client's agreement with the inclusion of the documents as soon as possible.

I have the right to represent myself 'on an even playing field'.

If I have not heard from you within one week, I will have no alternative but to take this issue up with the Tribunal.

Kind Regards

Janette Hirst (formerly Janette Castle)

From: spathclaims@sylaw.co.uk

Sent: 23 August 2013 16:38:51

To: janettehirst@hotmail.com

Subject: Castle V Kirklees College Case no:1800254/2013

Dear Mrs. Hirst,

I have made the position clear. The documents will be included in the bundle.

My client is neither agreeing nor objecting to their inclusion at this stage.

An amended bundle will be sent to you.

Kind Regards

Stephanie Path

I now have every piece of 'evidence' that Kirklees College has against me – which consists of a big fat ZERO.

Kirklees College has all my evidence. Surely, they will look through it with a 'fine-tooth comb' and realise that I can prove every claim that I have made????

1/9/13

Just over three months to go until the tribunal hearing. I need to observe some more employment tribunals, to see if I can get more tips on how to represent myself, and to make sure I'm as prepared as I can be.

5/9/13

I went to the tribunal today to watch a tribunal hearing where a man had been a HR manager and was claiming that he had been unfairly dismissed.

This was quite a good one to watch as the man was representing himself – and as he was a HR manager, he must have known about Employment Law, worker's rights, etc.

I thought that he represented himself quite well, but one thing I noticed was that when he was questioning his former employer's witnesses and referring to evidence in the bundle – he took a lot of time himself, trying to find said evidence in the bundle. This kept happening and made his questioning a bit disjointed.

I was glad I had seen this, so I could make sure that I was a lot more organised in this department.

27/9/13

I went to another session at the free legal advice service. I asked the solicitor for any advice about representing myself.

The solicitor was kind and helpful and made me feel that I did have a case.

One of the pieces of advice was to help prevent me from feeling too nervous, that I should look at the Judges when being questioned and address the Judges, (instead of Kirklees College's solicitor, who will be questioning me).

15/10/13

I went to another tribunal hearing today. A lady was being represented by a lawyer for unfair dismissal.

It was interesting to watch/listen to. The lady did not look at her former employer's witnesses or lawyer and instead looked directly at the Judge when she answered questions whilst on the witness stand.

This was what the solicitor at the legal advice service advised me to do, but it didn't seem natural to me – not to look at, and address the person who is speaking to you???? I think I will look at the solicitor when she questions me.

2/11/13

I feel nervous and anxious as usual.

I feel worried that all the cases I have watched at the Tribunal are unfair dismissal cases. None of them have been for Constructive Dismissal – and when I spoke to a solicitor at the tribunal, he said that he kept away from constructive Dismissal cases as he found them more difficult to win!!!!!

Surely, it's just facts? – and I have the facts to prove my case?

I am also worried as it gets near the hearing date that Kirklees College may make me another offer to settle out of court.

I think if they made me an offer Robert would probably want me to accept it, and to walk away.

This would just cause me more stress as:

I have come so far and now I want my day(s) in court.

I want to put all Kirklees College's management on the stand! I want to look into their eyes as I question them, and I want to prove that they treated me disgracefully.

I particularly want Ron Atler and Dale Rolland on the stand. I want to put them under pressure and show how unfairly and incompetently they treated me in front of their superiors (senior management at Kirklees College). They destroyed my career. I am unemployed because of them – and if I can make them pay, I will.

<u>5/11/13</u>

I started working again on the questions I will be asking Kirklees College's eight witnesses.

I write, re-write and re-write again until I am happy with each one. I refer to evidence in the bundle by page number and paragraph.

I think back to the mistakes I felt that the HR man representing himself made about referencing evidence in the bundle.

I have decided that when I type up my questions for the witnesses I will:

- Write all the questions in black ink
- Write references to where the evidence in the bundle is in blue ink (and I will write down what the evidence is (for my reference) – so I don't have to search through the bundle at the tribunal)
- Write any words I want to strongly emphasise in red ink

Because I am dyslexic (and I am worse when I am stressed), I will type the text in 'comic sans' and in-text size 14, so it is clearer for me to read at the tribunal.

<u>12/11/13</u>

I have completed and typed up my questions for Ron Atler, Dale Rolland, Jean Turrand, Anthea Mitchell, Paul McKant, Jen Walden and Alan Wiley.

I have completed and printed out my written statement and a closing statement which I think the Judges read at the beginning of the tribunal?

Even though I have no legal training or experience I think it is professional. It is six pages long and it covers everything that Kirklees College has 'done wrong' against me. I have referenced where all the evidence is in the bundle to substantiate my claims and I have also referenced what Regulations and Employment Law they have contravened.

I don't believe that I could have done any more or prepared any better – so whatever happens, I know I will have done all I could have done.

My written statement:

Case number: 1800254/2013 Miss J Castle V Kirklees College   *Page 1*

The written statement of Janette Castle

1. *I am here today to prove that I was constructively dismissed by Kirklees College.*

I aim to prove that Kirklees College failed in its 'Duty of Care' to me as an employee and that I had no alternative but to hand in my notice under The Employment Rights Act 95 (1) (c) on 5th of November 2012, due to the broken relationship of mutual trust and confidence.

2. *My problem originated from the unacceptable behaviour of my line manager. I was made ill by my line manager, so I put in a formal complaint. My illness was then made worse by Kirklees College:*

- *Not following their grievance procedure Pages 43 - 45*

- *Not following their investigation procedure Discussed and referenced later in this statement*

- *By NOT keeping me informed and up to date with proceedings Page 347 (bottom paragraph)*

- *Lack of confidentiality throughout my grievance Discussed and referenced later in this statement*

- *Making false accusations against me Page 306 (bullet points at bottom of page), page 307 (top 4 bullet points and 2nd bullet point from the bottom of page) Page 344 (paragraph numbered 5)*

- *Putting me back into the same section as Ron Atler (my line manager) was during my grievance, when the occupational therapist that Kirklees College sent me, to stated that, "Meeting her line manager would be too difficult and stressful at this time" Page 145 (first 2 lines of paragraph 5) Page 147 (last 2 paragraphs of email)*

3. *Kirklees College Grievance Procedure Pages 40 – 52 states that:*

- *Stage 1 should have taken 5 days maximum – it took 10 weeks and 6 days. I informed Kirklees College I wished to put in a formal complaint 31/1/12 Page 114. I was then made to wait until 24/2/12 to begin the process and didn't receive the outcome until 16/4/12 Pages 190 and 191.*
- *Stage 2 should have taken a maximum of 15 working days – it took 13 weeks and 3 days. I informed college I wished to move to Stage 2 on 18/4/12 Page 193. I was made to wait until 18/5/12 for Stage 2 Hearing Page 214 and didn't receive the outcome until 21/7/12 Pages 305 - 308*
- *Stage 3 was completed within the 20-working day maximum limit*
- *The Appeal stage should have taken a maximum of 30 working days – it took 9 weeks. I informed college I wished to appeal on 24/8/12 Page 348. I had to wait until 5/10/12 for Appeal Hearing Page 355 and until 27/10/12 for conclusion Pages 406 - 407*

All in all, it should have been concluded within 70 working days (which works out at 14 weeks)

I had to wait just under 37 weeks or <u>8 months and 27 days</u>.

Page 2

I made Kirklees College aware during the grievance process of my concerns about the length of time I was being made to wait, and that it was causing a detrimental effect to my health (I was off work due to Work-Related Stress).

There are 26 separate examples of such correspondence in this bundle. These are:

Page 118 (2nd and 3rd paragraph)
Page 145 (paragraphs 3 and 6)
Page 161 (Paragraphs 9, 11 and 12)
Page 170 (Paragraphs 4, 8, 10 and 12)
Page 173 (Paragraphs 1, 2 and 3)
Page 187 (Paragraph 2)
Page 198 (Paragraphs 1 and 2)
Page 200 (Lines 6, 7 and 8 from the top)
Page 201 (Second email – 2nd line)
Page 206 (Paragraphs 1, 2, 3, 4 and 5)
Page 209 (First line of email)
Page 211 (Paragraph 1)
Page 214 (3rd bullet point)
Page 216 (Paragraph 6, 7 and 9)
Page 303 (Lines 7, 9 and 10 from the top)
Page 305 (Paragraph 2)
Page 323 (Paragraph 7)
Page 328 (Paragraphs 5 and 6)
Page 343 (Paragraph numbered 1)
Page 347 (Paragraphs 1,2 and 3)
Page 348 (Paragraph 5)
Page 349 (Paragraph 1)
Page 365 (Paragraph 8)
Page 366 (Paragraph 6)
Page 406 (Paragraph 4)
Page 423 (2nd paragraph from the bottom of page)

4. *Kirklees College also contravened the ACAS Code of Practice 1- Disciplinary and Grievance Procedure*

It contravened the following parts:

Page 9 (Number 32)
Page 10 (Number 38 - evidence Page 190 and 191) and numbers 40 and 43)

5. *Kirklees College did NOT follow its investigation procedure. My colleagues and I were assured during Stage 2 of the investigation that our interview notes would be sent out to us for us to check and verify the accuracy. We would then sign and send them back. The notes would then be given to the panel for them to make their decision to Stage 2 of my grievance. Page 343 (paragraph numbered 2)*

Page 3

Mine and 2 other colleagues were sent out on or after the 18th of July 2013 (the same day that the panel reconvened to make their decision) Page 305 (Paragraph 3)
Page 301 (Date at the top)
Page 417 (Top 3 lines)
Page 418 (Top 2 lines)

The rest of my colleagues never received their interview notes back to sign and verify for accuracy (even though I brought this to the attention of the HR manager, both Vice Principles and the Principle of Kirklees College at Stage 2 and Stage 3 of my Grievance Page 329 (Paragraph 2). Page

357 (Paragraph 11 beginning 'There were questions…). The aforementioned promised me that this would be looked into and that they would be sent out)
Page 401 (First line of the email dated 24th August 2012)
Page 411 (First line)
Page 412 (First line)
Page 413 (Full email dated 9/11/12)
Page 414 (First line)
More proof that the interview notes were not sent out and signed are on Pages 222, 224, 225, 226, 228, 236, 239, 241, 243, 245, 246, 259, 277, 279, 283 and 303.

6. Kirklees College also failed to keep confidentiality during the investigation procedure

Page 260 (Top 2 paragraphs)
Page 265 (All of the email)
Page 266 (All of the email)
Page 332 (First line of the email dated 19th June 2012)
Page 334 (Top 4 lines)
Page 335 (Lines 7 – 15)
Page 336 (The top line)
Page 337 (Paragraphs 4, 5 and 6)
Page 338 (Bottom 2 paragraphs)
Page 339 (Paragraph 2)

7. My trust and confidence in Kirklees College were broken because of the above and also because:

(i)   My grievance was NOT upheld even though evidence gathered meant that it should have been. Stage 1 – Page 164 (no 1 at the bottom), page 165 and page 166.

(ii)   Stage 2 – *Page 289 (bottom half of page), page 293, page 294 (especially 4th paragraph) and page 297 (last bullet point from bottom). Page 346 (Last sentence of the last paragraph)*

(iii)   *Kirklees College did nothing but compound my illness - Doctor's notes Pages 141, 142, 143, 144 and 442. Clinical questionnaire forms Pages 113, 233 and 443 by the length of time the grievance took and NOT keeping me informed throughout. This was a massive shock to me as I had believed that I was a valued member of staff before this.*

Page 4

(iv)   *Kirklees College had protected my line manager when other colleagues had made complaints about him previous to me. It seemed that my line manager was 'untouchable.' I was certain that I would have been victimised if I returned to College as I had seen this happen to other colleagues who had moved sections within the college to escape being managed by him – Pages 120, 121, 133, 158 and 159. Other colleagues felt they had no alternative but to leave due to the treatment they and I had received Pages 122, 152, 153, 154, 155 and 156. At least 2 other colleagues had been made ill previous to me and had left and another member of my team was off work with work-related stress due to the same problem at the time I handed my notice in.*

(v)   I was told by my work colleague (Andrew Smithy)16/6/12 that I did not have a timetable for September 2012 as I was not expected to return Page 260 (Bottom paragraph)

(vi)   The false accusations made against me Page 306 (bullet points at bottom of page), page 307 (top 4 bullet points and 2nd bullet point from the bottom of page) Page 344 (paragraph numbered 5) shocked me to the core. I was threatened with 'appropriate action being taken against me' on my return to work. When I asked for written proof to substantiate these false claims the accusations disappeared Page 342 (3rd paragraph) – **But there was no explanation and no apology for making the false accusations!** Paul McKant in an internal memo asks if (accusations) are verbal or recorded Page 399

(vii)   Evidence was removed from my evidence folder by Kirklees College management at Stage 2 of grievance Pages 324, 325 and 326 and again when I retrieved it after the appeal hearing.

(viii) Examples of my confidence being shattered Page 217 (top paragraph), Page 434 (no 30, 31 and 33). This was also felt by my colleague's Page 338 (3rd paragraph beginning 'Obviously...') Page 423 (second paragraph from the bottom of page)

(ix)   Kirklees College making me promises that they did not keep (eg promising to investigate the lack of confidentiality Page 344 Paragraph numbered 6 and why the investigation interview notes were NOT sent out) Page 343 Paragraph numbered 2.

(x)   Kirklees College offering me counseling at Stage 3 of the grievance but then not following it up.

(xi)   Kirklees College withheld information Page 415 (1st paragraph) that I requested via the Freedom of Information Act 2000 (Page 372) even though the college states on its' website that it will respond within 20 days Page 370 (3rd paragraph).

(xii)   My Appeal conclusion letter dated 26th October 2012 stated that the rest of my team were much happier Page 406 (Paragraph 2). The line manager of the team only had 7 lecturers under him. 3 of these 7 lecturers handed in their notice and left the college and another of the 7 was on long term sick due to Work-Related Stress. This happened within a 2½ months of 2012. My confidence in the college was completely shattered and so was over 50% of my former colleagues.

Page 5

No 8. Kirklees College makes many untrue statements and/or assumptions in their ET3 form under the heading of 'Factual Background' Pages 14 to 18

No 11 states that 'the grievance was dealt with in line with Kirklees College's grievance procedures'. This is completely untrue as discussed previously in my statement.

No 28 states 'the respondent did acknowledge that Mr. Atler's management style was at times inappropriate....that he was referred for cognitive behaviour therapy .... for Ron to change his behaviour particularly around how he reacts under stress...' This proves that my accusations were proved to be correct, that Kirklees College knew Ron Atler did not have the skills required to manage staff appropriately but instead of redeploying him they decided to attempt to redeploy me.

No 29 discusses recommendations/suggestions made by Kirklees College as to how I could return to work Providing me with a mentor (from HR who I no longer had any confidence in), A third party present at all meetings with my manager (proving that I would not feel confident being alone with my line manager), Counselling (an admittance that I had been treated appallingly, that I had been made ill by the management of Kirklees College. The offer of counseling was made in my Stage 3 outcome letter Page 345 top bullet point). It was never mentioned again or followed up), Redeployment (why should the innocent victim be redeployed?), Acas intervention/mediation Page 375 top 3 lines (I responded that I would be happy to meet with Acas if I agreed to the Principle's decision to my appeal Page 398 Line 4 and 5 of my email to Paul McKant)

No 30 states 'it is contended that I was not prepared to try any of the interventions offered and that therefore Kirklees College was unable to support me back into the workplace'. Kirklees College paid 'lip-service' to the interventions offered. Nothing was followed up, promises were broken and my confidence in Kirklees College was broken. When I handed my notice to Paul McKant (the Principle), all he did was give me a distasteful look. He did not attempt to discuss the issue – so he accepted it without trying to put any interventions in place.

No 33 states 'Kirklees College went to great lengths to investigate my grievance' and 'went to great lengths to provide me with support'. Both these statements are completely untrue.

No 35 states 'Further the Respondent denies that it committed a breach of any express or implied term of the claimant's contract of employment.' My contact contract of employment Page 37 (no 16 Grievances) states 'A copy of the Grievance procedure is attached' and Page 38 (21.1) states 'This contract of employment and any documents expressly incorporated herein constitute the entire terms and conditions of your employment'. The grievance procedure was not followed so, therefore this is a fundamental breach of my contract.

No 36 states 'Kirklees College denies committing any act or omission which could have the effect of, either destroying or seriously damaging the relationship of trust and confidence between myself and college' This is absolute nonsense. How can Kirklees College measure this?

No 37 states 'that the incidents and allegations that I refer to are denied in their entirety or it is submitted that the incidents did not take place as described by me' I believe that I have given the tribunal the evidence and referenced the written proof to substantiate that all my claims are true.

No 39 states 'If, which it is denied, the Tribunal finds that there was a fundamental breach of any expressed or implied terms of my contract, the college submits that my resignation was NOT in response to the alleged breach' Why would I resign from a job that paid me over £31,000 per year when I didn't have another job to go to?

No 9. _Closing Statement_
Page 6

1. I worked for Kirklees College for 12 years and had an impeccable work record. Pages 53, 54, 108 and 168.

2. The length of time the grievance procedure took and the constant worry during this time that the career I had worked so hard for was slipping away made me very ill. I became a shadow of my former self. I suffered from panic attacks, was reluctant to leave the house and wouldn't answer the telephone. My doctor prescribed me with sleeping tablets as I couldn't sleep due to the anxiety and I was off work for the majority of 2012 due to Work-Related Stress. Pages 141, 142, 143 and 144

3. My doctor diagnosed depression due to my work situation Page 442 He wanted me to take antidepressants and referred me for counseling. I refused the antidepressants as I was frightened of being in even less control and felt that I had to try to stay as alert as possible throughout the grievance process.

4. Kirklees College has contravened Employment Law and Statutory Regulations including:

(i)   Acas definition of Employer's Duty of Care Page 465 (Bullet points 2, 6 and 8)

(ii)   Acas Guidance for Employees booklet 'Bullying and Harassment at Work' Page 76 (top paragraph) page 77 (bottom paragraph), page 78 (top paragraph)

(iii)   Acas Code of Practice 1- Disciplinary and Grievance Procedure (page 9 – no 32 and page 10 – no's 38, 40 and 43)

(iv)   Health and Safety at Work Act 1974 Page 78 (paragraphs 2 and 3)

(v)   Kirklees College's Values and Behaviours Policy Page 86 (1st sentence of 2nd paragraph from bottom) Page 87 and 88 (top boxes names 'as a college employee you can expect to')

(vi)   Protection from Harassment Act 1997. Section 1 (1) (a) (b) and 1 (2) and Section 3 (1) and (2)

(vii)   Employment Rights Act 95 (1) (c)

5. Kirklees College's higher management have admitted their negligence in letters to me and via internal correspondence Pages 343 and 344. Page 347 (Last paragraph). Page 395 (First 2 lines of Paragraph 2) Page 406 (First sentence of 4th paragraph)

6. For the sake of my health, I could not return to a section where the Investigating Officer at Stage 2 of my Grievance concluded the following about my line manager – 'there is cause for concern regarding Ron's behaviour in the form of **intimidation** as over half of the staff interviewed felt Ron was **intimidating**, a third of the staff felt Ron was unprofessional, a

*quarter felt Ron was **undermining and was a bully**, a staggering 10 out of 12 people felt that staff were **not treated equally or the same**'* Page 294 *(Paragraph beginning 'As shown in…')*

7. *Kirklees College's treatment of me has caused me to be unemployed long term for the first time since I started working in 1986. This has put me at a serious financial loss – not just short term, but in the longer term as my pension contributions have stopped.*

8. *My Mutual Trust and Confidence in Kirklees College was destroyed in 2012.*

I was constructively dismissed by Kirklees College

15/11/13

Today I have made a list of dates of all the 'breakdown of correspondence, missed deadlines and 'mistakes''. This is in case I need to refer to or prove anything, (whilst under pressure at tribunal), as it will help me find the evidence speedily.

20/11/13

Whenever I have been to watch other people's tribunals, I have noticed that the lawyers have small 'suitcases' on wheels, which they carry all their evidence around in.

Now that I have prepared all my evidence, it is quite heavy when I add it to the bundle and my folder of evidence. I think I will take everything in my smallest suitcase on wheels, as the car park I use is quite a walk from the tribunal place. I will be sweaty and harassed by the time I get there if I carry it in a normal shoulder bag. I want to arrive at the tribunal each day as calm, relaxed and comfortable as I can.

<u>24/11/13</u>

I am prepared but very, very nervous. I decided to ring ACAS to find out whether I will be put on the witness stand first, OR if I will question Kirklees Colleges witnesses first. I would prefer it if I was questioned first (to get it out of the way).

When I got through to the ACAS lady and asked her the question she replied, 'We are not here to advise you on how to represent yourself'.

I replied that I wasn't asking for advice, I was merely asking about the normal, standard process, and whether the claimant or the defendant went on the witness stand first. She wouldn't answer, and she was no help what so ever. I was annoyed when I got off the phone with her.

I telephoned John Forrest (my witness on the first day of the tribunal). I gave him directions to the tribunal. He sounds like he is looking forward to it (as he dislikes Ron Atler).

<u>30/11/13</u>

No offer of a settlement out of court from Kirklees College which is good news. I panic every time the phone rings in case it's them trying to offer me something so that I'll disappear.

<u>4/12/13</u>

How very strange?

When I opened my emails, I found that I had received a request to connect with Anthea Mitchell on Linkedin. I just kept looking at it confused? Anthea Mitchell is the only manager at Kirklees College that I have some respect for, BUT I can only assume that it's a trick – that if I connected with her, Kirklees College could claim that I had NOT lost my 'Trust and Confidence' in the College.

I don't trust them – so I won't connect. I will connect with her in person next week at the tribunal!

7/12/13

It's the last weekend before the tribunal. This time next week it will all be over. I just hope to goodness that it goes in my favour – if it doesn't, I have no idea how I'll deal with it.

8/12/13

Robert took me shopping in Leeds to try to take my mind off the tribunal.

When we got back Robert asked me again if I wanted him to come to the tribunal with me.

I said 'No,' as I don't want any emotion there. I just want to focus on what I am doing without any distractions. I am also conscious that if it starts going wrong, then I will be more likely to cry and be emotional if I have people close to me there.

My dad isn't happy that I won't let him come with me for support – but I am adamant that I want to be alone (except for John as my witness on the first day) and deal with it myself.

<u>9/12/13</u>

I got up as normal and tried to stay as calm and relaxed as possible. I decided mid-morning that I would watch day time TV to try to distract myself. I received quite a few text messages of support from people like Tanya, Kay and, Judith wishing me luck. I hope I have some good news to share with them in a few days?

At dinner time I got a phone call from the tribunal, informing me that my tribunal would have to be postponed due to one of the Judges being ill!!!!

I felt like I had been punched in the stomach! I couldn't believe it. I just felt sick!

I told them that this wasn't fair, that I had been postponed once already. The lady apologised and said that she would investigate - (as I had already been cancelled).

When I put the phone down, I started thinking about all the tribunals that I had watched – the claimants had only been dismissed a few months before their tribunal, whilst I had been waiting 12 months.

I telephoned her back straight away to 'fight my corner'. I told her:

- That I had been postponed once already
- That I had been waiting 12 months for my tribunal to be heard
- That as I had a 3-day tribunal – this would be harder to re-arrange at a further date than 1- day tribunals

I finished by saying that I didn't think it would be fair if my tribunal was cancelled and other people's tribunals went ahead that hadn't been waiting as long a time as I had. I stated that I had been cancelled once already – so I was already six months overdue for my case being heard.

I was polite but as firm as I could be, (but I also ended up quite tearful). The lady said that she would do all that she could and that she would ring me back before 4 pm.

When I got off the phone all I could do was cry. I telephoned Robert to tell him and he was trying to calm me down.

I had a dreadful afternoon waiting for the tribunal to ring me back. I just felt sick and couldn't believe that I was getting cancelled again – especially not the day before!

I kept thinking that Kirklees College would be laughing their socks off.

4 pm – The tribunal telephoned me to tell me that my tribunal would be going ahead.

I felt such a relief; but also felt sick and weak from the stress. How much more stress am I supposed to take?

I had started the day trying to remain calm and relaxed but had instead taken yet another 'smack in the teeth'.

At 5 pm I checked my emails to find that I had an email from 'Psycho,' wanting to know how many witnesses I would be taking to the tribunal, and informing me that their witnesses were Ron Atler, Dale Rolland, Jean Turrand, Anthea Mitchell and Paul McKant.

They have altered theirs from eight witnesses to five witnesses.

I replied to the email to say that John Forrest would be my only witness.

Stress levels shot right up! I now need to change my questions. Now that Alan Wiley and Jan Weldon are no longer witnesses, I will have to re-jig the questions I was going to ask them and put them into Jean Turrant's questions, (as they were all involved in some stage of the grievance).

I quickly made the tea and 'threw mine down my neck'. Robert got home from work, so I told him that he would need to take Indie out as I needed to alter my questions. I then locked myself in the room with my laptop and printer.

I hate the last minute! I am an organised person who likes to be prepared, so I am stressed beyond belief that I am having to alter things now – the night before the tribunal!

It took me until 10 pm to re-organise, retype, and reprint my questions for tomorrow.

OCD in overdrive! I checked and re-checked my questions, then put all my paperwork back in my suitcase, ready for tomorrow.

I had a cup of tea and tried to calm myself down, but it was impossible as I was completely stressed.

I went to bed, but it took ages to fall asleep. I slept for an hour then woke up. My mind was wide awake, so I knew I wouldn't be able to get back off to sleep. I got up and laid on the settee.

CHAPTER 9

Day 1 of Tribunal

I got up off the settee at 5.45 am. I had breakfast and a cup of tea. I made a protein shake, got bottles of water and my sandwich out of the fridge and put them in my bag.

I got all my evidence/questions/bundle out of my suitcase to check again. I made sure that all my questions were there, and in the correct order, then I put them all back in my suitcase.

I took Indie for a walk, came back, had a shower and got dressed. I tried to remain calm and I was breathing as slowly as I could.

I drove to Leeds, talking to myself to keep myself calm. I told myself how important these next three days were. That I had this one chance alone and that I couldn't blow it.

I parked in the car park, got my suitcase and bag out, and walked to the tribunal building. I tried to walk calmly and not too fast (so I would not reach the tribunal building out of breath, stressed and sweaty).

I was taking deep breaths as I walked up the road to the tribunal building. I looked up the road and noticed that walking down towards me and the tribunal building were Ron Atler, Dale Rolland, Jean Turrand, Anthea Mitchell, Paul McKant and another person (who I assumed was Kirklees College's lawyer, but it was a male – so not Stephanie Path)?

I wasn't going to let this phase me. I took a deep breath, stood up straighter, with my shoulders back and carried on walking towards them.

We met at the door of the tribunal! I walked towards the doors, head held high and they paused to let me through first, then they walked in behind me. I went to one lift, and they went to stand outside the other lift. Their lift came first, and they got in it.

John Forrest arrived whilst I was still waiting for the lift. I just hugged him and told him how I had bumped into the opposition outside. We got in the lift and I took John into the claimant's waiting room. I thanked John profusely for supporting me and explained what little I knew about what would happen.

Julian (the tribunal clerk) came in and asked me for my written statement as he needed to photocopy it for the Judges.

When Julian returned, he informed me that the name of Kirklees Barrister was Ranpump and asked me to confirm that I was representing myself. I replied that "Yes, I was and that I had assumed that Stephanie Path the solicitor who I had dealt with up to now, would be representing Kirklees College". Julian explained that a solicitor dealt with it at the preparation stage, but that large companies were usually represented by a Barrister during the tribunal.

This 'shook me up' some-what! All I could think was that although I knew I was in the right, how could a non-legal person with no experience fight a Barrister!!!!

Anyway, I decided I couldn't change anything, it was happening, so I just needed to try to remain calm and carry on.

At just before 10 am, Julian came to inform us that it was time to go to the tribunal hearing room. John and I went outside and waited in the corridor as requested until our Kirklees College opponents came out of the defendant's waiting room.

I made sure I stood up to my full height, with my head held high and followed Julian to the courtroom.

We all sat down in the tribunal courtroom. Three Judges walked in and spoke to us briefly. The main Judge asked me what issues I was claiming against Kirklees College.

I replied, "Breach of Contract and Loss of Mutual Trust and Confidence".

The Judge informed us that they needed some time to read through our written statements, so we would reconvene at 1 pm.

John and I wandered into Leeds and went to a coffee shop. We were there for a few hours, chatting about the old days (both working at college) and about what may, or may not happen when we returned to the tribunal.

At 1 pm we were back in the tribunal hearing room.

The main Judge started reading out what I thought were parts of my written statement. When he had finished, he looked at Kirklees College's Barrister and said, "You seem to be agreeing with everything that the claimant has said".

Ranpump sounded a bit flustered and made a few feeble excuses before John was called onto the witness stand.

Ranpump asked John about accusations that he had made in his witness statement and tried to make them seem minor and insignificant. John was on the witness stand for about thirty minutes. He remained calm, answered all questions honestly and without hesitation.

Next on the witness stand was me. As I am an atheist, I didn't swear on the bible, but instead, swore on the non-religious alternative.

Before Ranpump could begin questioning me, the main Judge addressed him and said, "I don't expect you to have many questions for the claimant as you haven't stated anything significant against her in your statement"

I sat down and faced Ranpump. Ron Atler was sitting directly behind him, so I could see him in my line of vision over Ranpump's left shoulder. The other Kirklees College witnesses were behind Ranpump to the right. All eyes were on me.

This didn't bother me one bit. Although it was nerve-racking to be on the witness stand in front of a Barrister and facing my opponents from Kirklees College, as I knew that I had done nothing wrong, my time had come, after two long years to 'say my piece'!

Ranpump started by asking me if I felt that Ron Atler treated me differently to the men at Kirklees College and if I was claiming that Ron was sexist. I replied, "No. Ron Atler treated everyone appallingly, it didn't make a difference whether they were male, female, black, white, etc"

Ranpump was happy with my answer and moved on quickly. (He had asked this question as if I could prove that Ron Atler was sexist towards me; then as a 'protected characteristic' I could claim an 'uncapped' amount of compensation).

I was just being honest – and stating that Ron Atler just treated everyone badly!

Ranpump went on to say that I had written at Stage 1 of my grievance that Ron Atler's email to me 'was the last straw' - (He was intimating that to claim unfair dismissal there has to be a 'last straw' and that my 'last straw' was in January 2012 – but I didn't resign until November 2012).

I looked directly at Ranpump as I answered him, "It was the last straw that made me unable to function properly! I had been feeling stressed for months, but I had still managed to go to work and carry on teaching, but that email just pushed me over the edge" I looked at him and said, "I just went like that!" and clicked my fingers to emphasise the point. "I went from being able to function to not being able to function and I couldn't go to work anymore. That is what I meant by the last straw".

Ranpump realised that he had not won this point, so quickly moved on.

Ranpump then asked me to turn to page 235 in the bundle. I started turning over the pages and when I got to page 229, I found that the next page I turned over was 246. I checked and double-checked then looked up at Ranpump and said, "Sorry, I can't find it, I don't think it's here, it goes from page 229 to page 246." Ranpump thought I was being stupid, as he walked over to the witness stand and started looking through the bundle himself. When he found out that I was correct, he went back to his seat and started looking through his copy of the bundle. He started looking uncomfortable and said that his bundle was the same. My Kirklees College opponents were looking through their copies and all of them had the same pages missing. Ranpump started apologising profusely to the Judges saying, "I'm so sorry your Honour's. Pages are missing. Can I go and make some copies please?"

He was feeling embarrassed. He was a qualified professional Barrister, but he looked like an amateur. The Judges told him we would have a 30-minute recess, whilst he sorted out the problem.

John and I walked back to the claimant's room. We were both sniggering when we got inside the room and John was laughing and taking the mickey out of Ranpump, saying, "What a Pumper!" and that's what we started calling Ranpump from then on – 'Pumper'.

We returned to the tribunal room and after Ranpump had thanked the Judges again, he started trying to make excuses for the length of time my grievance took - and this was because it was done thoroughly.

I replied, 'Kirklees College wrote the Grievance Procedure. I kept to the Grievance Procedure. I would have thought that Kirklees College should have been able to keep to their procedure – and the fact that they didn't, made me iller!'

Ranpump again moved on quickly.

Ranpump then started saying that Ron Atler had faced a very difficult task as the Electrical and Plumbing section had been performing poorly, had poor student success rates and had faced very negative staff attitudes. He then began reading from a sheet of paper and started 'spouting' about poor student success rates'.

I just looked at him with a puzzled expression. I said, "No. I don't accept what you are saying, can you direct me to where you are getting these figures from please"

Ranpump told me it was the document on page 367 of the bundle. I turned the pages over in the bundle until I got to page 367. (I had noticed this document previously and had realised that it was there for a 'reason,' so I knew the document 'inside out' – and I knew that it contained only 10 – 15% of our student numbers).

After looking at the document, I looked directly at Ranpump and said, "This document isn't accurate. This only shows Kirklees Colleges day release students, most of our students are JTL, who are block release and consistently have success rates above the national benchmark. JTL claims the funding for these students, so, therefore, Kirklees College cannot claim the student success rates which is why they are not on this document".

Ranpump just looked at me (a bit dumbstruck).

I carried on, "I taught mainly 1st year and 3rd-year JTL students. I was also the course tutor for 3rd-year day-release students who are on this document. I took over as the course tutor during the 2009/2010 academic year. As you can see, I took the student success rate from 75% to 82.98% and it remained consistent under me"

Ranpump just looked at me. He didn't know what to say as he didn't know what/who JTL was and if it was true what I was saying. He looked around at Anthea Mitchell and she nodded to confirm that what I was saying was true.

Ranpump tried to finish off by saying that the lecturers under Ron Atler were underperforming and that Ron Atler had had to be firm and make changes.

I kept looking directly at Ranpump and replied firmly, "I have NEVER underperformed!"

Ranpump realised that he was getting nowhere again so he gave up and said, "No more questions."

The Judges then asked me a few brief questions. The main Judge had a very calm, gentle voice which helped.

I left the witness stand and sat back down. I was so glad that part was over. I felt proud of myself as I had been calm, polite, clear and to the point.

The main Judge said that we would finish for today – and that I would be questioning Kirklees College's witnesses in the morning.

Ranpump informed the court that Dale Rolland had a hospital appointment tomorrow, so he wouldn't be able to attend – but he could be questioned on Thursday instead. The main Judge asked me if that was OK with me.

I was disappointed, but polite and replied, "My questioning won't be in the correct order as Dale Rolland was 2nd on my list, but yes, it's OK."

Ranpump also asked if Paul McKant could be excused in the morning, and just attend in the afternoon to be questioned. The Judges agreed to this.

John and I walked out of the courtroom with our heads held high. When we got outside, I started saying, "God, what happened there? It's all a blur!"

John was laughing, saying that I'd done a brilliant job. I was giddy and laughing also (I don't know if it was adrenaline/stress or both)? John was taking the mickey out of Ranpump and how he hadn't managed to intimidate me. He said he would ring Steve Clay as soon as he got home to update him.

We hugged, and I thanked him profusely for coming. He wished me well for the next two days and left.

I drove home, and my head was buzzing with what had gone on during the day.

When I arrived home, Marcus was there so I told him how well the first day had gone. I then telephoned my mum and dad. I told them how it had all seemed to go well, and that the Judges seemed to be on my side. I also told them that I was a bit worried – that it had gone so well today – would it all go 'downhill' tomorrow?

When Robert got home, I tried to tell him what had happened at the tribunal, but I was a bit manic. Bits of information from the day were just whizzing in and out of my head. My head was still completely buzzing so I was telling him what had happened in a completely haphazard manner.

I decided I needed to go on a walk to try to get rid of my excess energy and to calm my mind – I went on a decent length walk at a quick pace, but my mind wouldn't calm.

I came back, had a shower, checked through my questions for tomorrow again, then went to bed. I couldn't sleep for long, as my mind wouldn't rest, so I ended up lying on the settee from 2 am onwards – waiting for dawn to arrive.

11th December 2013

DAY 2

I got off the settee at 5.45 am. I ate breakfast and took Indie for a short walk. She didn't seem 'right' at all and wouldn't eat her breakfast. Really bad timing as I had enough worries on my mind without worrying about her as well.

I showered and checked through my questions yet again (OCD). I told Robert that I thought something wasn't right about Indie and, just as he was about to set off for work, I noticed Indie halfway down the stairs. I called her to come down (to try to tempt her to eat something), but she just stood there. I went towards her and realised that she couldn't move properly. I picked her up (she yelped in pain) and I carried her downstairs. I shouted Robert and said that she needed to go to the emergency vet. Robert telephoned the vet immediately and then took her over. My last words to Robert were, "Right, my phone will be turned off today, as I can't cope with this".

I'm sure Robert understood. I couldn't believe that this was happening, today of all days. I love my dog so much – and to have the stress of worrying about her, when all I should be doing today was concentrating on my very important day at the tribunal was terrible. Any other day and I would be with my dog, looking after her, whenever she needed me – it was an absolute nightmare!

I set off for the tribunal, trying to breathe slowly as I drove. I walked as calmly as I could to the tribunal building, walking slowly, breathing slowly and deeply as I went.

I arrived in plenty of time and went to sit in the claimant's waiting room. I sat with my back towards the door (so I couldn't see my Kirklees College opponents when they arrived).

I got my questions out and read through them again, just to feel as ready and prepared as I could. I felt that I had made the right decision in coming alone (no Robert or parents). I just wanted to remain calm and focused with no distractions.

I felt very nervous but ready. This was my time to question those who had put me through hell over the last two years. I was ready to question them – to put them under pressure. They could attempt to lie as much as they wanted – I had all the evidence to prove that they were telling untruths in their witness statements against me - and that they were in the wrong.

Just before 10 am Julian came to ask me to stand outside in the corridor, to wait for my Kirklees College opponents to accompany me to battle (or rather courtroom as they call it).

I waited for them, standing tall again with my shoulders back, keeping my breathing even. Today present were Ron Atler, Jean Turrand, Anthea Mitchell, Joan Horncastle (HR Manager) and their Barrister, Ranpump (Dale Rolland was at his hospital appointment and Paul McKant was due to arrive at dinnertime).

I calmly walked down the corridor in front of them, went into the Hearing room, sat down and got my paperwork out.

I was sat right next to the witness stand. I was glad to be so close – so I could look them straight in the eye whilst I questioned them.

The Judges walked in and, after the preliminaries, Ron Atler was called to the witness stand. Ron Atler sat down and was sworn in, and his right leg started twitching almost immediately. It used to twitch at work when he got wound up (so this pleased me, even before I started my questions).

Goodness was I ready for this! I looked at my nemesis straight in the eye and began my questioning.

I said, "In your witness statement (3g), you state that previous to taking over the section 'that staff had not received a Performance Development Review for years".

Ron Atler answered, "Yes".

I replied, "Can you turn to page 468 (of the bundle,) and look at the 2002 Appraisal meeting document please."

I waited until he had found the page and asked, "Is it true that what is now referred to as a Performance Development Review used to be called 'Appraisals'?"

Ron Atler agreed that it was.

I carried on, "Can you briefly turn to page 469 please, this is my 2003 appraisal....and page 471 is my 2005 appraisal....and then page 484 please, this is my 2007 appraisal."

Ron Atler started to look uncomfortable, and his twitchy leg was going 'ten to the dozen'. I then asked in a firm voice, "Will you now retract from your statement that staff had not received a Performance Development Review for years?"

"Yes, I will" replied Ron.

I then said, "In your written statement (4) you also say that 'under the previous management no lesson observations had been undertaken within the Electrical department".

Ron replied confidently, "Yes, none were carried out. I never had one when I was teaching".

I asked, "Can you turn to page 467 please." I waited until he had found it and then explained, "This is a copy of my 2002 lesson observation". I continued, "And now turn to page 470...my 2003 lesson observation... and page 483...my 2007 lesson observation, and then page 494 shows a copy of my 2008 lesson observation".

I paused to let this sink in and was pleased to see that there was no cockiness to Ron Atler. He was in the spotlight – and he wasn't enjoying it! I was looking straight at him as I questioned him. I was in control. Ron Atler's twitchy leg was facing towards the Judges (and it was screaming 'guilty' at them loud and clear).

I then asked, "Do you now agree that your statement about no lesson observations taking place was untrue?"

Ron answered, "Yes".

I continued, "Still on page 494 could you look at the 2nd to the bottom box labelled 'Comment relating to teaching' – does it say that I had a satisfactory lesson plan?"

"Yes" replied Ron.

I ask, "Now please turn back to page 483....Along the bottom of the first two boxes can you see where it says 'well-organised scheme of work and lesson plans?"

Ron looked at the documents...

I stated, "But in your statement (3b) you have said, 'There were no Schemes of Work or lesson plans in place, which are fundamental when teaching in FE"

Ron Atler looked down-cast but didn't answer.

I continued, "So do you now agree that I had Schemes of Work and lesson plans before you took over our section?"

Ron replied, "Yes".

I carried on my questions, "In your statement, you mention that I wished to reduce my fulltime position to a 0.8 post." Ron nodded, so I continued, "So having a 0.8 post would mean working four days instead of five?" I asked.

Ron replied, "Yes".

I asked, "Did I have a 0.8 post?"

Ron replied, "No"

I continued, "But in your witness statement you have said on two occasions (8 and 16) that I took every Wednesday off work?" I looked up at Ron with a confused look on my face before continuing, "If I took every Wednesday off work, this would mean that I had a 0.8 post which you are saying that I didn't have!"

Ron doesn't comment – he doesn't know where I'm going with this.

I ask him, "Can you briefly look through pages 510 – 534 please?" Ron flicks through the pages. I continue, "These are copies of my timesheets. There are 21 timesheets here that all prove that I worked every Wednesday"...I paused then said, "So why would you say that I took off every Wednesday when it is completely untrue?"

Ron Atler looks 'sheepish' and doesn't have an answer for me.

I am enjoying myself. I have waited for this moment for so long! I am proving that Ron Atler has made false claims in his witness statement about me – and all in front of his bosses!

I make sure that I don't show that I am enjoying myself. I carry on with my questions in a professional and business-like manner.

I continued, "You say in your witness statement (16) that 'you covered all open evenings and recruitment events, so that staff could be at home with their families'…Can you look at page 497 please"? I wait until Ron finds the page and then say, "this shows me covering enrolment on Monday evening, page 498 shows me covering Tuesday evening until 8.30 pm. Pages 516 and 525 are both Tuesday evenings also, and page 526 shows that I manned open evening on Thursday night"

I paused to let the information sink in and then said, "So do you now agree that I manned enrolment and recruitment events?"

Ron nodded and said, "Yes."

I continued, "Would you also agree that I was the person in the section who attended the awards and presentation evenings that celebrated student success?"

Ron said, "Yes" straight away. I think he had guessed by now that I could evidence everything I stated.

I then asked, "Would you also agree that I was the person in the electrical section who covered the practical assessments on Tuesday's until 7.30 pm (as shown on pages 495, 496, 520 and 522)?"

Ron again replied, "Yes".

I then moved on to a different topic and said, "You have said in your witness statement that I started work at 7.30 am as if this was something negative – can you explain why?"

Ron could NOT explain why and started mumbling something about 'it was earlier than management liked people to start'.

I stated, "I taught classes from 8.30 am each morning. I think it was professional of me to be prepared and organised for my classes".

No real response from Ron Atler, so I continued, "You also stated (16) that 'I would work through my breaks and lunchtimes so that I could leave earlier than was considered normal". I paused, then asked, "Does Kirklees College have a specific start and finish time for lecturers?"

Ron answered "No".

I asked, "So there was nothing written in my contract of employment about start and finish times?"

Ron repeated, "No".

I asked, "What hours did my contract of employment state I must work each week?"

Ron replied, "37 hours".

I stated, "My timesheets show that I regularly worked a 46 to 48-hour week - as shown on pages 495, 496, 497, 499, 500, 506, 507 and 508". Ron doesn't bother to look at the pages but the Judges do.

I have now completely disproved Ron falsely stating that I had Wednesdays off, didn't work out of normal hours and I have also proved that I worked for more hours than I was required to do so.

Ron Atler can't wait to get off the stand! His twitchy leg is going even faster! His bosses - a Director, the Vice-Principal and HR Manager of Kirklees College are witnessing him being 'torn apart' by me. Well, it serves him right!

I now ask, "Can you look at page 504 please and tell me what it is?"

Ron finds the page and explains that it is my lesson observation (that he did of me).

I ask, "What grade did you give me?"

Ron Atler replied, "2".

I ask, "What does Grade 2 signify?"

Ron Atler replies, "Good."

I then say, "Can you turn to page 511 please and explain what it is and what date it is from?"

Ron turns to page 511 and replies, "It's your annual review from April 2011".

I said, "So if you had any issues with me, then this would have been the document that you would have raised them in?"

Ron Atler's answer to this surprised me (and I imagine surprised the listening Kirklees College management). He said, "I didn't have any issues with you. I thought you were a good teacher, you worked hard, and you always did the best you could for the students".

I must have looked surprised! I don't know why he said this (even though it's true?) He either knew he was beaten – or was he trying to redeem himself???

I carry on regardless, "Can you turn to page 513 of the same document please". Ron does so. I say, "Can you see what you wrote about me in the middlebox under 'summary of strengths' – you wrote 'Commitment to learner success and wellbeing. Excellent organisational abilities. Good work ethic' "

Ron nodded. I ask, "Did you write anything under 'Areas for Development'?"

Ron answered, "No".

I read out, "Can you see under 'Any Issues Arising' – you have written 'Recognise sometimes when you need to share your workload'?"

Ron merely nodded again. I said, "That sounds like you thought I did too much work". I paused for effect and then said, "So, in April 2011 you thought that I was a good teacher, that I was committed, had a good work ethic and that I did too much work".

Ron nodded and muttered, "Yes".

I then said, "In your witness statement (3c) you stated 'classes were generally starting late and quite often lecturer's did not turn up for their classes'" I paused and looked directly at Ron before saying firmly, "Did you EVER know me to be one second late to teach a class – never mind not turn up for it?"

Ron Atler responded, "No, that was about other members of staff in the section, not you".

I had now disproved all of Ron Atler's false accusations and proved that I was a very competent, hardworking and reliable lecturer. I had nearly completed my task. I began finishing my questioning by asking him, "How many lecturing staff were you responsible for in 2012?"

Ron replied, "Seven".

I asked, "Apart from me, were any of the other six lecturers under your control off work with Work-Related Stress in 2012?"

Ron replied, "Yes, one other".

I asked, "Isn't it true that three out of the seven lecturers handed in their notice and left the college during the short period between the end of August and the beginning of November 2012?".

Ron Atler looked sheepish and quietly replied, "Yes".

I replied, "So, out of the seven lecturers, three left and one was off with Work-Related Stress within that short period". I paused, then ended with, "No more questions!"

I knew that I had done a really good job, but as soon as I had finished questioning Ron Atler I started shaking uncontrollably – all over, from head to toe; like I had DT's!

I had my back to the other Kirklees College management. Anthea Mitchell was sat directly behind me. They must have noticed me shaking – as it was so obvious. I tried taking deep breaths to calm myself down, but it must have taken at least twenty minutes for the shaking to stop.

Luckily whilst I was recovering, the three Judges were questioning Ron Atler themselves. Ron Atler started making excuses that he had not managed me as he should have done as he had been 'unwell' himself (as if this was a valid excuse for his treatment of me - my heart was bleeding for him as you can imagine – NOT)!

The Judges questioned Ron Atler for a further 20 – 25 minutes before he was allowed off the stand. He must have been so glad to get off there!

He stood up, head down and scuttled back to his seat without looking at me or his managers. I bet he wished the floor would swallow him up.

I had, by this time, calmed myself down enough to do battle with my next adversary, Jean Turrand (the 'Smiling Assassin' as she was called by some at Kirklees College).

The Judges called Jean Turrand to the witness stand and she was sworn in.

I first asked her to explain her role at Kirklees College. She replied that she was the Director of Higher Education, Development and Innovation.

I asked her, "Did I email you on the 18th of April 2012, to inform you that I wished to proceed to Stage 2 of the grievance procedure?"

Jean Turrand answered, "Yes, you did".

I continued, "Did you respond the same day to confirm that you had received my email?"

Jean Turrand answered "Yes" confidently, (smiling that sickly-sweet smile that she has).

I asked, "Were you the relevant Director that I should have sent my grievance form to?"

"Yes," she acknowledged.

I then asked, "Can you turn to page 44 please" I waited until she had found the relevant page of Kirklees College grievance procedure and then continued, "Do you agree that 4.3.1 of Kirklees College's Grievance Procedure states 'where a grievance cannot be resolved at Stage 1 or where a grievance has not been resolved to the satisfaction of the employee, the complainant will be required to complete a grievance form (Appendix 2), available from Human Resources'".

Jean Turrant answered, "Yes".

I asked, "Did I follow Kirklees College's Grievance Procedure and complete the Appendix 2 Grievance form on 18th April 2012?"

Jean Turrand replied, "Yes, you did".

I then made the point, "So I followed the Grievance Procedure" I paused, to let that point sink in and then said, "Still on page 44, can you go down to point 4.3.2... can you see where it says 'A panel will reconvene to hear the Grievance within 10 working days of receipt of the grievance form?"

Jean Turrand (still smiling) replied, "Yes" – clearly not knowing where I'm going with this.

I asked, "Did you follow 4.3.2 of Kirklees College Grievance Procedure, page 44 regarding the timescale for the panel to hear the grievance after receipt of the grievance form?"

I was expecting a "No" and an excuse as to why from Jean Turrand – but instead she surprised me by saying, "No, I tried to make it less formal, I wanted to get to know you better first before proceeding"

I replied, "I put in a **formal** complaint about Ron Atler at Stage 1. The grievance procedure started formally, and you should have followed the Stage 2 grievance procedure formally".

Jean Turrand again repeated, "I thought it would be better for you if it was more informal, so I could get to know what your issues were and what was bothering you".

I asked again firmly, "Did you follow 4.3.2 of the Grievance Procedure?"

Jean Turrand was evasive and would NOT answer my question – she just kept repeating how she had tried to keep it informal.

I asked her again twice more and, again, she was evasive and wouldn't answer. She looked so confident with that smug smile on her face!

I was feeling frustrated that she wouldn't answer 'Yes' or 'No' to my question – but I knew that I couldn't show that I was frustrated. After a quick think, I decided that by not answering my simple question – she had, in fact, answered it.

The Judges were capable of drawing their conclusions, so I decided to move on.

I said, "The Stage 2 hearing was held on 18th May 2012 – a month, or just over 20 working days after you had received my grievance form. At the hearing did I seem upset and did I mention that the length of time I had already waited during the grievance procedure was making my illness worse?"

Jean Turrand answered, "Yes, you were upset" (with a false, sympathetic look on her face).

I continued, "Do you agree that in your written statement (5) you say that at the Stage 2 grievance hearing (18th May) I had stated that 'I was concerned regarding the length of time taken, following submission of the complaints grievance at Stage 1'".

Jean Turrand replied, "Yes".

I then asked (in a firm manner), "So you agree that at the Stage 2 grievance hearing on May 18th, 2012 I informed you, Alan Wiley and Linda Anison that I was concerned about the length of time that had been taken so far with my grievance?"

"Yes, you did," replied the 'Smiling Assassin'.

I said, "Linda Anison from HR wrote to me on the 18th of May 2012. Can you turn to page 215 please," I waited until she had found the page and then continued, "Can you see the last sentence below the two bullet points where it says, 'I will ensure that you are kept up to date in terms of timescale of investigation and will communicate our findings once the investigation has been concluded".

Jean Turrand smiled and said, "Yes".

I stated firmly, "So, on the 18th of May, HR promised me that they would keep me up to date in terms of the timescale of the investigation – I never heard from her again!" I paused and looked at her before saying, "HR promised to keep me informed and yet I was completely ignored again after telling you at Stage 2 hearing how ill the waiting was making me!"

I looked directly at Jean Turrand and asked, "Do you think that was acceptable?"

"No" she quietly answered.

I said, "The panel reconvened on 18th July 2012 and you say in your statement (no 7, 2nd bullet point) 'the panel was satisfied that a thorough investigation was conducted in line with college's procedure.' Can you explain what that procedure was, please?".

Jean Turrand explained confidently, "All staff in the Electrical and Plumbing department were interviewed and statements were taken from staff. We then used these statements to come to our decision".

I said, "So all my colleagues were interviewed. What happened to the interview notes?"

Jean Turrand replied, "They were sent out to the interviewees for them to check, sign and send back."

I asked, "So you made your conclusions from these **signed** written statements?"

Jean Turrand confidently replied, "Yes".

I stated, "There were NO signatures on any of the interview notes!". Jean looked at me but didn't comment.

I asked, "Do you agree that the panel made their decision to Stage 2 of my grievance based on unverified sources of information?"

Jean Turrand answered, "We had done a thorough investigation" (not answering my question but I let it go).

I continued, "Can you turn to page 414 please". I waited until she was looking at the correct page in the bundle and then said, "The 2nd email on the page is from me to my colleague Jack Booth asking him whether or not he received his interview notes back from his Stage 2 investigation meeting. His reply at the top of page 414 states 'Janette, I did NOT, and I emailed them to that effect! Regards Jack'"

Jean Turrand looked up at me. I stated, "So Jack never received his interview notes back to check for accuracy. Jack contacted HR to inform them of this – and he still didn't receive his interview notes back".

Jean Turrand again just looked at me but didn't answer.

I carried on, "There is similar evidence from my other colleagues who were interviewed at Stage 2 regarding interview notes not being sent out to them on pages 413, 412, 411, 417 and 418."

The Judges turned to the relevant pages to check this information.

I then asked firmly, "Do you now agree that Kirklees College investigation procedure was <u>NOT</u> followed during Stage 2 of my grievance?"

Jean Turrand would not admit this outright and merely answered, "There doesn't seem to be any signatures on them."

I continued, "Can you turn to page 251 please, which is part of the minutes of the investigation meeting I had on 11th June 2012 as part of my Stage 2 grievance...if you look at the last sentence it says 'Jane Davis ended the meeting by informing Janette Castle that they would send Karen Watkin's notes to her home address as quickly as possible, <u>though it would probably be next week due to Karen's work pattern</u>. She checked that JC was happy to receive the notes at her home address and JC confirmed that she was. She thanked JC for her comments and assured her that they had received many positive comments about JC from her work colleagues'"

I looked directly at Jean Turrand and said, "So I was promised I would get them the following week, but I did <u>NOT!</u> **Can you see why my confidence in Kirklees College was destroyed during my grievance?"**

She quietly replied, "Yes."

I asked, "Do you agree that your panel's decision to Stage 2 of my grievance was made using unverified, unsigned evidence?"

Jean replied, "Unsigned yes."

I asked her, "Do you agree that the majority of my colleagues never received their interview notes back and that the three who did receive them, did so after the 18th of July 2012 when your panel reconvened to make your decision?"

"It seems so" she replied.

I then asked, "Do you agree that Kirklees College's investigation procedure was **NOT** followed during Stage 2 of my grievance?"

Jean replied, "Not fully, no."

I then asked, "After the Stage 2 grievance hearing held on the 18th of May 2012, did you follow 4.3.3 of Kirklees College Grievance Procedure on page 44 of the bundle, for giving me the written conclusion to Stage 2 which states that 'The panel will communicate their decision to the complainant, in writing, within 5 working days of the hearing'?"

Jean Turrand replied, "It took longer than 5 days due to all the staff who needed to be interviewed, we wanted to make sure we got all the facts."

I then asked, "If Kirklees College grievance procedure states that I should have received a written response within 5 working days – How long was I made to wait before I received my response from you?"

Jean Turrand responded, "I'm not sure of the exact timescale."

I replied, "Well it was the 20th of July 2012 – **2 months or 40 working days!**" I looked directly at her to make a point and she gave me a pathetic smile.

I then asked, "Do you still agree with the decisions you made on 18th July 2012 about Stage 2 of my grievance?"

"Most of them" she replied.

I asked, "Is it true that you decided that <u>no formal action</u> needed to be taken against my line manager Ron Atler?"

Jean replied "Yes."

I looked at her, then asked, "Did you carefully read the investigating officer Jane Davis' report before making this decision?"

Jean replied that she had.

I then said, "Can you turn to page 289 please." She found the correct page, so I continued, "12 of my colleagues were interviewed during the investigation. This page shows how many people stated that Ron Atler was the following:

Unprofessional (4 out of 12)
Undermining (3 out of 12)
Intimidating (7 out of 12)
Bullying (3 out of 12)
Didn't treat people the same (10 out of 12)
Lack of confidentiality (11 out of 12)
I continued, "Those findings sound serious – Intimidating 7 out of 12 and bullying 3 out of 12. Is that the kind of behaviour that you think is acceptable from a manager at Kirklees College?"

I looked directly at her again to make a point and she replied, "No."

I then said, "Can you turn to page 294 please,…. The 4th paragraph states, 'as shown in (see paragraph 6) there is cause for concern regarding Ron's behaviour in the form of intimidation as over <u>half of staff</u> interviewed felt Ron was intimidating, <u>a third of staff</u> felt that Ron was unprofessional, a **quarter felt Ron was undermining and was a bully** and a <u>staggering 10 out of 12 felt that staff were not treated equally or the same</u>'"

I paused for effect, looked directly at Jean Turrand and said, "So you read this and decided that **no formal action** was to be taken against Ron Atler and that I was expected to come back to work under Ron Atler!"

I couldn't see Ron Atler as he was behind me – but I bet he was wishing (again) that the floor would swallow him up by this point!

I carried on, "Can you turn to page 43 please, ….this is Kirklees College's Grievance Procedure. 4.1.12 states 'proceedings in all matters relating to grievance procedures shall be confidential'. Can you explain why there was a lack of confidentiality during the investigation procedure?"

Jean responded, "I don't know what you mean. It was conducted confidentially."

I calmly replied, "Can you turn to page 265 please" Jean Turrand turns to page 265, and so do all three Judges who were following every word I said.

I asked her to read the full email (to herself) from Andrew Smithy to Karen Watkins in HR. When she had read this, I asked her to turn to page 266 and read the email from another colleague (Steve Clay) to Jane Davis.

Jean Turrand and the Judges read the emails. I then asked them to read the last sentence from page 335 which was another email from Andrew Smithy to Karen. All three emails were from my former colleagues complaining about the lack of confidentiality during the investigation process. I had now proved this without a shadow of doubt in black and white.

Now I had got Jean Turrand's attention! She looked very uncomfortable and wary of what was coming next.

I said, "So that we can get a clear picture of what happened at Stage 2, can you please turn to page 338 please and find the email from Andrew Smithy to Joan Horncastle the HR manager." Joan Horncastle was sitting behind me (I wished that I had eyes in the back of my head to see her face as I read this interesting email out).

When Jean and the Judges had found the correct page I said, "The last two paragraphs of the email states 'Obviously all the denials and the College's complete disregard for the procedure at Stage 2 (after Jane Davis had assured us about the rigour of this process), can only have contributed to Janette's feeling that she was up against the whole College and not just her line manager. I was not the only member of staff whose comments found their way to Ron before they had been checked. I don't know by what route this (unverified) information travelled but it made the journey...and very quickly.'"

I looked at Jean Turrand and said, "So my colleagues were also very concerned about the procedure not being followed!"

No response from Jean, apart from an uncomfortable look.

I then asked her, "Would you say that Kirklees College followed Employment Law and all Statutory Regulations?"

"Yes" replied Jean.

I asked, "Which Regulation told you that it was acceptable to decide that someone was a bully and undermining 'based on the balance of probabilities' which you state on page 306 paragraph 2?"

Jean did not have an answer for this.

I continued, "You sent a letter to Ron Atler on the 20th of July 2012 explaining what outcome you had decided to my grievance against him…can you turn to age 310 please" Jean and the Judges did so I continued, "The top paragraph of your letter to Ron Atler states 'The panel is satisfied with the evidence put forward that the allegations of bullying and undermining are not upheld: however there is evidence to suggest that you need to make changes to your behaviour to effectively manage and lead the team, as evidence suggests that **you can display intimidating behaviour** towards members of the team'"

I looked straight at Jean Turrant and said, "So; he displays intimidating behaviour, BUT he is NOT a bully?" I paused and then asked, "Can you explain the difference between intimidation and bullying please?"

Jean Turrand made a feeble explanation that if a person intimidates someone, they do it subconsciously and don't mean it, whereas a bully means it.

I just looked at her in a confused manner, then confidently said, "I have looked up the definitions of both. The definitions are as follows:

Intimidation – 'Making you feel frightened or nervous, to make timid or fearful, frighten – especially, to compel or deter by or as if by threats, **to bully is to intimidate** through blustering, domineering or threatening behaviour

Bullying – 'Use superior strength or influence **to intimidate someone**'...

Bullying and intimidation are the same things!" I stated firmly.

I looked up briefly at Jean and said, "I told Kirklees College that I and the rest of my colleagues were being bullied. This was proved by yourself by admitting that Ron Atler displayed intimidating behaviour, - yet instead of protecting me and my colleagues as you should have **lawfully done**, you decided to ignore the situation and try to get me back into the section under my bullying boss who you knew had already made me ill!"

Jean Turrand's smile was now just a thin veneer. The cockiness had gone. She had underestimated me – and I had not finished yet – not by a long way!

I asked her, "Did you not think about my Health, Safety and, Wellbeing at all?"

No response from the (not so) 'Smiling Assassin', so I carried on.

I then asked, "Were you surprised when Anthea Mitchell who dealt with Stage 3 of my grievance overturned the majority of the decisions, you and your panel made at Stage 2?"

Jean Turrand was non-committal, so I continued, "You made several false accusations against me in your conclusion letter dated 20th July 2012 on page 307, three of which were:

- A general negative approach and attitude...where examples of underperformance were evident

- Falsifying completion dates on student tracking documents
- Internally verifying own work which contravenes all college procedures"

I looked directly at my nemesis and asked, "Can you point me to the evidence in the bundle that compelled you to write these accusations against me?"

Jean Turrand looked 'sheepish' and replied, "No"

I stated firmly, "So you had NO evidence!"

I continued, "Still on page 307, 2nd to bottom bullet point, you went on to say 'Examples of underperformance and falsifying of College documents to be addressed with individual members of the team and any appropriate action taken'"

I looked at Jean for effect and then asked, "Would you agree that that was quite intimidating - to send a letter to a person's house who was off work with Work-Related Stress. To make false accusations against them and to threaten them with appropriate action being taken against them!"

Jean Turrand replied, "That was relating to members of your team, not you."

I just looked at her and said, "Was I a member of that team?"

She replied, "Yes but it was about the team in general."

I stated firmly, "Was the letter addressed to me?"

Jean replied, "Yes" and looked away.

I then said forcefully, "To make false accusations against me is also 'Defamation of Character' which could, and in fact, may have harmed my reputation. The impeccable reputation that I had taken 12 years to achieve – and you destroy it through libel comments that you did <u>NOT</u> investigate to check for accuracy and merit."

I continued, "I asked Anthea Mitchell and Joan Horncastle to look into these false accusations at Stage 3 of my grievance. The accusations then mysteriously disappeared but I received NO apology or explanation" I looked at Jean Turrand and said, "Can you see how your false accusations made me lose my Trust and Confidence in Kirklees College?"

No comment from her, so I moved on to another point. I said, "In your statement (9 – last bullet point) you mention that I was requested to attend a meeting on Wednesday the 15th of August 2012. You have stated that I did not attend this meeting. Are you certain that I did not attend this meeting?"

Jean confidently replied, "Yes, you didn't attend."

I asked, "Are you certain that the meeting on Wednesday the 15th of August was not cancelled?"

Jean Turrand rather smugly answered, "No, it wasn't cancelled, and you did not attend.

Smiling inwardly to myself I said, "Can you turn to page 327 please" Jean and the Judges did so. I said, "This is an email from Joan Horncastle to myself. In the subject box, it says, 'Meeting on 15th August'. It is quite a lengthy email, can you read it to yourself please."

Jean and the Judges read through the email. When they have finished Jean Turrand looked crestfallen.

I said, "So the meeting on Wednesday 15th August 2012 was cancelled by your HR Manager at Kirklees College. Will you now retract from your statement that I did not attend a meeting that I was asked to attend?"

Jean Turrand replied, "Yes, it clearly states it here."

I feel extremely smug, but I don't show it. I'm extremely happy to see Jean Turrand's discomfort. It serves her right for her earlier smugness.

Joan Horncastle is here behind me (I just wish I could see her face). Don't these well paid 'professionals' talk to one another? Haven't they looked through their 'evidence' and checked through it???

I remained professional and ended by saying, "No more questions."

As soon as I finished my questioning I immediately started shaking again. The shaking was dramatic and obvious. It was a good job that I was sitting down or I may have fallen. It must have been all the adrenalin flowing through my veins!

I may have been shaking all over, but I knew I had done a good job - particularly for a 'layperson' with no legal training.

I had proved the bullying and intimidation. I had proved that Kirklees College did NOT follow the Grievance procedure or the Investigation Procedure. I proved the lack of confidentiality and that my Trust and Confidence in Kirklees College had been broken (which was one of the two things that I needed to prove to win my case). The other thing I needed to prove was 'Breach of Contract' – I felt I had more or less done this already, (I aimed to completely prove it by my questioning of Anthea Mitchell, Paul McKant and Dale Rolland later today and tomorrow; I would prove they, as well as Jean Turrand, didn't follow the grievance procedure – which was part of my contract of employment).

Whilst I sat there shaking it was now the Judges turn to question Jean Turrand. If she thought that I had given her a hard time, then it was about to get far worse.

I think the Judges were quite 'gob-smacked' at the length of time the Grievance Procedure went on for. All three Judges grilled her for a further thirty minutes, and by the end of it, she looked like she could burst into tears! I enjoyed this immensely, (but again, I was careful not to show my pleasure).

One Judge was stating "Miss Castle told you that the length of time the grievance procedure was taking was making her ill and you decided to ignore this and make it longer, by not following procedure." He was shaking his head in disbelief!

Jean Turrand tried making excuses, but the Judges weren't having any of it. They asked her why the Grievance Procedure took so long, why the investigation procedure wasn't followed, why it was not confidential etc. Jean Turrand had managed to be evasive with some of my questions, but the Judges expected answers from her, and wouldn't accept her excuses.

When the Judges had finally finished with Jean Turrand, she left the stand meekly and sat down.

This made me feel fantastic – she had so confidently walked to the witness stand, all smiles only to retreat all deflated and defeated.

The main Judge said that we would have a short lunch break and return at 12.30 pm prompt.

I put my questions in my bag and got ready to walk out. Ranpump was furiously shoving all his piles of paperwork (bundle and all), into his suitcase before he walked out.

This amused me immensely as I knew he was flustered, and that he had an awful lot of work to do during his lunch break, whereas I could relax, eat my dinner and remain calm.

I went into the Claimant's room. I ate my sandwich and then calmly read through the questions I was going to ask Kirklees College's next witnesses, Anthea Mitchell and Paul McKant. I took deep breaths as I read through the questions trying to remain calm and prepared for the afternoon ahead. I was thinking about Indie and wondering how she was – but I wouldn't allow myself to ring Robert. I kept my phone turned off, so I wasn't contactable – I couldn't cope with any bad news right now.

I was still nervous about my task ahead, but I felt immensely proud of myself as I knew I had annihilated Ron Atler and Jean Turrand before dinner. It felt fantastic on two counts – one that I had proved everything I was saying was true and two, that I had put them under immense pressure (that they fully deserved). They had seen me calm and in control today. I was in charge and there was nowhere to hide for them.

I put my questions away and began reading a magazine I had brought to take my mind off things.

At about 12.25 pm I heard someone ask if I minded if they had a word with me. I looked up and saw that it was Ranpump. I was a bit confused as to why he had come into the Claimant's waiting room but calmly replied, "Yes" to him.

Ranpump remained standing and said, "We've decided not to contest your claim any longer. We concede."

I just looked at him and gave him a slight nod. He then said, "When we go back in, I'm going to tell the Judges we don't wish to fight your claim any longer and ask if we can go straight to the Remedy (compensation), they may tell me to 'Bog off' and carry on, but we would like to move straight to the Remedy. Are you OK with that?"

I showed no emotion at all. I looked at him and calmly replied, "Yes."

As soon as he had left the Claimants room some of the other people in the waiting room, (who I didn't know) got 'giddy' and we're saying, "God, well done, I bet you feel great!"

Another was laughing and saying, "I bet he didn't enjoy coming in here and telling you that! Well done."

One lady was telling me to "Celebrate – Go, Girl!"

I replied, "They have seen me crying, they have seen me shaking – today they will see that I am calm and in control." I smiled at her and I think she understood.

After about five minutes Julian the steward came to ask me to wait in the corridor (to wait for my Kirklees College opponents to walk down to the tribunal hearing room together). Julian was smiling and said, "Well done, you must feel fantastic" I replied, "Yes, brilliant, but I'm not showing any emotion as I want them to see me calm and strong."

My Kirklees College enemies came out of the Respondents waiting room. I made sure my face showed no emotion. I imagine they may have expected me to be smug – but I felt that if I appeared calm and professional it would do three things; it would show them that I was in control, that I had great strength to take them to a tribunal and represent myself and remind them that they had lost a competent, honest, hardworking and professional member of staff.

We walked into the Hearing Room and sat down. The Judges came in and Ranpump informed them that Kirklees College no longer wanted to fight my claims and that they would like to move to the Remedy.

The Main Judge looked at me and asked if that was OK with me. I replied, "Yes" (again whilst showing no emotion). None of the Judges seemed surprised or questioned Ranpump as to why he (and Kirklees College) had suddenly conceded defeat. They knew from my questioning of just two of their five 'witnesses' that I had proved my claims with no area left for doubt.

The main Judge said, "Right, you need to prepare Mr, Ranpump, so we'll reconvene at 2 pm. Ranpump asked the Judges if it was OK if all Kirklees College staff could leave now, except for Joan Horncastle (HR Manager) and Paul McKant (Principal).

The Judges agreed, and we walked out. I showed no emotion and walked out with my back straight, head held high, and with a confident bounce in my step.

I didn't look at any of my opponents. I had won fair and square. I knew it and they knew it. More powerful I decided not to gloat, but to just disappear and leave them to think about what had gone on over the last two days.

I started to feel very emotional as I travelled down in the lift. Once out of the lift, I quickly walked across the reception and rushed out of the doors. I couldn't control my emotions any longer. I burst into tears and began shaking all over. All I could think was, "It's over! Two years and its finally over."

I was thinking about Indie too. I had no idea how she was – was she dead or alive? Indie had got me through two years of hell. She was my constant companion who had kept me going. She couldn't die today – not now everything else was OK.

I was walking around Leeds town centre, all alone – crying and shaking. Walking with my head down, trying not to attract attention to myself. It took me about an hour to stop crying and shaking.

It was such a massive thing - I just can't describe it....

The anxiety, stress and, tension that I have carried with me day and night for two long years just went..... It wasn't a matter of knowing the amount I would be compensated for what I had been subjected to, but in knowing I had achieved my goal. I had proved that I was constructively dismissed and that I had done nothing wrong. I now knew that my life was no longer 'on hold'. I would be able to move on (to hopefully a more positive chapter of my life).

I walked back to the Tribunal building, went into the toilets and tried to compose myself for what was going to happen during the rest of the afternoon (I had no idea what to expect).

When we got back into the Tribunal Hearing room there were the three Judges, Julian the steward, Ranpump, Joan Horncastle, Paul McKant and me.

Paul McKant started telling the Judges that I would have no problem finding another job as I had qualifications and experience in 'different fields. He said that as a qualified electrician I could work as an electrician. I could go back to teaching, and that my qualifications in health and fitness meant that I could work in that industry also.

Paul McKant went on to say, "The recession in the Construction trade is now over, so there will be more teaching jobs in the Further Education sector again."

I replied, "The recession took about four years to impact on us with student number reductions, so it will take approximately four years to build student numbers back up before colleges will need to recruit extra teachers again."

Paul McKant again repeated that I had qualifications in the Health and Fitness sector, so I could gain employment in that industry.

I replied, "The health and fitness qualifications that I have, are from the late 1980s. They are quite out of date as things have moved on in the fitness world," I added, "I am 45 years old. I don't think I could compete with all the 20-year olds in the fitness industry today."

Paul McKant and Ranpump were trying to make it sound like I could get another job tomorrow. Everything they said to me/about me – I had a sensible calm answer for (to contradict the points they were making).

Kirklees College was just trying to limit the amount of compensation they would have to pay me.

Paul McKant was amusing me (inwardly) as he was 'bigging me up' as this person with so many qualifications and experience that I would have no problem getting a job. I don't think he saw the irony – that he was telling the Judges how employable I was – when he had made me unemployed!!!

I felt that the Judges thought that my answers were honest and valid. They had no reason to doubt me when I had proved myself to be honest throughout the tribunal hearing.

The Judges explained to me that tomorrow I would go on the witness stand again to explain what I had done to try to find employment since leaving Kirklees College. They told me that I needed to bring in my teacher's pension information, as this would help them to decide the amount of compensation that they would award me.

I drove home and all I could think about was whether Indie was OK.

I arrived home, and Robert's car was outside. I rushed into the front room to find Indie on the floor in front of the fire and Robert on the settee.

All I was concerned about was Indie and what the vet had said about her. Indie looked very subdued. We discussed Indie for about twenty minutes and he updated me on what the vet had said regarding Indie, then Robert asked, "How have you gone on?"

I told him that I had won, that Kirklees College had given up at dinner time, but I didn't know how much compensation I had won, and that I had to go back tomorrow with my pension details.

I telephoned my mum and dad to inform them and was absolutely 'gagging' to tell my mates from Kirklees College I had won – but I decided I would wait until tomorrow when I knew the full facts and the amount I had been awarded.

I spent the first part of the evening trying to get my up to date pension record off the internet – but there was a problem. I couldn't access it, so more stress.

Indie started looking like she was 'going down-hill' again, so we ended up taking her back to the emergency vets at about 8.30 pm.

We returned home stressed and upset. All I could think was that Indie had got me through the last two years. Now I had won, she couldn't die and leave me! I loved her so much. I couldn't lose her now!

I didn't sleep yet again! I got up and just laid restlessly on the settee.

12th December 2013

DAY 3

I got up off the settee, had breakfast then showered.

Extremely stressed! Worried sick about Indie, and being unable to access my pension details!

Robert said he would try to get my pension details off the internet, then fax them to me at the tribunal.

I set off to the tribunal, and when I got there, I asked Julian for the fax number.

Day three was due to start at 10 am and I spent the first half-hour before that on the phone to Robert answering questions whilst he was trying to access my pension details for me.

He managed to fax them across to me at about 9.55 am. Just in time, but it didn't leave me any time to calm myself down before proceedings began.

Proceedings began at 10 am. There were the three Judges, Ranpump, Joan Horncastle and me.

I was called to the witness stand first, to be questioned by Ranpump about what steps I had taken to find work since leaving Kirklees College on 5th January 2013.

I told Ranpump that I had had a 'very up and down' year with depression, that the doctor had wanted me to take anti-depressants and to have counselling.

I explained how I hadn't felt well enough to get a job which entailed having a boss for the first six months of the year and that I had tried to start up my own business as a weight-loss consultant, but had not been unsuccessful.

I told him about trying to get into teaching fitness classes for people who had heart problems (with a company called Heart Beat in Brighouse), and that I had spent seven weeks throughout July and August 'shadowing' classes for free, but that there were no job vacancies at present.

Ranpump asked me about teaching jobs for electrical installation. I told him there were no jobs at my local colleges and that I had contacted Andrew Smithy (my ex-work colleague) who works at a local college – who told me there were no jobs there. I told him that there was a private teaching provider in Brighouse where another ex-colleague works – and that there were no jobs there either.

I told him that I was on the 'books' of agencies and had taught three days at Oldham College in September, but that there was nothing permanent.

I told him that I had attended an interview at College in Leeds as an assessor in October, but had not been offered the job.

I also told him that I had been looking at houses on the internet, with a view to property development – but that I didn't have the cash to finance it at present.

Ranpump asked me about my depression, and how long it had gone on for.

I answered that there was no pattern to it, that I might have had a few days feeling not too bad, followed by two weeks of being tearful and then four days feeling mildly down, a day or two feeling OK followed by a week feeling seriously depressed....

Ranpump asked, "When did you start to feel an improvement?"

I answered, "July, I managed to sleep for about three weeks during July." I looked up at the female Judge as I said this and smiled. She smiled back at me.

Ranpump commented, "That fits with the work at 'Heart Beat' in July/August and teaching at Oldham College in September."

I got the feeling that Ranpump believed me (probably because it was true), and because of this he couldn't interrogate me – which probably annoyed him no end.

The Judges asked me a few questions but nothing significant. I felt that they understood that I had been completely shafted by Kirklees College. That they had turned my world upside down, and that I had worked for over twenty-six years before this – so I was not work shy.

The Judges then informed us that they now needed time to work out my compensation award and that we would reconvene at 1 pm.

Ranpump and Joan Horncastle didn't look very happy. They knew it was in the hands of the Judges (and that they hadn't been able to make any case against me to try to reduce any compensation I might be awarded).

I left the building, walked around Leeds for a while, then returned to the Claimant's room to eat my sandwich.

My head was spinning – knowing that I had won (which was fantastic) but having no idea how much compensation I would be awarded.

My emotions were mixed. I was excited to find out how much compensation I was getting but very worried about Indie and whether she would be OK or not.

1 pm

We went back into the Hearing Room. Julian (the steward) sat in, taking notes.

The main Judge began explaining what they were going to award me. I looked up at the female Judge and mouthed, "Do I write this down?"

She smiled and nodded "Yes."

The Judge started stating figure after figure. I started to write the figures down, but I soon 'got lost' and was confused.

Ranpump tried to interrupt a few times and disagree with a few parts, but the Judge was having none of it.

Ranpump was seriously perplexed. Both he and Joan Horncastle looked seriously concerned. This amused me immensely (but I didn't show it).

I was totally confused dot com??? I knew it must be good for me if Ranpump and Joan Horncastle were so unhappy, but I had no idea what amount I had received in compensation. I think the female Judge could tell that I was 'lost' and asked me if I understood.

I replied, "No, I'm lost…what have I been awarded?"

The Judge replied, "£78,499"!

I calmly wrote £78,499 down on my note pad. Calm on the exterior, showing no emotion – but on the inside, I was ecstatic!!!

I fleetingly wondered if it would be Ranpump or Joan Horncastle who would have the pleasure (NOT) of informing Paul McKant that he needed to find just over £78,000 from somewhere! I would love to listen to that conversation.

It was now over and Ranpump and I began clearing our things away.

I remained expressionless. I thought it would hurt Ranpump and Joan Horncastle more if my face was calm and neutral (instead of smug). I also knew that Joan Horncastle would report back to my Kirklees College ex-managers that I had continued to be thoroughly professional. I would be the bigger person in this.

The Judges remained seated as we cleared up and Ranpump waited so he could walk out with me (I assume this is professional protocol)?

I wanted to thank the Judges before leaving, but I was starting to feel very emotional. I just about managed to say, "Thank you very much" to them all, and then addressed the main Judge by saying, "And your calm, gentle voice throughout really helped." My voice was 'cracking' by now and I was quietly crying happy, relieved, emotional tears as I walked out of the room and down the corridor with my head held as high as can be.

I walked back to my car and was just talking to myself in my head, saying, "£78,000! £78,000!" It felt fantastic.

When I got to the car, I decided I wanted to ring Robert before I drove home. He answered and asked how I had gone on.

I replied, "Great, I've won £78,000!"

Robert didn't respond. I said, "Well, what do you think, it's good isn't it?"

Robert replied, "I'd rather we didn't have the money – and that you hadn't had to go through what you've been through!"

I was quite surprised by Robert's response, but it just proved that he had been completely disgusted by what I had had to go through and that he had been worried sick about me.

I replied, "No. I'm happy with it. It's over now and I can move on"

Robert told me that we had to ring the vets at about 6.30 pm to check if Indie was OK to come home. I drove home feeling fantastic.

It was weird how it did feel like it was over. It felt as if a massive weight had been lifted off my shoulders. Two long years of that solid weight dragging me down mentally, emotionally (and even physically during the first year) – and now I felt positive, happy and excited.

When I got home my first phone call was to my mum and dad. They were ecstatic. They arranged to come down to my house in the morning, for me to go through it all with them.

I felt John Forrest needed to be my next phone call (as he had taken time out to support me and be my witness). When he answered I shouted, "I've won!"

John replied, Fantastic! Well done girl! How much have you won?"

"£78,000" I laughed, to which John responded, "Fucking Hell! I wish I'd been there to see it! Fucking fantastic! God, Ron's going to get it now! Wait till I tell Steve. I'm going to ring him. Fantastic – made my day"

John was so happy for me. We had a good laugh on the phone and arranged to meet for a drink to celebrate.

I telephoned Phil Carter next as he had been very supportive throughout, ringing me every single week that I had been off ill to check how I was. When I got through to him, he was working and with a student, so I couldn't talk for long.

I said, "I've just called to tell you that I've won"

Phil replied, "Oh, well done. What did you get?"

I replied, "£78,000!"

Phil's voice went up about ten octaves as he shouted down the phone, "Fucking Hell. I hope there's a pint in there for me!"

I assured him that there was and didn't talk much longer (as he was working). I agreed to email him later about a celebratory drink.

Next on my list was Tanya Brown (who had kept in contact and had been sending me supportive texts before and during the tribunal).

Tanya's response to my win – and the amount of compensation was the same as John's and Phil's. I received a very loud and excited, "Fucking Hell! Oh my God! Fucking hell! Fantastic!" down the phone. Tanya wanted to know all the 'ins and outs' of the tribunal, so I was on the phone with her for about thirty minutes. She was so happy for me.

Tanya finished by saying that she would telephone Amy Lamb immediately and that she was interested to find out what got said at work tomorrow.

Then it was Kay Ramsden's turn. She was very happy too and was also interested as to what would go on at work tomorrow. Seemingly Ron Atler had told someone at work that I would end up with some money – but that I hadn't won??? (Still telling 'porkies')!

I then telephoned Judith Hamilton. Judith is like Kay and doesn't swear. Judith was excited and proud of me for standing up to Kirklees College and then deservedly winning. She knew what I had been through. She had seen me at college and had seen me a complete wreck during one of the meetings she attended with me as my witness – so another very happy ex-colleague and friend.

Amy Lamb texted me as soon as I got off the phone to Judith. Her text read, 'Well done. You have done a fantastic job. Will ring you later xx'

Steve Clay then rang me. John had given him the good news and he was buzzing as he had been off work with stress due to Ron Atler's 'unique' management style.

Steve was praising me and saying, "You did it all on your own! You, against the whole College! You won without a solicitor. You should be so proud of yourself."

Steve told me how pleased he was for me. That it had made his year and that Kirklees College had finally got their 'comeuppance'!

We agreed that we would meet up for drinks and that I would tell him all the gory (but great) details.

I then texted my ex-colleague Andrew Smithy and John Schofield (my previous and lovely boss and friend from Kirklees College). John was ecstatic as he has very little respect for the management at College.

I then waited for Robert to get home so that we could hopefully pick Indie up from the vets.

Robert arrived home, gave me a massive hug and told me how proud he was of me. Whilst driving to the vets I filled him in on the day's events and all my ex-work mates delight at my win (and their excited swearing).

We drove over to the vets and picked Indie up. She was still subdued and not her normal self. We got her home, lit the wood burner and got her settled in front of it. We then both lay on the floor with Indie, stroking and comforting her.

It wasn't the evening I had imagined after winning my tribunal. No celebratory drink (I just couldn't whilst Indie was unwell). As Robert was working the next day I ended up 'sleeping' downstairs on the floor with Indie to keep an eye on her.

I didn't get much sleep as Indie was fidgety and took hours to settle down. My head was spinning from the last three days. I just lay there, next to Indie, thinking in my head '£78,000! WOW! I have won!'

13th December 2013

I woke up feeling very proud of myself. I couldn't do anything or go anywhere as Indie wouldn't settle unless I sat next to her on the floor.

Robert went to work, and my mum and dad came down for the full account of the past three days' proceedings. They were both so proud of me and ecstatic that I had won that amount of money.

I decided that now would be a good time for me to 'connect with Anthea Mitchell' on LinkedIn. I opened my emails and found the email that Anthea Mitchell had sent me just before the tribunal. I smiled and clicked on the 'connect' button. This amused me, (but I bet it won't amuse her). Tough!

The next four to five days were all about Indie. I slept downstairs with her Friday, Saturday, Sunday and Monday night. She thankfully started improving so life 'was on the up' in all areas.

Kay, Tanya, Amy and, Judith had been asking me if I could go out with them on Friday 20th of December and I had agreed that I would if Indie was OK. That was the day that Kirklees College broke up for Christmas and all staff went around Huddersfield. As Indie was better, I was looking forward to going out and to finally be able to celebrate.

20th December 2013

I met Tanya, Kay, Amy, Judith and a few other girls from Kirklees College at 1 pm for dinner/drinks.

They were all giddy, wanting to know everything that had happened. I explained what had happened throughout each day of the tribunal.

Tanya and Amy said that the day after the tribunal, one of their managers had been to a meeting where their boss informed them he had just been told by Dale Rolland that I had lost!

Amy said to her manager, "No, Janette told me herself that she won. Janette couldn't say that if she hadn't as she doesn't lie."

Unbelievable that Dale Rolland had said that. I suppose I shouldn't be surprised by now!

Kay works in the Construction Department (at Brunel House where Electrical and plumbing are along with builders, joiners, etc). Colleagues there had been aware of my on-going saga and were quizzing her on my Tribunal, as they knew she was my friend.

She said that they were all pleased for me.

After our dinner, we walked up to Wetherspoons, where we knew all the Construction Lecturers would be drinking.

As we walked towards the door, Gary, the joiner was outside on his phone. When he saw me, he gave me the 'thumbs up' and a knowing smile. We walked inside, and all the construction staff was congratulating me and asking me questions.

Phil and Paul (the plumbing and electrical technicians) were in and came straight over. Both were pleased for me, hugging me and trying to buy me drinks. They were laughing as I was telling them what had gone on throughout the tribunal.

James Tebb dared to walk over to me! He stood in front of me smiling as if we were mates. I completely ignored him, and he soon got the message.

John Schofield and Phil Carter met us around 5 pm.

John informed me that on the Sunday evening before the tribunal, Ron Atler followed him into the toilets at the Irish Club. Ron said to him, "That bitch won't win, and I'm going to discuss you at the tribunal"

John said Ron was drunk and aggressive, and that he answered him, "That bitch happens to be one of my best mates. Be careful what you say about me. Janette will ring me up and I'll come straight down to the tribunal and be her witness".

We celebrated in style. I had people who I didn't even know (who had previously worked at Kirklees College) coming up to me, asking if they could shake my hand and congratulating me.

A most enjoyable and long-awaited celebration.

1/1/14

Happy New Year to me. Feel good. Real good.

8/1/14

I received the Judgement Letter from the Tribunal. Great to have it in black and white:

Case No: 1800254/2013

EMPLOYMENT TRIBUNALS

Claimant: **Miss J Hirst**

Respondent: **Kirklees College**

Heard at: **Leeds On: 10th, 11th and, 12th December 2013**

Before: **Employment Judge Knight**

Representation

Claimant: In-person

Respondent: Mr. Ranpump, Counsel

JUDGEMENT

1   The Claimant's claim of unfair dismissal is well-founded

2   The Respondent is ordered to pay the Claimant the sum of £78,499.00 compensation which comprises firstly a Basic Award of £6,149.00 and, secondly, a Compensatory Award of £72,300.00. The Statutory

maximum has been applied to the Compensatory Award.

3   The Recoupment Regulations apply

4   The Prescribed Element is £20,364.00 and the excess in the grand total over the Prescribed Element is £58,085.00

Employment Judge Knight

JUDGEMENT SENT TO THE PARTIES ON

7th January 2014

FOR THE TRIBUNAL

NOTICE

THE EMPLOYMENT TRIBUNALS (INTEREST) ORDER 1990

Tribunal case number(s): 1800254/2013

Name of the case(s): Miss J Hirst V Kirklees College

The Employment Tribunals (Interest) Order 1990 provides that sums of money payable as a result of an Employment Tribunal (excluding sums representing costs or expenses), shall carry interest where the full amount is not paid within 14 days after the day that the document containing the tribunal's written judgement is recorded as having been sent to parties. That day is known as "the relevant decision day". The date from which interest starts to accrue is called "the calculation day" and is the day immediately following the relevant decision day.

The rate of interest payable is that specified in section 17 of the Judgement Act 1838 on the relevant decision day. This is known as "the stipulated rate of interest" and the rate applicable in your case is set out below.

The following information in respect of this case is provided by the Secretary of the Tribunals in accordance with the requirements of Article 12 of the Order:-

"the relevant decision day" is: 07 January 2014

"the calculation day" is: **08 January 2014**

"the stipulated rate of interest" is: 8% per annum

For the Employment Tribunal Office

£78,499 for compensation!   And 8% interest if not paid on time.

They haven't done anything else on time, but perhaps the 8% interest may encourage them to comply for once!

It made me very happy, and I had a big smile of satisfaction on my face as I read through the information a few times, to make sure that I understood when I should receive my money.

It seems that I should get paid within 14 days of their 'calculation day' which the letter states, is today. That means I should have my money by January 22nd – and if not, I can charge them interest.

Will Kirklees College pay within the correct timescale? It's a lot of money to find!

I know Kirklees College can't appeal against the decision (as they conceded defeat the at tribunal), but will they try to appeal against the amount of compensation they have to pay? Even if just to drag things out before paying?

18/1/14

I haven't heard anything from Kirklees College's solicitors – no surprise there! I would imagine they will either send me a cheque or ask for my bank details to pay the compensation straight into it. If they don't contact me soon, they won't be able to meet the January 22nd deadline.

I decided to ring the tribunal for advice (to see if Kirklees College can appeal the amount of compensation - just to delay things).

I spoke to Julian (the steward) and he was more than helpful. He informed me that the Employment Tribunal Judgement wasn't binding by law and that Kirklees College could mess me about and try not to pay the compensation that they owe me. Julian told me that I could (through a sheriff?), go to the High Court and have my Tribunal Judgement made legal, and then I could serve Kirklees College with a Writ.

This would mean that legally they would have to pay it fully, within the timescale and if not, I could charge them interest.

I have no idea what a sheriff is. I thought they were only in Wild West films? Julian made it sound quite a 'do-able' process, so I immediately started researching on-line about sheriffs, High Court and, Writs.

My research showed that everything Julian had told me was true and it sounded quite simple to do. It was by now 6 pm so I looked up the contact details of the sheriff of

Huddersfield. I wrote down the number and decided to ring him tomorrow.

21/1/14

I telephoned the number for the sheriff of Huddersfield. He answered, and I asked him if it was possible to get my Employment Tribunal Judgement made legal, and then serve my former employer with a Writ.

The sheriff asked, "Is your former employer still in business?"

I replied, "Yes."

He asked, "Do you think that your former employer has the funds to be able to pay the compensation?"

I again replied, "Yes."

He then asked, "Who is your former employer?"

I replied, "Kirklees College."

He said, "Oh, they should have some money" then he asked, "How much compensation have you been awarded by the tribunal?"

I replied, £78,499."

He was shocked and said, "Oh my God! No wonder they don't want to pay. That's the annual budget for a section!"

He then said, "They will have the means to pay, but it will be very uncomfortable for the person having to explain why they need over £78,000 extra budget, from the board of Governors!"

He briefly explained the procedure – I would have to send him a £60 cheque, made payable to the County Court (and a copy of my Tribunal Judgement). He would then go to court, pay them the cheque, show them the evidence and then obtain the Writ from them. He would then serve Kirklees College with the Writ.

He said Kirklees College would have to pay me the £60 it had cost me for the Writ on top of my compensation.

I asked the sheriff how much I would have to pay him for this service.

The Sheriff told me he charges 7% of the amount for his fee (and this is paid by the person owing the money). That means Kirklees College may have to pay the Sheriff nearly £5,500 (7%) on top of my £78,499!

I told the sheriff that I would need to discuss what he had told me with my husband and that I would contact him tomorrow.

I telephoned Robert and told him what the sheriff had explained to me. I felt very positive about it, but Robert was very cautious. His concern was that I would have to pay the sheriff a percentage of my compensation and that it would be a risk. I told Robert that the sheriff had told me that Kirklees College had to pay the sheriff's fees, and assured him that I would double-check the facts on line.

I began researching sheriffs/court writs online and it confirmed everything that the sheriff had told me – that I would have to pay £60 for the Writ (and this would be re-reimbursed to me later), and it stated that the sheriff got his expenses from the person/company that they served the Writ to.

I showed Robert the information online when he got home from work and we then decided that I would get the 'ball rolling' tomorrow.

24/1/14

I telephoned the sheriff and told him that I wanted to go ahead and that I was sending him the £60 cheque in the post today.

The sheriff explained that when he received the cheque, he would make an appointment at Court and obtain the Writ. He would then telephone me when he had obtained the Writ and would tell me when he was serving it.

I felt good, positive and highly amused. It was now over a month since the Tribunal and yet again it seemed that Kirklees College was prepared to ignore and disregard me.

22/1/14

The sheriff telephoned me to tell me that he had obtained the Writ from the court and that he was going to serve it to the Principal of Kirklees College (Paul McKant) this afternoon!

I started laughing and asked him if he could video it for me! He said he would ring me to let me know when he had served it.

I felt good and giddy with excitement! I must have shocked them in December, with how well I had prepared for the Tribunal and how easily I had won. I felt that once again I would prove that they couldn't just ignore me and the Judgement from the tribunal.

The sheriff telephoned me mid-afternoon. He said that the Principle and Vice-Principal weren't at the Huddersfield site, so he had had to serve it to one of the Directors of Kirklees College. A pity as I would have loved it to have been handed straight to Paul McKant — but I'm sure his mobile will have been ringing immediately after the Writ had been served.

About twenty minutes after the sheriff had contacted me, Kirklees College's solicitor telephoned me. She was extremely flustered, saying, "What have you done this for? We were going to pay your compensation."

I replied calmly, "The way you have treated me in the past makes it impossible for me to trust you, I am not willing to be messed about by you any longer."

I had just been about to leave the house (as I was going to view a house). After all the waiting Stephanie Path had put me through, I decided that 'the boot was on the other foot now' and that she would wait for me. I said to her, "I have an appointment in ten minutes, so I'll ring you back when I've returned." I was smiling as I said it. She would have to wait until I was ready to speak to her.

I went to view the house and then telephoned 'Psycho' upon my return. She thanked me for calling her back and asked for my bank details, so she could organise a transfer direct to my bank account. I gave her my details and then rang the sheriff to inform him. I was very amused at how flustered and under pressure 'Psycho' had sounded. She had probably forgotten all about me.

When I got through to the sheriff, he said that the funds would have to go through him. Kirklees College would have to pay him my compensation, plus £60 for my cheque and the sheriff's fee. When the funds cleared, he would then pay me.

So, another short waiting game - but it would soon be over now.

4/2/14

The sheriff telephoned me to inform me that Kirklees College had paid him my money!

The sheriff explained that he would have to transfer my money in three separate amounts over three separate days (some legal reason – money laundering?)

I thanked him and told him I would check my bank account tomorrow.

It must have cost Kirklees College well over £100,000 in total with their solicitor's and Barrister's fees on top of my compensation. If only they had listened to me right from the start. They could have resolved the problem, saved themselves a fortune and also saved my career. But, what's done is done. Hopefully, they have learned their lesson and no one else will suffer as I did?

5/2/14

I woke up feeling excited. I took Indie out and made myself wait until 11 am before walking on to the cash point.

I checked the joint account – and there in black and white was £50,000 credited to our account. I went home (walking on air) and telephoned Robert, then my mum and dad to give them the good news.

6/2/14

I checked my bank account again and another £20,000 had kindly been deposited.

7/2/14

I checked my bank account, and the final £8,499 had been deposited, so I had got the full £78,499.

I felt ecstatic. I have won fair and square. Kirklees College treated me badly and then went on to seriously underestimate me.

Well, I won – and I hope it hurts like hell!

10/2/14

2014 just gets better and better. I have been offered a job at a college in Leeds as an NVQ assessor for apprentice electricians. I have my compensation and am going to start my new job in April. WOW!

March 2014

I just enjoyed this month. I spent my time with Indie. She needs lots of short walks now as she is old and has 'slowed down' considerably, so I am making sure she is well looked after.

Someone from College suggested that I should put my story in the Huddersfield Examiner.

I now thought it might be the right time to serve Kirklees College their last piece of justice by putting what they put me through in their local newspaper.

My local radio station plays adverts about Kirklees College which states how fantastic they are. Every time I hear the advert it seriously winds me up.

31/314

I decided to telephone the Huddersfield Examiner and explained that I had an interesting story for them. I briefly explained what had happened to me and I was put through to their reporter called Robert Sutcliffe.

He sounded very interested and asked if he could come to my house tomorrow to interview me. I agreed.

<u>1/4/14</u>

The reporter from Huddersfield Examiner came to my house at 11 am. He interviewed me and took my picture.

I could tell he was shocked at what Kirklees College put me through, that I represented myself and that I had won that amount of compensation.

I showed him my documentation from the Employment Tribunal as proof.

When he left he told me that it would be on the front page of the Huddersfield Examiner tomorrow.

I spent the rest of the day feeling amused that the management of Kirklees College is in for a surprise tomorrow.

Kirklees College put me through two years of hell – now it's time for me to remind them that they must treat their remaining staff professionally and with respect.

<u>2/4/14</u>

I got up feeling giddy.

I sent a text to Tanya Brown which said, "You might want to buy a copy of the Huddersfield Examiner".

She texted back, "Why, are you in it?"

I texted, "Yes."

Ten minutes later she telephoned me. She had gone online and read it.

I then got a cheery phone call from John Forrest. He found it very amusing. One of his mates had contacted him about it, and it was only 9 am.

I got texts from Kay and Judith. Kay said they were all whispering about it in the Construction Department and that Ron Atler and Dale Rolland were not looking amused!

I walked on to the shop and bought three copies of the Huddersfield Examiner. I felt quite paranoid as my face was on the front page.

I took the paper home and read through it.

The heading on the front page was:

LECTURER WINS £78K FOR UNFAIR DISMISSAL

Tribunal victory for a woman who faced months of college intimidation

The full story was on page 5:

'A woman lecturer who says she suffered 'mental torture' whilst working at Kirklees College has won her fight for justice.

And she was awarded more than £78,000 after successfully pursuing a claim for unfair dismissal.

Janette Hirst of Brighouse, says she worked for the college's electrical section for just over 12 years but the career she had worked so hard for slipped away from her following a change in management during the second half of 2010.

In a written statement presented to an employment tribunal, she said: 'I became increasingly unhappy with the Curriculum Team Leader's unacceptable management style during 2011.

"In early January 2012, I was too ill to continue working and was absent for most of 2012 with work-related stress

due to my leader's intimidating behaviour. I became a shadow of my former self overnight. I didn't want to leave the house. I couldn't sleep and would not even answer the telephone".

Mrs. Hirst (nee Castle), said she also suffered panic attacks and was diagnosed with depression due to her work situation.

She said that the college failed to follow its grievance and investigation procedures and also made false accusations against her which 'shocked her to the core'.

Eventually, she says that despite having worked for the college for a long time and possessing an 'impeccable work record' she left.

She was determined to fight her corner and armed with a large amount of evidence took on the college.

She said, "I represented myself and cited constructive dismissal due to breach of contract and loss of mutual trust and confidence. The tribunal was due to last three days but Kirklees College's barrister conceded liability for unfair dismissal on the second day of the hearing. I was awarded the equivalent of two and a half year's salary and my nightmare had finally come to an end.

Janette is now looking forward to starting a new job shortly.

The reporter had contacted Kirklees College to ask if they had any comment – and when I read it, it read as quite pathetic and an admission of guilt:

Mandy Rook, Vice Principle at Kirklees College, said: *"This is the first time a tribunal judgement has been made against the college, and we have reviewed our employment procedures as a result. It is always regrettable when a situation arises between the college and a member of staff."*

They say that revenge is a dessert best served cold....

Yes...It seems so.

Acknowledgements

In memory of Indie, my beautiful (now sadly deceased) Weimaraner. My constant, loving companion who got me through the long, dark days of 2012 and 2013. Miss you 'baby girl'.

To Robert, Marcus, Mum and, Dad. Thank you for your love and support.

To John Forrest who stood up for what he believed in and was my witness on the first day of the tribunal. A genuinely good guy. Thanks, mate.

To Phil Carter who telephoned me every single week that I was off work with Work-Related Stress to give me support. I will never forget that. Thank you.

Dr 'Mattins' (now retired) who supported me through the darkest two years of my life, when I didn't know 'which way was up'. You are a fantastic doctor. Thank you so much.

To Judith Hamilton and Kay Ramsden. Ex-work colleagues and friends who supported me throughout. Your support and belief really helped me. You are lovely ladies. A special thank you to Judith who read through this book before I published it and altered my poor English and Grammar (and also took out lots of swear words).

To all my ex-colleagues in the electrical and plumbing department who told the truth during the investigation interviews – some of whom were then treated unfavourably because they spoke the truth. Thank you, guys.

In memory of John Schofield, my friend and fabulous ex-boss at Kirklees College from 2000 – 2010. I took your advice about 'Keep your powder dry.' Miss you 'daft lad'.

Hillside Legal Advice Service (no longer running, unfortunately). You guys gave your free time and gave free legal advice to people who couldn't afford to pay for it. You gave me sound advice and confidence that I did have a case. Thank you – much appreciated.

To a gentleman (who will remain nameless), who found out about my plight, contacted me, came to my house and gave me advice and explained some legal terminology which helped me understand how to prove 'Breach of Contract'. Knowledge certainly is power. I don't know if you are still employed by Kirklees College – but wherever you are, if you read this, you know who you are. Thank you for your help and best wishes for the future.

To Mick Clark. You took time out to visit me at home. You gave me advice and informed me that I could represent myself at Tribunal. Thank you.

Authors Note

I hope you enjoyed my book.

This is not a 'witch hunt'. It is just a story that I thought needed to be told -in the hope that it may help other employees going through similar situations and also for Management and HR of all Companies to understand how devastating such situations can be for employees.

This book is 100% true. I have altered most names.

Most of the Management and HR discussed in this book have now left the College and two others are no longer in management positions.

The Management and H/R who dealt with me during 2012 and 2013 know who they are. I hope they have reflected on their past actions and behaviours and now behave in a more morally acceptable manner.

They say mental illness affects 1 in 4 people throughout their lifetime. I always believed that I was a strong person, but I suffered badly throughout 2012 and 2013. I couldn't see a way out or any future for myself.

Luckily I knew that my mental illness was due to the behaviour of my employer and after I resolved my issues with said employer, my mental health improved immediately.

My heart goes out to anyone who is suffering right now. Speak to people and seek help. If it's work-related and you think you can deal with it – please try.

If not, look for work elsewhere. Your health is extremely important – more important than any job.

Take care xx

Printed in Great Britain
by Amazon